A Rising Tide

by

Iona Morrison

A Blue Cove Mystery, Book Thirteen

Dedication

Dedicated to my husband, Rob, who experienced an
extremely hard year including three major heart
procedures with resilience and resolve.
And to my three friends, Vickie, Tammy, and Judy who
supported us both through it all.

Chapter 1

Only a few more hours in the air, and she would be on the ground, in Matt's arms. Jessie sighed. She had missed him more than she imagined possible. At least the long flight, combined with the sound of the engine's steady roar, gave her plenty of time to consider how the last month had changed her. Ireland had opened her heart and mind to new possibilities. The Emerald Isle's beauty and magic gave her a sense of connection and a strong desire to belong. Matt had told her as much when he surprised her with the tickets. The man knew her better than she knew herself. She liked that about him. His honesty was refreshing, if somewhat annoying at times.

Placing all of her rich discoveries into some kind of order in her thoughts, she couldn't wait to tell Matt, and of course Reba, her mentor, about what she had learned during her travels. The experience as a whole was positive. She'd discovered more than a few love stories among her ancestors to satisfy the worst skeptic in her. And a major highlight for her was learning about a relative from several generations past that she not only looked like, but the woman had the gift of sight too. There were travelers, a few relatives who dabbled on the darker side, and enough craziness in her family line to fill several journals. Matt would be left scratching his head in disbelief when she told him the details.

"Can I get you anything?" the flight attendant asked her.

"A blanket for my grandmother would be nice." Jessie reached for the blanket from the attendant and placed it softly over Sadie who slept soundly.

"She's out." Peyton smiled at her.

"Must be nice." Jessie pulled the blanket over Sadie's exposed shoulder.

"Well, it's back to this book for me. I hope it makes the time go faster." Peyton pointed at the book in her lap and opened it to where her finger held the last page she had read.

"I hope it's a good one. As for me, I'll pass the time daydreaming like I normally do." Jessie chuckled.

What amazed her and Peyton both during their trip were the superstitions that surrounded the births of some of those relatives. A strongly held belief at the time was if a baby was born at midnight or the twilight hours, the child would have the gift of sight. And if a child was born during the chime hours, an unknown term to her, the beliefs became more fanciful. She later learned that tradition taught that the chimes rang at three, six, nine, and midnight, and the designated hours only held true between Friday and dawn on Sunday. Those children would be able to see ghosts and spirits that others could not see. What had seemed strange to her at that piece of news was that she was born during the chime hours and so was Peyton. Even stranger yet, their grandmother and Peyton's sister, Madison, were too. Jessie had no idea if there was any truth in the ancient belief, but three of them could be considered positive proof of the ancient theory. They weren't sure about Madison yet. "We'll find out soon enough," she mused.

With a quick peek at her watch, she calculated the hours left in their flight time. New York sounded good at the moment. Matt had promised to meet them at the airport, and she found herself counting the minutes. Jessie leaned her head back against the seat. Her heart belonged to her hunky cop and to him alone. He wanted a wedding date, and they would figure the day and time out together. She didn't want to do life alone anymore or make any major life decisions by herself. What she knew for sure was she wanted to spend whatever time she had on this earth with Matt. How or when wasn't as important as the fact that they would.

Jessie glanced at Sadie sleeping beside her. Her grandmother was a wonder to her. She had discovered new facets to the amazing woman she called Grams resting peacefully in her seat. How would they ever repay Matt for the adventure he had given them? Sadie had loved every moment and enjoyed meeting family she had never got to meet before. She kept up every step of the way and often dragged Peyton and Jessie in her wake.

Jessie smiled to herself at the memories of one particular day in Dublin. After a long day of touring, they stopped for dinner at a place recommended by the locals. Grams had surprised them both as she danced with an older gentleman at the pub. Later that night, back at their hotel, they had all laughed like teenagers and Grams had even blushed.

"Do you know, girls, how long it's been since a man told me he found me attractive? I found his attention a bit thrilling. Because it's been a long, long time, I can assure you. Line or not, I'll admit it was nice." She fanned her face playfully, her dimples on full display in her wrinkled cheek. "When he took me in his arms, it was magic. Not since your grandpa Max, have I had such a moment. The dance took me back in time, and it seemed like I was dancing with my Max one more time." She wiped a tear forming in her eye.

And then Grams quickly reminded them both that her Max would always be the one and only true love of her life. That moment was special in many ways. Sitting in rapt attention in their PJs, with hot cups of tea in hand, they had listened as Grams told them about how she met their grandpa. Jessie thought she knew their story, but she had never heard the entire version told like this before. She didn't need to hear another love story after she heard Sadie's rendition. She couldn't wait to tell Matt all the details. Their story was swoon worthy.

How Grams could sleep with all the noise was beyond her. She glanced at her cousin Peyton on Sadie's other side. Her book must have turned out to be a good one. She seemed lost in the pages. Jessie could never sleep or read on a plane. Travel seemed only to hype her. Her mind refused to shut down. She wanted to remember everything she needed to tell Matt. Although she had already shared many of the highlights from their trip with him over the phone, some things were best said in person. As great as the trip had been, she had faced some troubling realities along the way too.

One area she hadn't disclosed to anyone, not even Matt, was also the one she had fought the entire trip. She refused to let her recurring dream spoil her travels, but it hadn't been easy. Each night she determined to think only happy thoughts, but the nightmare swept past any defense she erected, taking her on its strange journey. As soon as sleep claimed her, she found herself fighting to survive as the storm unleashed its fury. Waves crashed against the shore until the water swelled surging toward where she stayed. Water poured in all the windows and doors while the raging sea threatened to swallow her whole and take her out to sea in its retreat. No wonder she didn't want to close her eyes. She had tried to brush the premonition off, but the effects of the constant rain falling most days took their toll on her mental state. It was hard to maintain being happy when she had no idea what the dream meant.

The problem was, it wasn't only the dream that bothered her—there was more. No matter where they went, from the airport in the city or overseas, short-tempered people seemed to be screaming the loudest, and with them came pushing and shoving. More than once, someone had rammed into her or Grams without a single word of apology uttered. She could live with the bumps, but when their rudeness involved Sadie she wanted to confront the person, which would have only escalated the situation. Like a rising tide, people seemed to be caught in a season of discontent. More than one rude person waited on her in airport gift shops. She told herself that it was simply a feeling on her part and not anything she could put her finger on or had any proof of, but people everywhere appeared to be on edge.

Most of the people they met were hospitable and wonderful. Except for a few they ran into in the train station or airport, they were treated cordially. Maybe she was losing her mind. But it was what she couldn't see that troubled her most. Her whole view was changing. The sensation wasn't only in Blue Cove, or her country, but in each of the countries they made short jaunts into.

Every time she thought about all the great discoveries she had made during their travels, the nagging dream would arise to steal her joy away. When she factored in the strange sensation that someone was following them everywhere they went, she was more than ready to be home.

On one of her morning runs, she swore there was someone not only watching her but running near enough for her to sense his presence. No amount of reasoning seemed to persuade her there was no one nearby. She had searched, but she couldn't shake the feeling. On more than one occasion she asked Peyton to run with her, not wanting to jog alone.

Now, more than ever, she needed Matt's reassurance that everything would be fine. Another one of the many reasons to put on her list of why not to put off personal happiness. Especially when she could be enjoying every moment with her man and those she loved. That thought kept her calling her parents on a regular basis. Her mother was beginning to get suspicious of all her many calls.

At night, when sleep eluded her, her computer was her companion. Jessie read every article she could find on storms and the effects of waves. Several articles mentioned the real danger during hurricanes or typhoons didn't come from the winds but the wave action that surged during high tides, propelling great amounts of water onto land. People often were caught off guard by the quickly rising water and its destruction.

These were facts which made her dream all the more troubling. Was she seeing some subtle undercurrent affecting events not yet understood in the world? Did it impact all the nations or was she exaggerating what she saw? She glanced at the other questions and notes she had written over the past month. She had enough on her plate dealing with her corner of the world to avoid getting involved in the bigger picture.

"Grams has been sleeping for a while. She looks beyond sweet and peaceful." Peyton's voice interrupted her thoughts. Peyton placed a bookmark in her book and closed the cover.

"Poor thing. I think we tuckered her out." Jessie smiled at the sleeping woman beside her. "The last mad dash we made in the airport to make our flight after the delay in customs didn't help either."

"I hoped reading would make the time move faster. It didn't work. I'm ready to see Jaxon, and I can't wait to get home." Peyton scrunched her face and placed her book in the seatback pocket. "It hasn't lived up to hype, but our trip sure did. I'm sure we will be reliving it over again many times."

"Exactly what I was doing while you were trying to read." Jessie glanced at the flight attendant handing a pillow to the lady in the seat in front of her and returned his smile. "We have a lot to assimilate."

Peyton frowned, tapping her fingers on the arm of the seat. "I hear you."

"What?" Jessie asked noticing her cousin's expression.

"I loved every moment of our trip, and yet something is bothering me, and I wish I knew what it is."

"We need to talk." Keeping her voice soft so as not to wake up Sadie, Jessie explained her dream. "This has to be between us until I talk to Matt."

"Wow. Your dream describes my feelings at various times this past month. I thought I was suffocating, but I couldn't see any reason to feel that way." Peyton pursed her lips and leaned her head back against the seat. "Now I have something to think about." She closed her eyes. "Is that why you didn't want to run alone?" Peyton asked.

"As crazy as it sounds, I felt like someone was following me, and that was my real reason. Although, I always like when we run together."

"Dang, cous, I wish you would have told me." Peyton opened her eyes and glanced at her. "That gives another answer to the questions I've had this past month."

"I wasn't sure if it was real or my reaction to the dream," Jessie mused.

"We both know better than that. We can't discount what we sense no matter how impossible it seems." Peyton closed her eyes.

Jessie leaned her head back against the seat and did the same. Before she drifted off to sleep, she peeked one more time at her sleeping grandmother and beautiful cousin. She loved Peyton, but the past few months she was troubled by her own envious feelings that surfaced without warning once in a while. Ever since Peyton had gone back in time and lived for a moment in their great-great grandmother's life, Peyton seemed self-assured when it came to the gift of sight they possessed while she still seemed to flounder without an anchor. It wasn't Peyton's fault of course;

Jessie loved her to pieces. It was her own insecurity that needed an adjustment. This trip helped her in that department. She had wanted to find out who she was in the great scheme of things. In other words, why her? A big part of that question was answered for her.

The next voice she heard was that of the captain telling the flight attendants to begin to prepare the cabin for landing. When she glanced at her watch, she realized she had slept for three hours, a first for her ever on a plane.

"I thought you girls would never wake up." Grams patted Jessie's hand. Her eyes were bright, and she looked well rested.

"I don't know what happened. I never sleep on a plane. Besides, you went to sleep before we did." Jessie rubbed her eyes and tried to straighten her hair. Matt would be waiting, and she didn't want to look like a total wreck when she rushed into his waiting arms.

"If you ask me, we all needed it. We have been on the go for weeks, and I, for one, was more than happy to settle down for a moment." Sadie smiled. "I feel refreshed, but with the drive we still have to make, I'll be ready for bed again. This time in my own bed."

"Home sounds wonderful, doesn't it?" Peyton asked.

"Especially the part with my own bed in it. I can't wait." Jessie raised her seat to the upright position.

"Jaxon texted me before we left and said he was on his way to the airport with Matt. I'm ready to see my guy. He said it's been storming in the city, and he hoped our flight was smooth." Peyton pulled her purse out from under the seat and placed it on her lap.

The ride got a bit bumpier as they got closer to

their destination. The seat-belt sign flashed on, and the captain told them to take their seats. "Folks, please remain seated until we reach the gate. We're in for a bit of a rough ride during our descent, and there are a few planes in front of us." The intercom clicked off, and the flight attendants started to collect pillows and blankets.

A flash of lightning lit up the night sky followed by several more. As the plane started its descent into New York, it circled several times in the bumpy, choppy air before the pilot finally told them they were cleared to land.

Jessie was grateful. If they would've had to go around one more time dipping and turning followed by banking to the side, she would have screamed. As it was, a few passengers had when the plane seemed to drop and lurch forward. Thankfully, the captain set the big bird down nice and easy in an uneventful landing. The spontaneous cheers brought a smile to her face as she unclenched her fingers one at a time from the arms of the seat.

"Well, my dears, that was a tense welcome home. That's the roughest few minutes we've had the entire time." Sadie patted her granddaughters' hands. "We can breathe now."

"I know I was holding mine." Peyton stood when the plane finally came to a stop at the gate. "From all the cheers, I think it's safe to say we weren't the only ones a bit nervous." She reached in the overhead bin and pulled out Jessie's small carryon and Sadie's bag. Stuffing her book into her purse, she sat down again as everyone started up the aisle to exit the plane. "Boy, am I glad I don't have to drive home after that."

"Me too. I would stay in the city for the night

rather than drive." Jessie grabbed her purse and stood, stretching her legs. "I think the rush is over, and we can follow the crowd to customs." Jessie moved into the aisle behind Sadie. "I can imagine the stories people will have to tell about their trip into New York tonight." Including us, she thought to herself. Matt and Jaxon would soon hear their version when they made it to passenger pickup. Of course, she would embellish the rough ride in the air to get as much attention as she could get from Matt. A month away from him seemed like forever. His concern was exactly what she wanted right now.

After they picked up their bags, they made their way to passenger pickup, where Matt and Jaxon said they would meet them. Matt texted her that he had borrowed his brother's van, and there was plenty of room for everyone, including the luggage.

****

Matt pulled into a place to park near the passenger pickup to wait for Jessie's text. He could see the doors from the space in case she forgot to message him. He checked out every person that came through the doors when they opened. He couldn't wait to see her. He would love to tell her everything had been calm and crime free while she was gone, but that wasn't going to happen. The fact was that the opposite was true. Something was up, and he couldn't put his finger on what they were looking at, but he had bent Jaxon's ear the entire drive. The agency must have also noticed an uptick of online chatter and threats. In the past month, many warnings had come across the wire at the station from the FBI and top law enforcement agencies warning them of certain credible threats. Matt couldn't remember getting this many notices and alerts in such a short period of time. Jaxon said the same was true at their field office.

"I had an interesting report come across my desk about the increase in mass shootings. I'm sure your office got one too." Matt turned in his seat.

Jaxon nodded. "What was your takeaway?"

"The report said that in a fourth of the cases the shooter was motivated by hateful ideology or conspiracy theories. We have definitely seen an increase in the rhetoric in that department. The recommendation was to monitor the local chatter in our area. Thankfully, we have Gary, but we're a small department and can't monitor chatrooms twenty-four-seven. Blue Cove's mayor has already had a couple of death threats." Matt shook his head in disgust.

"That's nuts about the mayor, but the same statistic stood out to me. The FBI has a whole department which spends its days following online chatter searching for credible threats and still a lot of it slips under the radar." Jaxon stretched out his legs. "Another item that struck me in the report was that shooters are often motivated by personal grievances. To me, that's a bit harder to track. Some guy could be going along seething and do nothing for months and then one day—boom—he snaps." Jaxon glanced at his phone notification.

"I hear you. At least we can keep our eyes on recent arrests. The stats are high that they are a repeat offender. A quick check of our database from time to time might help. But how can you possibly know which one will become the next loner to go off the rails?" Matt's brows furrowed.

"The dilemma of our times. If we knew the answer to that, we could prevent the next mass shooting. Wouldn't a little foreknowledge be nice?" Jaxon leaned his head back against the headrest.

Matt glanced at the incoming text on his phone. "Jessie says they're headed our way now from baggage. They were able to make it through customs without a hitch." Matt stuck his phone back in the holder and drove to an open space in the line of cars to pick up passengers.

"Yeah, Peyton messaged me the same thing." Jaxon took off his seat belt and opened the passenger door as soon as Matt stopped. "I'll open up the back for their luggage." He smiled at one of the security officers who walked past him.

"Thanks. We got a nice space in the nick of time. Here they come." Matt jumped out of the driver's side to go help. Instead of luggage he found his arms full of Jessie, which was all right with him. "Welcome home, sweetheart." He kissed her and then reached around to bring Sadie into their hug. Jaxon would take care of Peyton.

Chapter 2

After their long flight and what seemed like an endless drive to Blue Cove on a rain slick highway, Matt delivered Jessie safely home with a promise of seeing her tomorrow. A few kisses later she said goodbye, locked her door, and headed to her bedroom, grabbing her travel case along the way. The ride home with rain blowing sideways on the windshield was almost as tense as their arrival in New York had been. She was happy to be home. The suitcase could wait until morning.

Jessie sighed as she finally stretched out on her familiar mattress, shut off the bedside lamp, and closed her eyes. A few minutes later she opened them again. She was wide awake. How was that even possible? Her body felt exhausted, but her mind was ready to solve the world's pressing problems. Obviously, the time change was affecting her again, which probably meant Peyton and Sadie were awake too.

Determined not to get up, she closed her eyes and willed herself to rest even as sleep eluded her. "Dang," she whispered into the dark room. "Wide awake and nowhere to go." She rolled over onto her side. Matt sure looked good to her, and she wished they could've spent time together, but he had an early morning tomorrow and so did she. She was anxious to hear how things in town were going, or if Matt and Jaxon knew anything that might account for how troubled she felt during the trip. Were there any warnings out there she needed to know about, or better yet, how were things at the store?

A month was a long time to be away from her business. Even though she talked several times a week to Audrey, who assured her that business was great, Jessie was still concerned. She worried about all the strange things that could happen when it came to her store. From ghosts tossing books to strange people who came from a different time and place, she knew all too well her store could be a happening place. All that was common to her now but not to her employees. Tomorrow she would know for sure if everything was truly okay.

The longer she lay there, the greater the sensation pulsated through her that some unknown monumental event was changing the world around her and not in a good way. Would she come face-to-face with the man who had followed them? Restless, she tossed and turned until exhausted by all the movement and a fitful sleep overtook her.

She walked along the shore on what appeared to be a picture-perfect day. The scene was comforting and familiar. Her favorite spot to go to on a hot summer day. Gazing out into the cove as she had done countless times before, she watched the gathering storm clouds off in the distance. Instinct told her she needed to get to the safety of her cottage as the wind picked up in intensity. Fearful and yet fascinated, she couldn't make herself move. Suddenly, the ocean churned and roared, its waves reaching heights she had never seen before. And though she tried to run, her feet were weighted like encased in cement. The waves grew and took on the appearance of angry claws reaching out to grab her, creeping ever closer with each push from the sea. One latched onto her foot, threatening to pull her out into its dark depths, but she fought against its powerful force and managed to escape, only to be seized by another. Weary from the struggle, she almost gave in to the water as it rushed in once again. Hearing the screams— they seemed to come from every direction—she found new strength to fight. "I will live." The words reverberated through her, drowning out the sounds of the crashing waves and cries. Breaking free, she scrambled up to the top of the hill and turned back for a moment to see all the many people not as lucky as her being carried out on the crest of the waves.

Jessie awakened, overwhelmed with a powerful emotion of fear. She pulled the covers up tight around her as the AC kicked on. The same blanket she had kicked off earlier now gave her security with its warmth and softness. The full meaning of the dream would reveal itself in time. She didn't want to close her eyes again. The sight was too horrible to relive. If she were mesmerized by the coming storm, knowing the possible damage, what would happen to those who couldn't see its approach?

****

As he stretched out on his bed, the man recounted all the places he saw over the past month while he traipsed through several countries following the three women. The blonde nearly discovered him when he got close enough to snatch her. On more than one occasion, he had almost run into her, literally. Not that he thought she would know him. His appearance had changed many times over the years, and yet she seemed to sense his presence, which was a bit disconcerting. He had used many people to fulfil his mission over the span of too many years to count. Wherever there was evil involved, you would find him or one of many others like him somewhere in the shadows of their thoughts, if not hidden in their lives or acting out in some way through their bodies.

There was a strong awareness on her part of his presence. He saw her looking over her shoulder, and their eyes had met in a passing glance several times. Yes, he could sense the strength that surrounded her. He shuddered. Defeat had overtaken him before when he met such strength. The aura around her was strong, and he needed to get to her before she understood her own strength. He plumped his pillow behind his head and leaned his head back against it.

She wouldn't be easy to tame. The old lady might be a way to get at her, but that wasn't how he liked to work. Damn, he needed a plan. The problem was he never knew what he might do at any moment. His personality could change with the wind or with the body he had or by an easily influenced human. It always took him time to work through a new personality.

He patted his protruding belly. "Hopefully, you'll hold up long enough for me to set my plan into action." He snickered. The young joggers did his bidding because this body would never have made it. He snickered. "Not attractive and an old man to boot, which suits me fine at the moment." He raked his hand through the few hairs left on his head. Who would suspect him or his nefarious ideas? He closed his eyes. This body definitely needed its rest. A tight-lipped smile lingered on his lips. After midnight, the pain that squeezed through his chest shot him to an upright position. He made a call to the front desk right before he passed out.

****

Matt found himself still wide awake. After his talk with Jaxon on the way to pick up the girls, he was concerned. His first sight of Jessie brought a sense of relief followed closely by a need to protect her. But from what? He shook his head and stretched out on his bed. Stacking his hands behind his head, he decided this would be a night for thinking. He hadn't told Jessie about the one unsolved homicide and a shooting victim. There would be time to discuss that another day, after she was rested.

For one of the victims, a woman, he already knew who the prime suspect might be. Her husband was at the top of the list. Matt was waiting for the results of the autopsy and toxicology to figure out the exact cause. Casey and Ria Craven were married for four years. Her sister Hazel told him during an interview that she had never liked Casey from day one. Ria feared him, and now she understood why. Lewis, the coroner, pointed out the bruises on Ria's neck and a couple of strange needle marks too. Casey fled the scene to the sound of the sirens, racing into the neighborhood after his neighbors called police when they heard Ria scream.

His team hadn't caught up to Casey Craven yet, but they would in time. He might need to call in Frank and his tracking dog Carlene. The other case he was working on was a young victim whose name was still unknown at the moment. Shot in the chest, his body was dumped along the highway. Once he was stabilized, he was flown by air ambulance to a trauma center in New York. Matt would still like to know what happened to the guy. He was a young one. It seemed the victims of gun violence were getting younger all the time.

Matt couldn't point to a single overarching issue and say this is the reason for his unrest, but the sensation nagged at him, nonetheless. Numerous possibilities kept him up at night, which didn't bode well for his town. Matt didn't like surprises, but the past year had brought too many to count. But hey, it also brought Jessie into his life, which was the biggest surprise of all. She walked into the town and his heart before he could stop her. Now, he couldn't imagine trying to. He liked her there. She belonged and made his life exciting. Protecting her was the first item on his agenda. All he had to do was figure out why. She wouldn't want to hear him say she needed him, but he knew she did.

All the signs were pointing to something big, but what did any of them mean? This wasn't the first time for an uptick in crime and probably wouldn't be the last. Still, national alerts had started filtering down to local PDs in the past several weeks, to keep their eyes open in the areas they served. The biggest threat wasn't coming from outside the country but rather from within. The same seemed to be true in many places in the world. Matt couldn't wait to talk with Jess to see if she was picking up on anything. She was better than any random unspecific warning issued by the higher-ups. He turned off his light, rolled over, and went to sleep.

The next morning, Matt walked out the door early

with the uppermost thought of stopping by the coffee shop on his way. He smiled to himself. Where else would he go? He needed coffee after his sleepless night and Jess was finally home. With any luck he might catch a glimpse of her before he had to go to work.

****

Jessie couldn't wait to get to her store. Audrey had reassured her on several occasions that her store was doing great, but she wanted to see for herself that the building was still standing. Of course, the fact that everything was peaceful while she was gone wasn't lost on her. No action meant she was the main reason for all the craziness that took place in her store over the past year. After coming face-to-face with the reality of her ancestors, she knew she shouldn't be surprised. Jessie simply planned on embracing the oddity of her life and family and somehow incorporate them into her normal.

The moment she walked in the door, she smiled, and a sense of contentment flooded her. Ahh, her world at last. She turned around in a circle. And she had plans to make the store even better. Turning to the door that led to Joe's coffee shop next door, Jessie waved at Molly, whose baby bump definitely grew while she was gone. Molly looked too cute. After making a quick check of the store ledgers, she concluded that Audrey was correct. The store had ticked along quite nicely while she was gone. The tourists and summer hours gave the accounts an extra boost, and she would accept the results gratefully.

A tap on the door broke her concentration. She smiled when she saw who was on the other side.

"I didn't expect to see you here so early, but I was hoping to. Coming to Joe's wasn't the same while you were gone." Matt stepped through the door she held open, with two cups of coffee and a bag.

"I was excited to get here. Besides, my sleep clock is off for a bit. I'm sure it will correct itself soon. At least it'd better." She shut the door and went to sit beside him at the table.

"I brought you a coffee and your favorite." He pulled the blueberry scone out of the bag and placed it on a napkin.

"Thank you." She took a bite. "I forgot how good Molly's scones are. At least scones were easy to find on our trip. I can't wait to tell you everything, but right now I want to savor this quiet moment with you. I missed you, Mr. Parker." She reached for his hand.

"I know the feeling. I can breathe again. Dylan can tell you I wandered around like the lost without you. I won't be sending you anywhere again unless I'm by your side." His thumb rubbed the palm of her hand. "Agreed?"

"Yes, agreed." She took a sip of her coffee. "Hmm, this is so good." She closed her eyes for a brief moment. "I've drank more tea in the past month than all the many months of my life combined. Who knew a simple cup of coffee would hit the spot? Another thing I missed was good old American-style pizza. No one makes it quite like Angelo's. It's not the same in Italy, but there was other great food. I especially liked the French profiteroles at a small sidewalk café in Paris."

"Profiteroles?" His brows rose.

"I thought I told you about or short ventures into France and England." She saw him nod. "Profiteroles are a wonderful French pastry like our cream puff. The small sidewalk café we stopped at in Paris served them with a warm chocolate ganache sauce over the top. They were yummy. Sadie loved our short tour of Paris. She said she'd probably never get back there again."

"I'm glad you girls enjoyed it." He laced his fingers through hers.

"It was wonderful. You'll never know how much it meant to the three of us. I learned more than I dreamed possible about my family. And best of all, my grams was the biggest revelation of all. I have a lot to tell. I'm warning you to prepare because I'm going to bend your ear."

"As long as I'm with you, I don't mind how much you talk." He stood. "I need to get to the station, but we'll have dinner tonight at Angelo's. Your reprieve is over, sweetheart." He kissed her on his way out the door she held open.

Boy, it felt good to be home. She got to work on her opening routine. Dusting and straightening books made her happy. Vacations must be good for the soul even when trouble seems to be everywhere. She opened the doors into the coffee shop, waving at Molly, and went to unlock the front door. She wasn't surprised when Reba pulled into the space in front of the store. She turned the sign around and held the door open for her mentor and friend.

"Hello, dear lady." She kissed Reba's cheek.

"I heard you were back. I knew I had to get here to see you first thing this morning. Sadie told me you had a fabulous trip. I can't wait to hear your and Peyton's sides of the details." Reba sat down in her favorite spot at the table in the center of the store. "Peyton will be here soon, I hope."

"She will be. She's helping out this summer for a

few weeks until school starts. We've been busy, if my sales receipts are any indication." Jessie pulled out the chair across from Reba and sat.

"Every time I came in to check on things, the store had customers mingling about. Meanwhile, without you here the store was quiet, if you know what I mean, but not the church or the town. The activity has been unlike anything I've ever seen before." She stood. "I need some tea. Would you like some?"

"No, thanks. Matt brought me some coffee, and I still have some left. Peyton should be here when you get back."

When Reba walked into the coffee shop, Jessie went to get her phone. Checking texts and emails had become her lifeline when traveling, and she wasn't about to break the habit now.

"Hey, cous. I hope you slept better than I did," Peyton said as she came in the back door. "I think it will take a few days to get back on track. I stayed up most of the night, reading a manuscript. It was quite good, actually."

"At least your time wasn't wasted." Jessie shook her head. "Me, I had another intense dream. I'll tell you as soon as Reba is back. She went to get tea."

"What are you having?" Peyton asked.

"Coffee, and it's nice for a change of pace."

"What, no tea?" Peyton laughed "Your decaf is only glorified tea. I was thinking about real coffee since I woke up. I'll be right back."

Once the three were settled at the table, Jessie smiled. "At least for the moment, all is right in the world. It's good to have things back to normal again."

"Yes, dear. But how long will this good feeling

last? Not long if I'm correct." Reba placed her napkin neatly on her lap.

"I'm sure you are," Jessie told her with a sigh.

"Did you learn more about your gifts?" Reba looked over the rim of her cup of tea at them.

"You could say that." Peyton explained what they had discovered about some of their relatives and about being born during the chime hour. "Which seems a bit farfetched to believe in the twenty-first century, but we seem to be living proof of the theory." Peyton chuckled.

"Not strange at all. I could have told you as much, but it was much nicer discovering the idea for yourself, wasn't it?" Reba patted Peyton's hand.

"Yes, it kind of was." Peyton agreed.

"Let's get down to business. There is something else you need to tell me. Something that might explain all the heavy supernatural activity in the area." Reba dabbed at her lips with her napkin.

"Everywhere we went people seemed to be on edge." Peyton frowned. "I've never encountered as many angry, rude people in my life."

"I agree with Peyton. Plus, most nights I have had the same recurring dream." Jessie told her about the dream. "Last night, the dream went a step further. I saw many people succumb to the force of the water and carried out to sea." Jessie shook her head, trying to dispel the image that came rushing into her mind. "I'm not sure what all the details mean yet, but I would describe it as a rising tide of discontent. I'm not sure if people recognized what was happening around them." She explained about being spellbound by the storm and almost trapped in its waves.

"Hmm, that's something to think about," Reba

said. "People overtaken before they know what's hit them."

"I can see the possibilities of that." Peyton sipped her coffee.

"We've seen rising movements before in history. But I wonder how the restlessness and displeasure you sensed will play out in everyday life. Does it mean greater acts of violence? I believe we're about to find out." Reba looked over the rim of her cup at them.

"That's not welcoming news." Jessie pursed her lips.

"We are living in uncertain times, my dears, and our gifts will be needed more than ever. Buckle up," Reba told them.

"It looks like our vacation is over, cous." Jessie waved at some of the mystery-book-club women who walked in from Joe's. "We were warming the chairs for you." Jessie stood and walked with Reba to the door and kissed her cheek. "I'm sure we'll talk more another day." Jessie joined in the conversation Peyton had going with the women. Smiling to herself, she was happy to enjoy this moment of sanity in her store.

Chapter 3

"Hey, did you hear that someone attacked the FBI field office in Hanover?" Molly rushed through the open doors from the coffee shop. "The news said the man was heavily armed with an assault rifle and a high-capacity magazine. According to his rants on his social media post, he went there with the intent to kill a lot of agents. His car was loaded with more weapons and explosives too." Molly leaned against the counter as she talked. "The story is all over the news."

Peyton's face went pale. "Was anyone hurt?"

"No. They stopped the guy in a shootout before he could kill anyone. Thankfully, an observant receptionist gave a couple of agents the heads-up before the man made it in the door. She had been watching his nervous actions and thought he was up to no good." Molly glanced at Peyton. "Don't worry. Jaxon is okay, and I bet you hear from him soon." She touched her friend's shoulder.

"I hope so." Peyton reached for Molly's hand and squeezed it.

"That's getting a bit too close to home, don't you think?" Molly asked. "Oops, someone's ready to check out. I thought you would want to know." She stepped through the open doors back into her coffee shop.

"Thanks, Molly," Jessie called after her and hugged her cousin. "He's okay. Take a deep breath. I guess we'd better get ready because it looks like Reba is right once again."

"You never think it can happen to you or someone you love. To me this is another wake-up call to appreciate what I have while I have it." Peyton took a deep breath.

"That's why I've decided to set a wedding date. You can't say anything yet. I still need to talk to Matt." Jessie moved behind the counter. "I've had way too many reminders this past year that life can change in a moment. It's time to quit dragging my feet."

"Your secret is safe with me." Peyton smiled. "A wedding and a baby." Peyton sighed and pointed into Joe's. "Isn't Molly's baby bump cute? She is a good friend."

"She looks great. It's time to plan a baby shower." Jessie smiled.

"A baby shower and your wedding is exactly what we need to take our minds off all the anger around us."

"To tell you the truth, I had already decided I wanted to get married before we left for Ireland, but our trip along with my dreams encouraged me to seize the moment."

"I'm not there yet, but if Jaxon asked me to marry him, I would seriously consider the offer." Peyton sighed. "He pushes all the right buttons. Speaking of my guy, he texted me to let me know he's okay." She held up her phone.

"He's a good guy and a millionaire to boot. What's not to like?" Jessie chuckled. "We'd better get back to work." She smiled at the two women who walked in the door.

"And with the help of his financial adviser he's

already growing that million. It's all a bit overwhelming to me." Peyton sighed.

"How so? You've got a great guy, and he'll be able to take care of you. That seems like a win-win to me." Jessie lowered her voice and patted her cousin's hand.

"True. But after living with so little growing up, and finally learning to plan a budget down to the dollar, it is overwhelming to think of all that money. It seems to me, one shouldn't spend every penny simply because they have the means when many don't," Peyton said.

"Think of all the ways you might be able to help someone. I would think that's an upside to being rich." Jessie walked toward the women to see if she could help them find something.

The rest of the afternoon went fast. At five, Jessie was ready to turn the store over to Audrey for the next three hours. Matt was picking her up for dinner at six. She drove home and changed her clothes. She glanced at the text Matt sent, saying Jaxon and Peyton would be joining them.

She was hoping for some alone time with her guy, but she understood Matt's logic after what had happened earlier in Hanover. The two guys would talk shop and Peyton and Jessie would keep each other company.

Jessie ran a brush through her hair and put on her lip gloss. She sat at her desk and turned on her computer while she waited. The first thing that caught her eye was the breaking news about the man who planned the attack on the Hanover FBI office. They had found his social media sites and were quoting from some of his many rantings. She was shocked to see all of the weapons that the authorities had found in the suspect's car. How on earth was one person able to amass so many weapons? She knew the answer—each one could be obtained legally, or not, in some cases. But she still found the need for so many a bit strange.

Yep, she knew what the conversation would center around tonight. Maybe she would be able to slip in some information about her dream and Reba's words earlier. Matt might have some insight for her to consider.

She opened the door to let the warmish summer breeze in through the screen. She would never tire of seeing this view of the cove. Living so close to the water meant the ocean breeze made any humidity bearable. Before long, summer would be winding down, and she wanted to enjoy as much time running outdoors as possible and hanging out at the private beach down from the inn.

Ireland was beautiful, but the weather was a tad cool for summer temperatures than she was used to. There's a reason they call the country the Emerald Isle. All the rain meant green everywhere. But the same dampness that made the country beautiful made all the curls on her hair grow exponentially bigger and frizzier with each day. She tried to tame her mane, but most days she had to pull it into clips or some other strange arrangement to look halfway decent. Her run each day amid the beautiful views everywhere she looked made any hair struggles worth all the work.

She liked to think of herself as a four-season girl. Each one held their own beauty and delights to be discovered. She took a deep breath of the sea air. Matt would be here soon. She glanced at the clock, closed the front door, and turned the lock when she heard the knock at the back door.

"Are you ready, sweetheart?" Matt asked when she opened the door. He pulled her into his arms and kissed her soundly. "I've been wanting to do that since I saw you this morning."

"Is that right?" She strutted past him and out the door while he set the alarm and locked the door. "I love the gardens this time of year." She inhaled the fragrance of all the flowers in bloom.

"They're almost as pretty as you." He reached for her hand. "I hope you don't mind I asked Jaxon and Peyton to join us tonight."

"I figured after the attack on the FBI field office, you would want to spend time talking with Jaxon."

"Since he moved into his own place, I don't see him as often as I used to. Besides, I want to hear your take on things." He opened the car door for her.

"I understand. You can always come back to my place after dinner." Jessie slid into the passenger seat and latched her seat belt.

"I want to hear all about your trip." Matt got in and shut the car door. "I don't ever want to go through a month without you again. Next long trip we'll be together, but I've already told you that, haven't I?"

"Yes. Does that mean you missed me?" She grinned at him.

"You bet I did." He pulled her head close and showed her how much.

"Well, I missed you too, and I especially missed this." She kissed him back.

He started the car. "If we don't leave now, we won't be going anywhere. You're too tempting." He backed out of the parking spot and drove past the inn.

"It's nice to know I've still got that thing." She laughed.

"You've got it, all right." He glanced at her before he pulled out onto the highway into town.

"What makes certain people attracted to others? I've often wondered. I mean, what attracted you to me?" Jessie asked him.

"We'll need more time to answer that question. I might need to prove some of my responses. Do you have a safer topic? You're making this hard on me." He grinned at her.

"What do you consider safe?" she asked.

"The cost of groceries or gas. That might work." Matt stopped at the red light. "Looks like Jaxon is already here. That's his new car." Matt pointed at the sports car in the parking lot of Angelo's.

"You're off the hook." She patted his hand. "Man, is that one sharp car." She jumped out and went to get a look when Jaxon stepped out of his car.

"Wow, you've got good taste." Jessie waited for Peyton to get out of the car. "How does she handle?" She saw Matt smile when she asked the question.

"Don't get him started. I want to eat sometime tonight." Matt laughed.

After they ordered and waited for their meal, Jaxon told them about what he knew about their suspect. "He had a damn arsenal in his car. The man had big plans. Thankfully, our receptionist felt something was off about the guy as he paced outside the office. She notified a couple agents, or this day might have ended differently." He reached for Peyton's hand. "It's true what they say—every day you get is a gift. You never know what a day might bring."

"What have you learned about the suspect, if anything, yet?" Matt asked.

"They have his cyber footprint and his social media accounts in research. We'll have a complete profile on him soon. What I do know is we might need to have a domestic-terrorist law on the books. This trend doesn't seem to be going away."

"I hear you. We've already had more mass shootings than days this year. Something is definitely up." Matt thanked the waiter who placed a salad in front of him.

"I'm proud of you," Jessie leaned close to Matt.

"Why?" he asked.

"For eating your greens." She smiled at him.

"I'll eat salad as long as it's followed by pasta." He patted her hand.

"I'll remember that in the future," she whispered.

"You do that." He gave her a lopsided grin. "Tell us some of the highlights of your trip."

Over spaghetti and lasagna, Jessie and Peyton told them about some of the beautiful places they had visited on their trip. Dublin, the Irish countryside, and Paris were mentioned by both of them.

"It's hard to pick my favorite place. Spending time with Sadie and seeing everything through her eyes was absolutely the best." Jessie took a sip of her iced tea. "What can I say? The whole trip was amazing in more ways than I can count."

"The same tension we can sense in our country seems to be a world-wide phenomenon. I encountered more rude, angry people than I ever hoped to bump into. Bumped is the optimum word. Grams got knocked into more times than I could count. All with no apologies or a simple 'excuse me'." Peyton frowned. "And Jessie had a dream she needs to tell you about."

"Okay, Jess, let's hear it." Matt reached for her hand.

"Almost every night I had the same dream." Jessie told them the details. "Last night, the dream went to the next level." After she explained the new parts of the dream, she asked, "What do you think it means?" She touched her lips with her fingertips.

"I have no idea," Matt said. "The question is, what do you think it means?"

"First, you need to know the whole trip was glorious. But there were times it felt almost suffocating. Peyton described it the same way to me. But after last night, it almost feels like people are getting sucked into the turbulence around them and might not even realize what's happened until it's too late." Jessie lifted her glass to lips.

"I've often wondered how some of the worst events in history could have happened without people putting up a fight. Now, I can see how it's possible. People are swept up in what's ensuing around them." Peyton shook her head. "It's almost like a cloud covers our mind and we refuse to see anything but what we want to see. We follow the one who speaks to our personal grievances and never take the time to listen to anyone who says anything different."

"True, and we seem to forget how to talk or disagree with any civility. And when you can see your neighbor as your enemy, then you think nothing about turning on them; it's all justified." Jessie placed her napkin on the table.

"How can you fight what is trying to divide us?

Especially, when we pick sides and come out swinging. It's an impossible task." Jaxon frowned. "That guy today saw us as his enemy."

"It's hard, but not impossible. Our world wouldn't exist if we hadn't found a way to settle our differences each time they threatened to destroy us." Jessie squeezed Matt's hand. "Although it may get worse before it gets better, if history teaches us anything. We can only take it one step at a time and try to be alert to our surroundings." Her brows rose. "Did I mention that I had the strangest sensation during our trip that someone was following us."

"I never felt it, but I know you did." Peyton frowned at Jessie.

"I told Peyton I found the idea hard to believe because it didn't seem probable. I was sure I was overreacting because no one knew we were going to Ireland. But now, when I think about how real it seemed at the time, I wonder if maybe there really was someone."

"She didn't even want to run by herself, and you know how much she loves running. I'm not as dedicated as she is." Peyton shook her head. "Reba posed the question earlier—would this season of time produce more acts of violence? Our takeaway was that we'd soon find out." Peyton glanced at Jaxon. "That was before Molly told us what happened at your office, and add the possibility of someone following us on our trip, and well, you get the idea." Peyton shivered.

"Jess don't hold anything back while you second-guess yourself. I always take your hunches under consideration." Matt covered her hand with his. "Ladies, you need to keep us up-to-date on any premonitions or any of your intuitions. I think we're in for bumpy ride." Matt paid the bill, and they left the restaurant. "Jaxon, call me later if you find out any more info on your suspect. I want to know if he's a lone wolf or part of something bigger."

"Will do. Goodnight, you two." Jaxon opened the car door for Peyton.

"See you tomorrow, Peyton." Jessie waved and slipped into the passenger seat. She laid her head back against the seat and closed her eyes for a moment. She went over in her mind what she wanted to say to the man beside her when she finally got him alone.

"Are you, okay, sweetheart?" Matt started the car.

"I'm better than okay." She smiled to herself, happy to get that piece of information off her chest. At least Matt knew what she had experienced.

Chapter 4

He had waited for what seemed an eternity for her to get there. It was time he took matters into his own hands. He found a point of entry and dismantled what puny security she had. The cop should have done more to make her safe from him. He laughed, smiling at the maniacal sound of it. No one he ever knew would believe how he looked now. Black suited him, and a young body was nice for a change. He had had a few disgusting ones over the years. He knew one thing for sure—she wouldn't know who he was, but he knew of her. Knowledge of one's opponent made the game all the more thrilling.

Tucked out of view, he positioned himself in a spot where he could see both doors, reached in his pocket for the candy bar he had stuck there earlier, and leaned against the wall to wait. He couldn't wait to surprise her and her cop boyfriend with the fireworks he had planned. He strained to listen until he heard their muffled voices. The gun lifted, he checked the clip, and his body tensed, ready to spring into action. No, Jessie didn't know him, but he would keep her guessing. He loved a good rabbit trail.

****

"A penny for your thoughts," Matt said as they walked the path to her cottage.

"After the trip you gave us, you don't need to pay a

cent for any of them. I think I owe you." She smiled and placed her keys in his outstretched hand.

He reached around her in one smooth move to unlock the door, pulling her close to kiss her as he pushed the door open. The keys slipped out of his hand as he deepened the kiss. The clang of them hitting the ground almost covered the sound of the bullet which grazed his arm and narrowly missed her head as he pushed her to the ground. Several shots came in rapid succession, ripping through the screen and sending pieces of screen and metal flying through the air, raining down on them where they lay, covering their ears.

"Here we go again," she grumbled and started to lift her head.

"Stay down." He pulled his gun out of his holster. "That came from inside your house." He strained to hear any noise that would alert him to where the shooter was. The suspect was inside her house. Damn, he had been off his game. They were sitting ducks where they were. "Jess, we need to get out of his line of fire. Stay low to the ground, and I'll cover you." He fired a shot when he saw a quick movement inside her cottage. The rapid return of fire confirmed his fear. Their assailant was well armed. Hell, the alarm didn't go off.

"How did he get in?" Jessie crawled a few feet away and sat leaning against the wall. "Matt, you're bleeding," she whispered.

"Damned if I know." He wiped at the blood trickling down his arm. "Stay put."

"Be careful," she pleaded, watching him crawl toward the side of her cottage before he slowly stood.

"I will." He held the gun ready in his hand and

waited. Every muscle in his body tensed at the thought of someone waiting for her inside. He didn't want to even think about what could have happened if he hadn't been with her. The security light at the front of her cottage suddenly illuminated the front of the cottage. Matt crept quietly along the side exterior until he caught a visual of their attacker. He exchanged gunfire. Several rounds went back and forth, with two striking too close for Matt's comfort. If he wanted to get the guy, he would need help soon. As he reached for his phone a flare of bullets kept him pinned against the side of the house, shredding the wood siding and sending pieces of wood flying through the air like shrapnel. From the other side of the cottage shots rang out, and the hooded figure fired several times as he raced into the dark cover of the woods.

"Are you okay, Matt? I came as soon as I heard the shots. More help is on the way," Dylan told him.

"I was trying to call you, but couldn't get my phone out of my pocket. The damn light made me a target. He could see me, but he was far enough away that I couldn't see him."

"Should I pursue him?" Dylan asked. "You're in no condition to do so." He pointed at the blood running down his arm.

"It's a scratch. You can't go in that woods without lots of backup and daylight. By then, he'll be gone. Our suspect was sporting some form of rapid-fire weapon. I need to check on Jess."

"I think she's shaken. She was leaning against the wall holding her side when I rushed past her."

"Jess, sweetheart, are you okay?" Matt walked up beside her.

"How did he get into my house?" Her voice trembled. "I need to know. I saw you set the alarm."

"I have a crew on the way to help figure that out." He slipped his arm around her shoulder.

"Matt, you're still bleeding!" Her face paled when her hand touched his wet arm, and she glanced at the blood that covered her hand.

"I'll let them check me out as soon as they get here. Let's get you inside." He opened the door for her.

"Is it safe?" she asked.

"Dylan has already checked it out He went in the front door, and he's waiting for us inside. Besides, we'll be safer in there than we are standing out here. The guy could double back around."

"Of course you're right. We should go in." She shivered. "I have no idea why I'm so rattled." She frowned. "It's just that I had planned a special evening and never imagined a night like this. I didn't include being nearly killed into my plans for the evening or you being shot." She walked in the door he held open. "He was waiting in my house." She rubbed her arms. "My space has been my safe haven. I'm not sure I'll ever feel safe in here again."

"That doesn't sound like my girl. You've taken on a couple of suspects right here in your house. Have you forgotten? You're tough, and we'll get through this together."

"I remember, but I don't want to." She shuddered. "I've tried hard to forget those moments. Right now, I'm stunned, but I'm sure I'll be mad before long. He ruined our evening."

After the crew arrived, the medic cleaned and bandaged Matt's surface shrapnel wound. His team went over the house, dusting the doors and surfaces for prints.

"Matt, we found the entry point." Matt followed Kip into Jessie's bedroom. "He pried open a window in her room and then disabled the alarm." Kip pointed at the smashed unit with its wires hanging out. "The alarm should have alerted the company anyway when it was tampered with. I'm not sure why it didn't. Unless he had the code to disarm it first and then did this for show."

"How would he get the code?" Jessie asked.

"Maybe he hacked into the system," Gary said. "It's possible he did an override on your security system. I'll check it out for you."

"Someone can do that?" Matt asked.

"Yes. Thankfully it's not that easy to do. He would have to know his way around a computer or know someone who does." Gary whistled when he saw the smashed panel. "If we design a stronger security system, someone will find a way around it. That's the downside of the internet."

Matt had Jessie search her house to see if anything was missing. He didn't believe it was a robbery but wanted to make sure. He also wanted to keep her busy with less time to think. The next few hours were spent securing the house and establishing a security detail for the night.

"Jess, I would feel better if you didn't stay here tonight. Dylan said you could stay at the inn tonight. You look tired, and we won't be done here for a while yet."

"I'm spooked, and believe me, I don't want to stay here alone. I'll pack a few things. I don't want to come back unless you're with me." Jessie went into her room and packed what she needed into her small case. She picked up her computer and was ready to go.

"Katie has a room ready for you," Dylan told her.

"I'll walk her over." Matt reached for her hand. "We'll decide where you'll stay tomorrow later. I want you to rest. I have a couple officers at the inn too." He kissed her when they reached the back door of the inn. "I love you, Jess."

"I love you, too." She walked in the door and closed it.

Matt walked back to the cottage. They had both come close to losing their lives tonight. If he hadn't paused to kiss her and instead sent her in the door first as he held it open like he usually did, the night would have ended differently. Those keys slipping out of his hand had them both bending down at the right moment. Another one to add to the list of those strange occurrences that saved their lives.

As soon as he walked in the door of Jessie's cottage, Kip called out to him. "Matt, you need to see what I found."

****

Jessie stretched out on the large comfy bed. Her legs trembled beneath the covers, and pesky tears flowed from her eyes. No matter how hard she tried, she couldn't control either reaction. Her mind rushed through how the night had played out. The dropped keys that might have saved their lives followed by the awful sound of the gun and the wood splintering around them refused to leave her memory. The sensation and sound replayed through her mind every time she started to relax. Sitting up, she turned the bedside lamp on and glanced around the room, hoping to calm her teetering emotions. She had forgotten how lovely the inn was, which didn't seem important at the moment. Her place of refuge had become a nightmare for her.

Katie had tried hard to soothe her rattled nerves. Her friend hadn't lectured her as she had on other occasions but seemed genuinely concerned. Katie wrapped her in a huge hug and brought her right up to the room with a cup of tea, reassuring her every step of the way that she would be safe. They cried together until she could find a measure of control. The simple memory of her friend's kindness sent her emotions careening again and threatened to start the tear deluge all over again. She took a deep calming breath with hopes that it might help. She reached for another tissue.

Was this awful stifling feeling of her dream coming to reality? She knew this sensation. She had experienced the manifestation before. Could he be back in another form, or was it someone else? *Think, girl. He threatened that you would meet again.* In the current atmosphere, anything was possible.

She closed her eyes, remembering the case. It was her first experience with inter-dimensional travel. A highly anticipated trip to a booksellers' convention in Boston had led her to a beautiful B&B outside of the city. She was there to see the latest books and to learn marketing tips for her new bookstore. Matt was going to join her for the weekend, but boy, were their plans upended. Jessie sighed. Flexible seemed to be optimum for her and Matt's dating life.

The first night in her room, a mirror fell off the wall—more like it was thrown from the wall—which was only one of many strange things that happened. A couple of nights, Jessie was awakened by a beautiful young woman crying while pleading for her help from inside a mirror. The experience both fascinated and scared her. But the investigator in her was determined to find out the woman's identity. Thankfully, Matt understood her need to follow a story once she was hooked. But even she had no idea where that one would take at the time.

Awakened once again, she picked up an antique key from the strange-looking bureau in her room and found herself being lifted, pushed, and pulled through a portal to another dimension to solve the murder of twin sisters, Kimberly and Hope. It was an experience which changed her life and altered her thinking in so many ways. Jessie shook her head. Up to this point in her life, she had been somewhat naïve.

Garrett Massey, an odd little man staying at the inn, followed her through the portal into the sixties and a strange hippie commune where she had landed. She met Skylar at the commune, who would one day be Garrett Massey. Trying to sort through the moving pieces even now seemed as strange as they were at the time. The more she learned about both of the men, the stranger that case became. Massey had died at in the same hospital as Skylar. Skylar jumped into Massey's body when he died. Even thinking about the possibility of it caused her to doubt the whole sordid affair ever happened, and yet it had. If what she sensed tonight was correct, a traveler might be back and sporting a new body. Skylar in Massey's body had told her he would be back to fight again. In her new world anything was possible, so it would seem. Tonight, the atmosphere seemed similar and yet different. She wasn't making any sense. It was that difference that left her shaking her head.

If Matt could go through all the strangeness of the past year and still love her, she had found a keeper and the right guy. But she couldn't help wondering what he would say when she told him it was possible that Skylar was back, or possibly someone like him. She still had a lot to learn about the world in which she found herself.

The hippie commune where she first met Skylar was her first experience of the sixties. To say it was a culture shock was an understatement. A frown marred her face when she thought about how Skylar manipulated all the girls, like Clover and Essence, who followed him. He groomed them to become one of his wives. He enticed them in with his strange religion and enslaved them in servitude to him. He had tried the same with her, but thankfully Clover helped her escape.

During their investigation, she learned that at some point Skylar had brought one of his grandsons through the portal when the young man was old enough to make it on his own. Corbitt followed in his grandfather's steps and now was in prison. A bad actor like his grandpa. Jessie helped to put him behind bars for running a sex ring that enslaved young women, also like his grandfather. She would never forget how Skylar had convinced those girls at the commune to serve him and follow his self-serving religion.

The sixties were both strange and awesome. Besides the cool clothes and the women's rights movement her favorite highlight was seeing Bob Dylan and Joan Baez in concert. It was a special connection she shared with her grandmother who was also at that concert. How many people could say they shared the experience of life in the sixties with their grandmother? After seeing the photos of Grandpa Max with his long hair and hearing about him living on a commune, she understood him better and why Grams loved him so much. At one point, he even lived in a tree house in the redwoods. She couldn't wait to tell Matt that part of the story. The part about Skylar possibly being back, she might need to wait to tell him until later when she was sure.

Chapter 5

"That bullet could have killed her. If I hadn't dropped those keys…" Matt shook his head as the shivers raced down his back.

"Truth is, you're both lucky. Bending down had the same effect as ducking at the right moment. It saved both of your lives." Dylan clapped him on the back. "What do you want to do about the note Kip found? She'll have to know. Maybe it will make more sense to her than it does to us."

"I have a theory about its origin, but I want to hear what she says first. My idea is far out of my normal thinking." Matt frowned, still feeling a bit shaky.

"Maybe that's a good thing. When it comes to Jessie and her cousin, nothing is out of the realm of possibility," Dylan said. "You need to go home and get some rest. Jessie is safe, we're almost done here, and there's nothing more for you to do tonight. You can hit the ground running in the morning."

"I want the woods searched tomorrow. He'll be long gone, but maybe he left us a few clues."

"One can hope. Now go home." Dylan nudged him toward the door. "I'll call Tom Maxwell. We'll need the FBI labs on this one, and maybe some help."

"Sounds good. If he has any questions, tell him to call me." Matt glanced at Dylan, "For me, it was déjà vu. I've been here before." He raked his hand through his hair. "There was something familiar and yet unlike anything I've ever experienced before. One thing I'm sure of—if he had wanted us dead, we both would be. There was nothing stopping him from killing us. No dropped keys, no screen door, not even I could have done anything if he meant to kill us. We would be dead. We were outgunned, believe me. He shot over us. There's no way I could have stopped him, and that will eat at me. I was caught completely off guard."

"All of us would be. Don't be too hard on yourself, man," Dylan told him. "Familiar how?" Dylan's hand fisted at his side.

"Like the note says, he's back to finish what he started. Maybe when she reads his words it will trigger a memory. Knowing her, she's already analyzing what she sensed." Matt opened the screen door and paused. "Hell, he's familiar to me, but I have no idea how. I couldn't see him. Call it a gut feeling. He's been around before."

Matt walked out the door. His evening hadn't gone as he had planned, and damned if he hadn't almost lost her in the process. Jessie was right when she said that there was a rising feeling of discontent worldwide. The warnings coming from the FBI director were enough to keep him up at night. Throw in the strange that often came with Jessie, and he had no idea what the next days or weeks would bring.

He started his car and glanced toward the inn. At least for the night, she was safe. He needed to hear her voice to be sure. "I hope I didn't wake you," he told her when she answered his call.

"No, I couldn't sleep. I've been thinking."

"I figured you might be, and that's why I risked

calling you." Matt turned onto the road into town. "Tell me what you've got so far."

"I've sensed dealing with a situation like this before. Not the gun, of course. That was scary. I've had the strangest feeling that he wasn't trying to kill us, or we would both be dead. At this point, he's giving me a message. We will meet."

"He said as much in the note he left you. I'll let you read it tomorrow. Try to get some rest. I'll stop by your store in the morning. I will make sure we have eyes on the bookstore. I don't want any surprises."

"As much as I appreciate those words, I think we are bound to have more than a few surprises in the next few weeks. The best we can hope for is that it won't be too rough of a ride. At least, I have some good things to share with you about our trip. And we still need to talk about our future." She paused. "If we have one," she mumbled under her breath.

"I didn't catch that. What did you say?" Matt asked.

"Nothing important. Just complaining. I'll see you tomorrow."

****

Jessie was sure when she closed her eyes that she wouldn't be able to sleep. The sounds and smell of that gun would remain with her for a lifetime. Did people ever really get over the trauma of what they went through? She had seen too many news stories, and now she had seen the power of that gun. She was still alive, but only because the gunman hadn't intended for her to die yet. How she would love to be back in Ireland, if only to escape the madness of the moment.

She glanced at her notepad before shutting off the

lamp and let her mind wander to try to settle the angst she could still sense threatening to overtake her. Jessie's ancestral look-alike, according to the record they discovered, was Johanna Campbell, who married Patrick Murphy and lived in the Kilkenny area. The one image, a painted miniature which was found among some keepsakes of Johanna's, showed she had curly hair like her own. The records mentioned her date of birth, her wedding date, and the date of her death. Johanna had been the mother of two boys and three girls.

The trip to Kilkenny was one of the highlights of the trips for Jessie. She could imagine Johanna walking in the places where she now walked. Of course, no gleaming cosmopolitan city would have existed there then, but her mind was able to push that aside. Jessie read through her musings.

Kilkenny is a modern city, in the heart of Southeast Ireland and situated on the River Nore. Today I learned there was a monastery on the site dating back to the sixth century. A bit mind-blowing for me to understand. My country is young in comparison. In the twelfth century when the Normans invaded this part of Ireland, they built the castle that I was standing in front of and admiring. I admit I got caught up trying to imagine the people who might have lived behind those walls over all the many years. The knights, lords, and ladies who found their way behind the castle walls. Impenetrable, the walls stood strong to this day. I can't help but wonder how many had found refuge there.

The town simply grew up around the beautiful castle and left intact many of the medieval buildings peppered throughout the city. I would describe it as a modern city with an Old-World feel. All the generations who must have seen some of the very same sights, including Johanna, made me feel small and yet connected to every human in that moment. The idea gave me goose bumps.

We ate at the Inn Kyteler after a day of touring. The story goes that the Dame Alice Kyteler was the last witch in Ireland. She was born in Kilkenny in 1280. Widowed four times, she was accused of poisoning all four of her husbands. Shivers ran down my back when we learned that the inn where we were eating was situated on the site of her former home. Interesting stories followed us wherever we went, and I found the idea of the strange, unusual, and magical being at home all over this beautiful country somewhat comforting. I'm not so strange after all.

We stayed at a lovely B&B with the kindest hosts, who knew the history of the area well. Our stay included dining at a few fine restaurants in the area as well as several great cozy cafes recommended by the locals at all of our stops. Throw in a couple of the famous pubs and listening to live music, and we got our fill of the people and the culture of the area. We saw much of this beautiful area, but I will expound on a few of the gems that stand out to me.

During our time in Kilkenny, we took several tours including one to the Cliffs of Moher, one of my favorite spots, and to the Kilkenny Castle with its beautiful grounds and gardens which Peyton loved. She told us it was the perfect setting for a medieval romance novel, and I agreed. Another special highlight was the tour of Jerpoint Park, a deserted twelfth-century medieval town. The caretaker was engaging and an amazing storyteller. Grams said he could really spin a yarn, and she was right. It was such a great place for traipsing through ruins and lost places. With the tombs of noble families, the tomb Effigy of St. Nicholas, and the impressive ghostly imprint of the lost town, we were made to see the magic of the place. I love history, and even more so after this trip. But it was at the Cliffs of Moher that the vision of the rising tide first appeared to me. The dream came each night that we were in the area. The whole experience made me wonder what Johanna had experienced in her time. I have sensed a connection to my distant relative, as though she still roams the area.

Jessie rolled over onto her side. How any of what she read fit into what happened to her tonight she had no idea. But time would tell if it did at all. And if any of the facts aligned, then Matt would need to hear about it. Gosh, with all the madness of the evening, she still hadn't had time to tell him her decision or the highlights of the trip. Mostly they had talked about her dream, which was all right, but there were so many positive things too. She didn't want him to get the wrong idea about what had truly been a life-changing, amazing trip. They would definitely have to go there together.

Jessie's ringing phone stopped her thoughts. She glanced at the caller's ID. "Hi, Peyton."

"I heard what happened. Dylan filled Jaxon in on your evening. How are you?"

"Truthfully, I'm still shaking. It was awful." Her voice quivered as she reached for another tissue.

"We got home a while after you. Jaxon took me to see his house since he moved in. I'll tell you about that later. I can't believe the guy was in your house. Do you have any ideas on who it was? Jaxon said it didn't sound like it would be a robbery."

"I don't think it was." Jessie explained her theory about the gunman.

"Then what I'm about to tell you will blow your mind—or maybe not," Peyton told her.

"I'm not sure anything will surprise me anymore."

"My sister called me earlier. She told me about something strange that happened at the hospital. The doctors and nurses involved are still all abuzz about it. She wasn't on the floor at the time, but had taken a dinner break. She had seen both of the people involved when they were first brought in." Peyton exhaled. "I've never heard Madison this rattled."

"What happened?" Jessie asked.

"Well, it seems that a man listed on the hospital records as Edwards died soon after arriving in the ER, from a heart attack. All attempts to revive him failed. Right before him, a young gang member arrived by air ambulance at the hospital and was rushed into surgery barely clinging to life. He had a gunshot wound to his upper stomach area. In the end, the surgical team couldn't save him. Both of their deaths had been called minutes apart. Someone from the morgue had come up to take the young man's body. Before the attending nurse could unhook all the wires from the young man, the heart monitor started to beep again and recorded a steady heartbeat."

"Let me guess. The doctors who worked on him all were saying there is no way the young man could have survived."

"Exactly, and that's not all," Peyton told her.

"I know," Jessie said. "His bloodwork didn't appear to be the same, and they are totally baffled by it."

"You've got that right. While they were poring over the test results, the young man took off the heart monitor and hospital gown, stole someone's clothes, and left. It sounds like that report you had me read about Garrett Massey. Add to that, the heart attack victim was wearing a red ball cap. Does that remind you of anything?" Peyton asked.

"Are you talking about the Edwards guy in the Arizona case who had the blood of a man who died before him?"

"Yes, he had worked as a custodian at the station and was one of the shooters that night. He always wore a red hat, and that was never found. Maybe he simply jumped bodies and took his hat with him, which sounds weird even to me. The guy that died was a big man though, and Edwards wasn't, so I'm not sure if he's the same man. Madison told me the hospital staff is still talking about it. What do you think?"

"If I have to venture a guess, we have a traveler who could have been a nondescript criminal in Arizona maybe. Now he's a gang member with a gun, and he was in my house using that weapon tonight."

"Now what?" Peyton asked.

"I'm not sure. I was thinking about how Ireland showed us that the strange and magical was real and how comforting that was. I can't help but wonder if the man from the hospital was the one following us in Ireland. From the sounds of it, he couldn't have been a jogger, though. Of course, there are other travelers out there, and it might be someone new that we don't know of yet. That is the downside of the travelers. But as much as I want to say I felt this before, this time feels slightly different."

"You could have gone weeks without telling me that. You're right, of course."

"The truth is, you never know when one of these bad dudes is going to show up and take it all to the darker side. But there must be an upside to being on the side of good." Jessie repositioned the pillow at her back.

"There has to be or why else would we need this ability at all? If in the end, evil were to prevail and good was to fall by the wayside, what would be the purpose of all this? Nope, I can't believe that. I'm a firm believer that good wins, at least I hope it does. Kindness once given is never wasted, as Grams often tells us. But having said that, what are we going to do about a man who may or may not be a traveler with a gun?" Peyton asked.

"Good question. I have a theory though. If he had wanted to kill us tonight, we both would be dead. I think he was announcing his arrival. Now all we have to do is figure out who he is and why he's here at all."

"Whew, that's a small feat," Peyton said with a touch of sarcasm.

Chapter 6

After Peyton hung up, Jessie pulled the covers up tight around her. The air was warm in the room, but the shivers she had running down her arms were real. It didn't matter whether he meant to kill them or not. The sound of the gunfire erupting around them sending pieces of the screen door and glass spraying down upon them was more than enough to convince her that she didn't want to stand up against that gun again anytime soon. She had no idea of the traveler's identity or why he would come back at this time, but the atmosphere seemed conducive to him being here. An angry, manipulative man from the past running around with a high-powered assault rifle was the stuff nightmares were made of, along with endless wakeful hours of trying to figure out the whys.

"But not tonight, girl." Jessie glanced into the darkness and yawned. As soon as the words left her mouth, the thoughts raced in again. There had to be a reason that included far more than revenge on her. Was he here on some kind of mission? She could try reasoning it out, but as Reba always said, it would reveal itself in time. "Enough is enough." She rolled over onto her side and sighed. "Just once it would be nice to have a few of the answers up front," she muttered. Simply thinking about that sound of the gun had the power to stop her in her tracks. She pulled the blanket over her head.

****

Matt tapped on the glass pane. He knew when her head jerked around with her eyes wide open and her lower lip drawn between her teeth that his girl was still a mite jumpy. Truth be told, so was he. He had faced a lot of tough situations in his job, but had never experienced such a helpless feeling as he had last night. He would have to find a way to remedy that soon. He never wanted to be at such a disadvantage again. He wanted answers, and he'd find them. He waved at her as she recognized who was standing there. Her smile was real enough, and he gave her one back.

"Why are you here so early?" she asked as she opened the door.

"Good morning to you too, sweetheart." He kissed her cheek as he passed her. "I wanted to check on you before I went to the station. Were you able to sleep at all?"

"I finally nodded off. How about you?" She watched out the front window as a man rushed past the store and then glanced back at Matt.

"Same, but it was a short night." He reached for her hand. "We'll have eyes on your store in case of an unwanted visitor, but you can relax. You won't know we're here."

"That's good," she said absentmindedly.

"Are you okay, Jess? You seem distracted," Matt goaded her. "You seem listless."

"Well, duh." She pointed her finger at him. "I think I might have earned the right to be a smidge distracted after last night." She poked his chest.

He grabbed her finger. "Yes, as long as you don't

lose your fight, but I can see it's still firmly in place." He grinned.

"Sorry, I tend to get riled up when a man challenges me, or when I'm shot at. I honestly believe I need to keep a list of all the times someone thought they could point a gun at me. Not only people living in the here and now but those who keep popping back in my life after I think they're gone." She slapped her hand to her head. "What's up with that?"

"I thought your mind might be going there. It's a bit hard to plan for someone who could come around again looking quite different from year to year. Tell me your theory on how he came to us in a gangbanger's body." He led her to one of the chairs and pulled it out for her. He nudged her to take a seat. "I'm sure it's bound to be interesting," he mumbled under his breath.

"It's not just a theory. This time I have the testimony of hospital staff, all thanks to Peyton's sister Madison." Jessie told him about the strange happenings at the hospital where Madison worked in New York. "The crazy thing is we think the man Edwards, who everyone thought had died in Arizona, who was one of the shooters that night Peyton was hit, might be the man in the hospital who died a few nights ago. But he doesn't sound like the same man. Labs and blood tests may or may not confirm the fact. The man arrived at the hospital wearing a red ball cap, which was a clue from the case in Arizona, but lots of people wear red ball caps. The same name may be a coincidence. Anyway, I digress. The man named Edwards died soon after he arrived at the hospital. I think it's possible he jumped into the body of a young man identified as Bobby Bristol, who was dying, and who the team of docs couldn't save. The doctors said that there was no way that he could've recovered. The bullet had torn through too many vital organs, and he had lost too much blood. We're talking about another crazy mystery." She twisted one of her curls around her finger. "The one fact we know at this point is we are dealing with a possible traveler who is now named Bobby, who may be Skylar, or Edwards, or someone else from the past or possibly the future even. A traveler or something worse, armed with a weapon of war."

Matt frowned. "I was sure you were going there, but knowing the possibility doesn't make the facts any easier to swallow. How can this situation be fought logically? I'll add another fact that might take it up a notch. We had a young man shot and dumped at the side of road who, once he was stabilized, was transported by air ambulance to a hospital in New York. I'm wondering if he's the same guy."

"I have no idea on either count." Jessie glanced at him. "How can you find out?"

"I can trace down what hospital he was sent to. I'm going to do it as soon as I get to work. He had a weapon on him when we found him."

"Speaking of guns. You do understand how potent that one was last night. On the battlefield from five hundred yards away it was made to do unbelievable damage to a human. The bullets expand as they move through the body to cause maximum harm. He was shooting from inside my house from only a few feet away. I want to know why we weren't killed."

"I'm wondering the same thing. Police are seeing more of the big guns than we used too, Jess. There is also the problem of the unregistered and untraceable homemade weapons called ghost guns. They can be made with a 3D printer or from a kit. And they are impossible to trace. How many of those guns are out there, it's hard to know." He pushed his chair back and started to stand. "Not to change the subject, but did you have anything good happen on your trip? I could use some good news." He smiled when she nodded.

"Our trip was amazing. I have lots to tell you. I wrote the important details in a journal."

"Of course you did. I look forward to hearing them." He gave her his hand as she went to stand. "If it's okay with you, I'd prefer that you didn't stay at your house alone. At least while the repairs are going on. You can stay at the inn, or I have a guest room. You can choose. I'll go with you to your house after work to pick up some more clothes."

"Sounds good. I would prefer not to stay alone either, for now. At least, until I know what the guy is up to. I'll think about where, but I'm not sure I want to put the inn in the crosshairs either." She followed him to the door.

"Jess, be careful. If you see anything or sense something out of the ordinary, let me know the minute you do." He opened the doors into the coffee shop. He gave her a brief kiss. "Wait for me before you leave after work."

"I will." She locked the doors after he closed them.

****

As soon as Jessie opened for the morning, Reba pulled up in front of the store, followed close behind by Peyton, and after them, several customers. Her day was on the fast track. The rush was over an hour later. Jessie was happy to finally sit in the chair across from Reba.

"You've had quite a rush of customers this morning. You girls haven't had a minute's rest. I'm sure that's good for your bottom line, but I was hoping we could chat leisurely. Not that I'm in a hurry. What's up with all the customers?" Reba closed the magazine she had been reading.

"I have no idea, but I'm glad for the business." Jessie smiled.

"Before we know it, the summer will be over, and it will be back to working at the school for me. I've enjoyed talking to grownups and love to watch Sadie read to the children." Peyton sat next to Reba after she checked out the woman she had been helping.

"Being gone for a month has made the summer seem shorter to me," Jessie told them. "Speaking of Grams, she'll be here in an hour to do a children's story hour."

"We don't have a lot of time. Earlier, Peyton told me about the close call that you and that handsome man of yours had last night." Reba patted Jessie's hand. "Are you okay? Does Sadie know?"

"Yes, I'm okay, but Grams doesn't know yet." Jessie lowered her voice. "The truth is, I'm convinced that if he had wanted us dead, we would be, which has me wondering what the guy's end game is."

"Well now, that's something to think about, isn't it?" Reba pursed her lips. "He's from the past, as you know, and yet is part of the present equally. Both of you girls have dealt with him on some level without understanding his purpose for being here. I think this is more about a mission than wanting to kill you. Time will reveal his real motive. In the meantime, he will be a menace and cause more harm than good. Matt will have his hands full. Like in your dream, troubled waters are rising. With each wave, anger and violence are rushing in with the tide."

"There's a comforting thought." Jessie frowned. "I want normal again."

"Me too," Peyton chimed in.

"I'm afraid, my dears, there's an upheaval in the world, and I'm not sure if anything will seem normal again. Change happens and our normal often shifts with it whether we want it to or not."

"I'll go on record as saying I don't want a new normal." Jessie stood when another customer came in.

"No one thinks they do, my girl, but sometimes we need a better normal and an alteration is in order. Look at all of the changes that have come your way this past year. Tell me, if you can, which one wasn't for the better in your life in some way."

"You're right, of course. It's anticipating what might happen that makes the whole concept unacceptable. I'm sure we'll make peace with the idea over time. But for now, I don't want to think about the topic anymore." Jessie went to help another customer.

Later as she listened to Sadie read to the kids, she almost forgot about the night she had experienced and what Reba had said earlier. There were moments like the present one that allowed her to believe her kind of normal was a possibility and not far from her reach. Grams loved the kids, and they loved her. She was patient during their many interruptions and with the odd subjects that the simple story aroused in their active little minds. Jessie found herself smiling more than once at their all-consuming questions and how imaginative they were. She could listen to them all day.

But Reba's words pushed the children's questions out of her mind and brought reality crashing back on her along with the memory of her dream. Last night was unusual on too many levels to count, and she wished she could figure out what made it feel different. It wasn't only the gun. It was the challenge the gunman had sent her way. Was he Skylar, returned for one of his nefarious reasons? But why would he pick this time to come waltzing back into her life, if at all? Why now, when she had finally decided she wanted to marry Matt and was ready to set the date? Were the two connected? Only time would reveal the answer. And how would Matt take the news if Skylar could be here to challenge him for her? Clover had warned her when she helped Jessie escape, Skylar never gave up when he wanted something. At this point, what she thought she knew was way too complicated for her to grasp. She was letting her crazy thinking run away with her. Enough was enough! All she had to do was get through the rest of the day until Matt got here.

Chapter 7

Matt had spent most of the day dealing with angry skirmishes all over town. He couldn't remember a day when there were these many irate people fighting with one another for the dumbest reasons. There were several domestic violence calls, which left him wondering if no one worked anymore. What were all the men doing home during the day? After a day like today, he could see why Jess struggled with the idea of marriage. There were some real losers out there.

Most officers, including his own, didn't like to find themselves in the midst of domestic calls. Matt didn't like dealing with them himself.

Kip knocked on his open door.

"Come in. You look like hell." Matt pointed at the chair in front of his desk.

Kip plopped into the chair. "Funny you should use that analogy. I feel like I was in the middle of it. That was the strangest family situation I've ever been in the midst of." Kip shook his head.

"How so?" Matt asked his lips turning up at the corner despite his good intentions.

"The girl's parents wanted our help to get their daughter out of the house and away from her husband. Here's the kicker—she wasn't legally married to him because the man was still married to what she thought was his ex-wife. We're talking bigamy. Of course, the parents got there first, and the man wasn't at work like they had hoped he would be. It was a hell of mess."

Matt chuckled. "Sounds like it. What happened?"

"I'm glad you can find some humor in it. Although, there was nothing funny at the time. I arrived on scene as the man was doubling up his fist to hit the girl's father, who had tried to shove the man's hands away from his daughter. We are talking about a middle-aged man taking on a big guy. I mean, bodybuilding type. I stepped in and pushed the father out of the way and then had to duck quick myself. That guy's fist went into the fridge door, and I swear it dented it. The damn door has his fist permanently etched into it. I hate to think what it would have done to my face."

"What happened to the girl?" he asked.

"She went screaming and crying with her parents, who were threatening to sue the man through their expletives." Kip grinned. "I can laugh now, but it wasn't funny at the time."

"No, I imagine it wasn't." Matt smiled. "Where's the man now?"

"He's in a jail cell cooling his heels after he tried to take another shot at me. Dylan cuffed him." Kip stood. "No more domestic calls for me today, thank you. I'm still shaking from this one. Not only was the guy big, but he was also strong. I can only imagine what his fist was capable of. I hope they can keep their daughter far away from him."

"I'm glad his fist didn't connect with your good-looking face." Matt laughed.

"Yeah, yeah." Kip left Matt's office.

He hoped Jessie's day was faring better. Jaxon said the Hanover police were calling their office in frustration, wanting to know if there were any credible threats in the area. At least for their two towns, the tensions were heightened. Some days were like that. He hadn't had many since becoming chief, but the cove had had more than its share of crime since Jessie came to town. No, he wasn't blaming the rising crime rates on her. It was obvious to anyone who did their research the criminals had been operating there for a while and Jessie was the one that found them. He couldn't wait to hear what she had to say when he told her about his day.

He texted Jessie to let her know he was on his way. He put his phone in his pocket and stopped by the holding area to take a look at the man pacing inside the cell. Kip wasn't exaggerating—that guy had some big biceps. Kip's face wouldn't have fared well. He stopped by Dylan's office to see if there was anything new on the investigation from the shooting the night before and gave him the name Bobby Bristol. He filled Dylan in on what Jessie told him.

"This could be another strange case, and I thought you might need to be prepared. I want you to be lead investigator on this one. It hits too close to home for me," Matt told him. "I ran him through the system. He's the same guy that was transferred by air ambulance out of here, and that's where the story gets more interesting. Bristol was raised by a single mom after his dad left. His father is serving time for armed robbery. There's more to the story." He told Dylan about Madison's account from the hospital. "I have a call in to the docs who worked on him. I want to hear their take on the story." He put his hand up to stop Dylan's question. "Don't ask me how any of this is possible. I have no idea, but you get it."

"Keep me in the loop on what they tell you, as well as anything Jessie senses. I've been around long enough to know how this works. She's in the know. I've been thinking about it most of the day. You were right when you said if he wanted you dead you would be. Still, I can't help wondering why here and why now?"

"You and me both. If you're headed out, I'll walk with you." Matt glanced at his phone and stuck it in his pocket.

"Sounds good. Katie is worried that if the guy knows Jessie is at the inn, he might come there looking for her. She doesn't want to put the guests' lives in jeopardy. But I know Jessie'd be safer there than at her cottage."

"I agree with Katie. I'm concerned for Peyton too. If he realizes they are cousins, who knows what he might do? I think neither one should stay in those cottages. I told Jaxon that earlier. I think I'll bring them both to my house. They can keep each other company, and Jaxon and I can watch over them."

"They won't like it." Dylan chuckled.

"I know, but I'll ask. I think Jessie is scared enough to play it safe even if she doesn't like it. At least, I hope so. I don't want to fight her."

They talked as they walked out to their cars. Matt was confident in Dylan leading the investigation. Hopefully, Jessie would be good with his suggestions as well.

****

Jessie was waiting for him when he pulled in beside her car. "I've been thinking that maybe Peyton and I should stay at your place. I don't want to put the inn in the center of anything. Katie would never forgive me if anything happened to one of her guests."

"That's sounds like a good idea. Why Peyton?" he asked.

"If Bobby is anything like Skylar in the past, he has a thing about pretty women, and my cousin is that. I already talked to her, and she agreed it would be the smart thing to do. Jaxon is going to follow her over. They are getting her belongings now. I have some in the car, but I need to get a few more outfits in case I'm at your place for more than a few days."

"Sounds good. Let's get it done and get out of here." They walked hand in hand to her cottage. The screen door had been removed and was leaning up against the siding.

"It looks like they're already starting to clean up." She walked through the open door where she could see the damage the bullets did to a few of her belongings. Her sofa would need to be replaced, along with her desk. She made mental notes on her way to the room to pack a few more outfits. Way too many holes to count in the drywall and window. Pillows and cushion stuffing made it look as though it had snowed in her living room. Her fists clenched. This guy had messed with the wrong person this time.

After she packed the last pair of shoes, she rolled her suitcase into the living room where Matt was talking to someone from the FBI crime lab. "Are you ready?"

"As ready as I'll ever be." She handed him the handle to her case. She reached for a few items in one of her desk drawers and stuffed them into the bag she carried in her hand. "Let's go."

"I'm sorry you're being upended again." He put her case in her car and opened the door for her.

"It's not your fault. It is what it is." She slid into the driver's seat.

"I'll follow you and see you at the house."

"Sounds good." She started her car when he closed the door.

She had wanted to make it easier on Matt. She knew he was sweating the idea of telling her she needed to stay at his place. He had given her the choice, which was really sweet of him, but she knew Katie well enough to know it would be the end of their relationship if Bristol showed up at the inn. She didn't want to risk it. Peyton was another thing, Skylar from the past collected girls like some men collect their toys. She didn't want to risk her cousin being one of his victims. This was the smartest plan all the way around. She felt relief when she pulled into Matt's driveway and saw Peyton and Jaxon standing there. She had no idea when Skylar and Edwards crossed paths or if Edwards was Skylar, or who was in Bristol's body. He was the one that had shot at them last night. She also knew according to Madison that Edwards had died when Bobby came back to life. "Try to put that in a report," she muttered while shaking her head. Matt opened the car door, and she slid out and opened the back door to get her suitcase.

"Well, cousin, here we are again. At least this time I'm okay with it." Jessie hugged Peyton.

"I am too."

Jessie turned to look at the moon shining over the cove and took a few steps away from the others. No matter how many times she had seen a similar sight the past year, it still felt brand-new. She loved any moments of peace she could sense when the world seemed to be shaking around her. Blue Cove was her home, and she had no regrets about moving here. The past year had been challenging, scary, and a bit over the top, but she loved the town. And no one could take that away from her.

Chapter 8

"Earth to Jessie. Are you coming?" Matt put his arm around her shoulders.

"Sorry. I was thinking." She leaned her head against his shoulder.

"I figured as much. About what?"

"Watching the moon glowing over the cove never gets old. I love living here, and I'm not going to let anyone take that from me." Her chin edged up. She glanced at him. "This is one of those precious few calm moments in the midst of the storm. I have to grab each of them when I can."

"I understand. Believe me, I do." He kissed her. "We should go inside. We can make dinner and get you girls settled for the night." He grabbed her suitcase and laptop case. "I want to hear more about your trip."

"Both of us have a lot of stories to tell. The trip was almost perfect. The only way it could have been better is if you had been there to share it with me." She took his free hand that he offered her.

After dinner, Jessie loaded the dishes in the dishwasher while Peyton cleared the table and the guys talked shop. Jessie wasn't paying attention to their talk tonight. She didn't want to chat about the shooting or her theories anymore. The more she thought about what she understood so far, the stranger it became and the less sense the details made. What she needed more than anything was to clear her mind and let what was happening reveal itself to her.

Jessie excused herself early and went into the room she would call home for the duration of her stay. Peyton's room was next to hers. They would share the Jack and Jill bathroom where Jessie placed her toiletries bag on the counter. She flopped down on the bed and turned on her computer. Her first stop was the hospital site where Madison worked. Digging through the information with the list of links that Madison had given her, she read about the two patients. She learned about when they were admitted and their times of death. Madison had sent her the attending physician's reports on each man. The more she read, the more it sounded like the doctor's report on Garett Massey and Skylar. There were similarities yet subtle differences too. Had Matt heard from the attending doctors or read their reports yet? She needed to ask him.

The knock on her door interrupted her thoughts. "Come in."

"Are you busy?" Peyton asked. "Jaxon left and I wanted to see how you are doing before I turn in."

"Have you read the report your sister emailed us?" Jessie asked.

"Not yet. I'll do that before I go to sleep." Peyton sat at the foot of the bed.

"Not light reading. Tomorrow, you can let me know what you think. It's nothing if not interesting." Jessie frowned. "I've been here before and so have you."

"Where is this going? Do you have any idea?" Peyton stood.

"No idea. I only know something big must be up,

but what it is a whole other topic."

"Matt wanted me to tell you if you were still awake, he wants to talk with you. I've done my job. I'll leave you to your research and to Matt, of course." Peyton hugged her. "Sweet dreams."

Jessie stood and stretched her arms over her head. She went in search of Matt. "Hey, handsome. Peyton said you wanted to talk." She stood beside his chair.

"I'm sorry Jaxon and I got to talking. I didn't mean to run you off." Matt reached for her hand.

"That's fine. I wanted to do some research and read over the attending physician's report that Madison sent me. It reads something like Garett Massey's did. I still find that one hard to believe, and I lived it. There were a few notable differences." She squeezed his hand and let him pull her into his lap. "Did you ever contact them today?"

"I did. Bristol was the victim transferred from the Cove Hospital. Both doctors tried to make sense of something that wasn't medically possible. They did their best to spin their findings and sent me their reports." He pulled her tight against him. "I'm not sure where this is going, but I'll do my best to keep us both safe." He stroked her head as she leaned against his shoulder. "Do you have any ideas yet?"

"No. But I wonder if Bristol did any more damage when he ran into the woods. Have you had any calls?" she asked.

"It's odd that you should ask that right now. We had a missing person's report that came in a couple of hours ago. A mother called to say her daughter and her boyfriend had never returned from their run last evening. A team of officers searched the path from the marina and found a severely injured young male in a bush and the girl is missing. I'm waiting for an update from the hospital about the boy. He had lost a lot of blood and was delusional but knew enough to say his girlfriend was missing. He's in surgery now."

"I hope he makes it. I was worried that maybe that's why the guy showed up at this time. He could be a collector of pretty women." Jessie shuddered. "A good starting point, but way too easy."

"For this case, let's call our suspect Bobby Bristol from this point. I know where you're going with this, but no one else will." He touched the dark circles under her eyes. "You need to get some rest. We have someone watching the house, and Jaxon will be also be staying here for a few days starting tomorrow."

"Sounds good. I'm tired." She stood.

"It's not far but I want to walk you to your door. Tomorrow, I want to hear about your trip." He pulled her to his side and walked her down the hall to her bedroom door. Framing her face with his hands, he kissed her goodnight and pushed her gently inside the room and closed the door.

Jessie sighed. How she loved that man. "All you need to do now, girl, is live long enough to set the date and marry the man." She changed into her nightclothes. Stretching out on the bed, she turned back and forth to find a comfortable spot, closed her eyes, and was carried off in her dreams.

She stood gazing out at the sea from the Cliffs of Moher but she wasn't alone. A woman stood there beside her, weeping. Her curly hair reminded Jessie of her own, but her clothes were from another time. When the woman turned to look at her, Jessie felt like she was looking in the mirror. She knew that she was seeing Johanna Murphy.

They reached for each other at the same moment and held tightly. As they watched, the sea began to churn. Each woman saw the troubles visiting their world in their time. The fierce wind swirled around them, chilling the air and sending shivers running down their spines. Each pulled their garments tight around themselves as they clung together. The waves grew in size. and the scene changed before them. Jessie saw those who stormed the land, pillaging Johanna's village as they came, destroying those in their path. Johanna had seen it coming. Jessie could relate. Johanna saved her family and any who listened to her warning, but many others were lost in the tumult. Jessie watched as Johanna grieved the death of her youngest daughter to a fever that killed many in her village, and later as she mourned the death of her eldest son, killed defending his homeland. Standing beside Jessie, holding tightly to her hand, was a woman who had gotten knocked down, known pain, but rose again to touch the lives of all those she came in contact with. Jessie was moved and knew in her heart Johanna was a great woman though unknown to most. How many others were like her? The castle, which seemed beautiful to Jessie when they toured the site on their trip, was a constant reminder to Johanna that her people were oppressed and ruled by outsiders. She saw no romance when she looked at the people who came and went decked in their finery from the lowered drawbridge, only those who stole what belonged to her people.

"I've been allowed to share this moment with you to strengthen and encourage you for your tasks ahead.

You are a woman for your time. We each were given a gift to aid our people. All we can do is make our place in the world better because we've lived. We can't change everything, nor should we try. We can only see and do what we can, but your life can make a difference. Embrace your gift, love lavishly, and help where you can. You will be all the richer for it."

They stood together talking above the roar of the sea for what seemed like days. Jessie didn't want the moment to end. She asked every question that came to her mind. Johanna answered her with great patience, smiling often. Jessie thought she must have sounded naïve, and in truth, she was. The gift was new to her, but having seen the scenes from Johanna's life, she could see how positive this part of her life was and what a blessing she had been given through her family line.

"I must leave now, but you will not forget this time we have shared. I or my words will return to you often when you need them the most." Johanna hugged her tightly and then was gone.

Jessie awakened, her eyes wet from the tears she had cried. The dream seemed as real as when she stood on the cliffs not long ago. Maybe it was real.

****

Matt finished listening to the news. He was tired but his mind refused to shut down. As he walked past Jessie's door, he heard her crying. He knocked. "Jess, can I come in?"

"Yes," she replied softly. She sat up, pulling the covers up to her chin.

"Are you okay?" He flipped on the light. "Damn," he swore under his breath when he saw her tears.

"What's the matter, sweetheart?" He sat at the foot of the bed. Her tears upset him, and he never knew quite what to do to comfort her.

"Don't worry. These are happy tears mingled with a bit of awe, to be exact." She reached for a tissue to wipe her eyes.

"I've never understood how women can cry when they're happy." He raked his hand through his hair.

"You know me. Crying comes easy for me, but tonight it's for a good reason." She smiled at him.

"I remember that about you. I guess I need to learn to deal with your tears better." His fingers tapped on the blanket covering her feet.

"At least you don't pound me on the back." She chuckled. "Do you remember when I told you about Johanna Murphy, who is my ancestral twin?"

"Yes, she was from Kilkenny, right?" he asked.

"Right. Well, tonight we met." Jessie told him about her experience. "It might have been a dream, or real. I don't know at this point. All I know is she seemed real, we hugged, and I saw several events that impacted her life. She was a great woman." Jessie caught the sob rising in her throat, but there was no stopping the tears.

"Here I thought you were upset from what happened last night and finding your life upended again. I wasn't expecting this. You never cease to amaze me. You don't need my comfort at all." He smiled. "I will leave you to process your experience. I'm sure at some point you'll tell me how this fits together with everything else going on." He walked to the side of the bed and kissed her forehead. "Goodnight, sweetheart."

Matt shut off the light on his way out the door. He hadn't known what to expect when he heard her crying, but he would have never guessed what she told him. He lived a fairly tame life compared to hers, and he was good with it. He'd probably cry too if he saw half of what she had since moving to Blue Cove. He wondered how many more women alive were like his girl.

When Matt finally stretched out on the bed, his tired body won the battle against his active mind, and he slept.

Chapter 9

Jessie wrote down everything she could remember of what Johanna had told her. She couldn't help but wonder what it would be like to live in her life for a few days like Peyton had their great-great grandmother Kathryn. What a life they were living. That, of course, was one of the highlights while being chased and shot at was on the downside. Life, it seemed, was a balancing act with just enough good mingled with the bad to keep you pushing forward.

How many times had she felt challenged to keep going all so she could see how this part of her story would end? Was life one big story with each person having a part to play? Choices had to play some part in how a person's life played, didn't they? No answers came; only more questions filled her mind as she got dressed.

She ran the brush through her hair and finished with her favorite lip gloss. A quick glance in the mirror told her there were no visible signs left from her tearful night. The aroma of bacon sizzling rushed her out the door toward the kitchen.

"Good morning, sleepyhead." Matt stood at the stove.

"Something smells good. Who knew I would catch a man that not only looks good in the morning but can cook?" Jessie smiled at him.

"Your coffee is in the carafe with the brown lid. Decaf as you like it. One or more?" he asked, pointing at the bacon.

"One, please." She reached for the plate he handed her and placed a piece of toast and spoonful of scrambled eggs on it. "Has Peyton eaten yet?"

"No." He sat beside her at the table. "Did you get any rest?"

"It took me a while to get there, but I finally did. How about you?"

"I did. I went out almost as soon as my head hit the pillow." Matt placed the rest of the cooked bacon on a piece of paper towel.

"Good morning. Jaxon said hi, and he'll bring dinner tonight." Peyton filled her plate. "This is what I want most." She poured herself a cup of coffee.

"Jaxon will be staying here for a few nights until we see what Bristol is going to do. I thought we could use the help. Because of the young girl who was kidnapped, the FBI will be working this case with us."

"Tom Maxwell is sending Jaxon, right?" Jessie sipped her coffee.

"Affirmative." Matt chuckled. "Jaxon is doomed to work with my department yet. I, for one, am happy to have him." He reached for Jessie's hand. "Did you tell your cousin about what happened last night?"

"Not yet." Jessie glanced at him over the top of her cup.

"Fess up, cous. I knew something was up. I was sure I heard you crying last night." Peyton took a bite of her toast.

Jessie told her about standing on the Cliffs of Moher beside Johanna. "I experienced life through her eyes and then we talked." Jessie told her a few of the wise words that Johanna had shared with her.

"No way," Peyton said. "That's totally awesome."

Matt took their empty plates and loaded the dishwasher. "Ladies, if you're ready, I'll be taking you both to work this morning."

"Why?" Jessie asked. "I'm capable of driving."

"I know that. I'm trying to keep you both safe until Bobby Bristol shows his hand. Work with me, Jess. You can leave your car here in the garage for now. I pulled my truck out to make room for it."

"Sure, whatever." Jessie jumped up. "I'll be right back. I have to get my purse," she said as she headed for the hall and then stopped. "I want to go on record as saying I can keep myself safe and would rather not be at work without a car."

"Me too." Peyton followed and stood beside her cousin.

"Duly noted," Matt told them. "But it doesn't change anything. I'm still taking you both."

****

Matt grinned as he heard their grumbles as they walked down the hallway. He loved that Jessie had someone close in her life who would stand with her in solidarity. Peyton looked like her avenging angel standing beside her, and he knew the reverse was true also. There wasn't anything his girl wouldn't do for her cousin. Both of their lives were in danger until he figured out what Bristol wanted and where the girl he kidnapped was hidden—or if she was still alive. The young boyfriend was lucid enough to talk but wasn't out of the woods yet. His condition was upgraded to serious this morning.

"Are you girls ready? Let's roll. I have a busy day ahead of me." Matt reached for his keys and called them. He picked up his briefcase from the counter and placed his phone in his pocket.

"Wouldn't it be safer if we had a car in case we need a fast getaway option?" Jessie asked, smiling at him.

"Kenny or Gary can be your chauffeur if you need to get away fast. Now quit stalling and get a move on." He gently nudged her in the back. "I have to get to the hospital."

"I take it the young victim is still alive." She saw him nod. "That's a relief. I was worried he might not make it. His situation didn't sound promising last night."

"Don't forget Jaxon is bringing dinner tonight," Peyton said when she joined them. "Whose situation didn't look promising?"

"Come on. I'll tell you all about it in the car." She grabbed Peyton's arm. "Matt is not a patient man when he's waiting." Jessie sauntered out the door he held open, yanked the car door open, and got inside.

"Seems to me, I've been more than patient waiting on you to make up your mind." Matt glanced at Jessie and frowned. He pushed the garage door opener and backed out.

"Now, children, let's behave." Peyton chuckled.

Matt checked the store out before he left them for the day, including the upstairs area that wasn't in use. At the moment it was more of an attic space, but Jess had dreams about enlarging the store and making the upstairs addition a children's section. He thought it was a great idea. Her store seemed to be thriving and made a great place for townsfolk to gather.

After leaving the store, he went straight to the hospital. Jaxon met him there. Matt wasn't sure how they would find the girl, especially if Bristol was a traveler from another time period as Jessie suspected. Jaxon was about to get immersed in the truly bizarre on this investigation. He had already been through a couple of strange cases with Peyton and would do fine. *Maybe he can help me.* Matt chuckled to himself.

Kyle Simpson's injuries may have left him weak, but his recall of detail was admirable. There wasn't a doubt in Matt's mind that the man who shot at them that night also shot Kyle and abducted his girlfriend, Ashley. And the man was Bobby Bristol.

"Did you notice how agitated our victim became when he talked about Ashley? He's concerned for her, and rightfully so. His description of what he saw when he saw the shooter up close would give anyone pause." Jaxon walked with Matt out of the hospital.

"Cold eyes with no sign of life in them doesn't bode well for her safety, and he knows it." Matt shook his head. "It's a damn shame what they went through. How are we going to find the suspect or the girl before he kills her?"

"Good question. Where do you want to start?" Jaxon asked.

"You need to contact the hospital in New York that treated him. You will find his story hard to believe. I've already heard it. Bristol first showed up here half dead from a gunshot wound and dumped on the side of the highway. He was transported to a hospital in New York where Peyton's sister works. The story gets more bizarre from there." Matt told him what Jessie had learned from Peyton's sister. "He fled the hospital only to end up back here, shoot at us, and abduct Ashley. Don't ask me how."

"A good place to start will be to talk to the attending physician." Jaxon shook his head. "Looks like I'll be thinking outside of the box on another one."

"Such is our life. Believe me, the doctors aren't sure what to say about this one either." Matt chuckled. "I could almost see him scratching his head as he told me the details as he knew them."

****

"I forgot you had an upstairs area until I saw Matt coming down the steps earlier. Do you still want to expand up there?" Peyton asked.

"I do. I think it would make a great place for a children's section with books, some toys, and small tables and chairs. I've already talked to a contractor to give me a bid. I will have to put in an elevator, which means I will lose some of the back storage area, but it has to be done according to the city code."

Peyton walked to the front of the store to turn the sign around to open. "Reba is on her way over to see us from the church. Looks like something is up. She's a woman on a mission."

"She'll have to stand in line with the ghost who came in when I opened the doors from the coffee shop. Maybe we shouldn't tell Molly that small detail." Jessie went to greet Reba when she walked in the door. "How are you, dear lady?"

"The question is, how are you?" Reba made her way to the table and sat in her favorite chair. "Something tells me you've learned a few more details since I last talked to you girls."

"You could say that. Peyton can fill you in while I wait on my customer." Jessie went to the front of the store to talk to the woman who had walked in. "May I help you with something?"

"I certainly hope so. I need all the help I can get." The woman glanced at her. "My name is Olivia," the short, dark-haired woman told her. "I've heard several stories about you, and I've come to find out if any of them are true."

The woman hadn't been kidding. She had come armed with many questions that left Jessie shaking her head in wonderment. Where did these people come from?

Chapter 10

"What was that all about? You talked to her long enough. Not only did I bring Reba up to date on Madison's report, but we had time to order goodies and eat half of them too." Peyton lifted her cup to her lips.

"We did save you a scone, dear, but you'll probably have to reheat your tea." Reba pushed the cup toward her. "Microwave it and then fill us in on what your conversation was about."

Jessie carried her mug into the back room to nuke it. How would she explain the conversation she had with the woman? It felt like it was the follow-up to the conversation she had in her dream with Johanna. As hard as it might be to explain, all things in life seemed to be connected when she took the time to see those connections. How merrily she'd tripped through life, never understanding this truth until now. One event was linked to another from one generation to another.

She carried her hot cup of tea back to the table where Reba sat. "My conversation with that sweet woman was a confirmation of sorts to something that happened to me last night. She said she had read some of my articles and wanted to meet me." Jessie smiled. "It's nice to know someone is reading them."

"What happened last night?" Reba asked,

"I'm not sure if the event actually happened or was simply a dream, but it seemed vivid and real to me. I stood on Cliffs of Moher, and my ancestor Johanna Murphy stood beside me for a moment. I saw life in her times through her eyes. We cried together and she expounded several truths that resonated with me, and today, this woman reiterated a few of those same things as she encouraged me. The woman just told me to continue on the path that I'm on." Jessie glanced around the store. "It makes me wonder how many people who come through those doors are otherworldly, making us not so unique."

"I'm sure more than you realize." Reba took a tissue from her purse. "My dear girls, you've been given amazing gifts." She dabbed at her eyes.

"I know that now. It's taken me long enough to figure it out, though." Jessie did a face-palm. "Last night I shared a moment with Johanna, and she spoke in such a way that encouraged me to embrace this strange gift that has been given to me. I asked her many questions, which she patiently answered for me. The awesome thing is that woman who I just talked to encouraged me the same way."

"What kind of questions did you ask Johanna?" Peyton asked.

"Oh, you know—the basics. How did you handle the interruptions to your life, how did you come by the gift, and how did it impact your family?" Jessie sipped her tea. "She answered them by showing me scenes from her life. Her life was normal for the most part until it wasn't, but she said those times rarely affected those around her. Her husband, Patrick, had learned to live with the interruptions because he came to know how special his wife was. Those moments we shared taught me no one's life is normal, whatever that means.

Hardships are a part of life, and it's how we face those times that matters."

"That sounds encouraging." Peyton smiled at her.

"It was, but some of the town's people thought she was a witch. She told me to embrace my life, love lavishly, and help where I can, and my life would be richer for it. Sounds like what Reba has said to us, eh, cous?"

Reba smiled. "I could say I told you so, but I won't. Some truths you must discover for yourself in the best way you can. Now, about the woman who kept you busy all morning. How does she fit in?"

"Good question. She asked about information on certain subjects which made me think at first she was here to ask about books on those topics, but then she told me that I was in this place and time to bring attention to the plight of those who had no voice. I knew then she wasn't an ordinary customer. She also told me my life can make a difference, and with that said she left."

"Cool," Peyton said. "I'm still amazed when that happens."

"These events in our life may be cool, but they aren't the norm for most folks. Think about the ghosts who randomly roam around the store. I want to believe there's a darn good reason for all of this." Jessie scrunched her face. "That's the investigator in me. I need facts."

"You know the truth, girls, even if it's not what you planned for your lives. We must figure out why you've been given two similar messages. There must be a reason. Premonitions and visions are not given for ego only. They are to help change situations for the better.

I'm here to encourage you, and the others are here to prod you to make a difference in your world. Time will reveal how you can be a part of the solution to the dilemma we are facing in our time." Reba drank the last sip of her tea. "I can't wait to hear how Johanna's story fits in with what is happening in Blue Cove and how the knowledge she shared helps you deal with it."

****

Matt and Jaxon had spent time talking to Kyle Simpson at the hospital. He was improving and Matt wanted to get all the information he could about Ashely. He had her photos and physical description. Her parents were willing to help in any way that they could. Matt asked Frank to bring Carlene to town for a track tomorrow. The sooner they could begin the better. The trail might still be warm enough to discover some trace of her location.

What troubled him most was that Jaxon told him earlier about another missing girl in Hanover. Were the two girls' disappearances somehow connected? If the investigation went the way of the others in the past, they were only at the beginning and they would learn of a link sooner rather than later. In his gut he knew their suspect was the connection. But unlike Jessie, he wasn't ready to accept their gunman was someone from the past. He needed more to go on than a feeling.

Jaxon agreed to meet him for lunch armed with new information about the man who came into the field office and more information on the missing girl from Hanover. Starting tomorrow, Jaxon would be working out of an office in Matt's station. The man may as well come to the cove and work permanently with him. Tom Maxwell sent him often enough, and Matt found it rewarding to remind him of the fact often. Matt grinned. Jaxon took it all in stride.

Any time he could meet someone at Joe's for lunch was a win-win for Matt. Jaxon was always keen on the idea too since Peyton was working at the store with Jessie for the summer. Matt would go whenever he could. Jess was the perfect way to break up a stressful day. Besides, knowing her, she probably had something strange happen today at the store and was itching to tell him. Did he want to know? It always dealt his logical brain a major blow even when it moved the case forward.

When all was said and done, he could live with the strangeness as long as it was Jessie seeing all the weird and bizarre and not him. She knew how to spoon-feed the supernatural to him in such a way that he could handle the peculiar along with the way it altered his cases. At least, he thought he was handling the whole process well. Jessie might have another take on the situation.

Considering the fact that a little over a year ago he knew nothing about ghosts and time travelers, he thought he had risen to the occasion quite well for the skeptic that he was. Jessie, on the other hand, must question her sanity every day. After all, she was the one that went through the mirror. Not to mention her latest experience of standing on a cliff in Ireland next to an ancestor from who-knows-what time period. But, damn, she was right every time, and he was learning to listen to her. Trying to, but not without grumbling and feeble attempts to talk her out of her theories. If she kept up her track record, his job would soon be obsolete. His ego had taken quite a blow a few times over the past year. It hadn't killed him, though, and they had taken some scary dudes off the streets.

He pulled his car into an open spot down from Joe's. Jaxon was already waiting outside of his car on the phone.

"Maxwell says hi," Jaxon told him as he approached.

"Ask the old man when he's going to come himself instead of sending a junior agent." Matt laughed.

"I heard that, Parker. I'm swamped over here. Have a little compassion. I'll be there if you need me," Tom promised.

"We'll talk soon." Jaxon disconnected the call. "The agency has its hands full at the moment. We're spread thin helping a couple of local PDs."

"I bet. I have officers going every which way in town. We have more skirmishes than I've seen in years. With our missing girl and a murder case under investigation, we've been hopping."

"Sounds like we both could use this lunch break. I have some new info to give you, and I hope you have some for me." Jaxon opened the door into the bookstore.

"Hey, sweetheart." Matt gave Jessie's shoulder a squeeze. "How's your day going?"

"You wouldn't believe what's been going on here this morning. Go eat your lunch. I can tell you all about it this evening. The day isn't over yet, and for all I know, I may have more to share with you later." She gave him a nudge toward the open doors of the coffee shop. "Don't forget you left us without a car."

"Oh, sweetheart, I could never forget you." He kissed her cheek and followed Jaxon into Joe's.

Chapter 11

"Sometimes I'm scared by the way my mind works." Jessie leaned her hip against the counter.

"Why?" Peyton asked.

"I'm never sure what might happen next, and yet somehow I'm accepting of that fact. Doesn't that make me strange? I seek to analyze each event while waiting for the next shoe to fall." Jessie shook her head.

"I'm right there with you. What does that make me, your student? I've learned to think outside the box often enough not to know where the box is anymore. I wonder if we are the ones who make the box and draw the lines. I mean, there's a whole lot we don't understand in our world. Better yet, in our universe." Peyton got busy straightening the basket of bookmarks.

"True. We have certainly moved the lines in the past year. It does make me wonder whether that's a good thing or bad. Where might we end up? I had my little world figured out before, and now I know I didn't understand anything. I have many questions about the bigger picture." Jessie moved away from the counter when the bell above the door rang. "Time to get back to work."

She was always happy to wait on customers to get out of her head for a while. Every now and then, she glanced into the coffeeshop and could see Matt and Jaxon in serious conversation. If the lines on Matt's forehead were any indication, he didn't like what he was hearing. How well she knew that feeling. She could try to guess what their conversation was about, but she would learn soon enough if he wanted her to know.

With that settled, she turned her attention to straightening the book table. What would she do if she weren't constantly having to straighten books? She moved several books around. They never seemed to make it back to the right place. The small details made her life seem almost routine and average, just like everyone else. It was the same for Johanna. When she viewed some of Johanna's memories, Jessie could recall seeing ordinary moments with her family mixed in among some of the more dramatic events of her life. Such was life. A bit of a roller coaster even without ghosts or premonitions. Highs and lows all mingled together in a mixed bag.

"You're quiet, cous. You've been standing in the same spot for the past several minutes."

"I like straightening books." Jessie smiled at Peyton. "This routine is one of the more-normal things that I do on a daily basis."

"I hear you. That's why I like to teach. Working here is okay too. Although, the ghosts who randomly show up remind me our lives can be challenging from time to time."

Jessie glanced in the coffee shop again. "I wonder what they're discussing."

"I have no idea, but from the looks of it, they are deep into their conversation. Maybe I should slip in there and check up on them." Peyton headed toward the open doors.

****

Matt grinned. "I wondered how long it would take for one of them to come in and find out what we're talking about." Matt had noticed Jessie glancing his way several times.

"You two have been here a while. Have you solved the world's problems yet?" Peyton asked.

"A few, maybe," Jaxon told her as he stood. "I'll fill you in later. I need to return a few calls." Jaxon took her hand "Walk me to the car."

"I'll tell Jess goodbye and meet you back at the station." Matt walked into the bookstore where he spotted her looking out the front window. She seemed lost in thought as he stole up behind her and slipped his arms around her waist. He pulled her close. "What are you looking at?"

"I'm watching the man creeping through the cemetery followed by a couple of ghosts."

"Where?" Matt looked where she pointed. "I'll be damned." He flew out the front door and headed across the street. The man took off running. He followed him through the cemetery keeping him in his view. The man ran, weaving among headstones until he got beyond the cemetery. Matt lost him in the wooded area behind the church.

"What was he doing when he caught your attention?" Matt asked Jessie who watched him from the sidewalk.

"I noticed the supernatural activity around him, which usually means something is off. Angry ghosts rarely show up without cause." Jessie pursed her lips. "Makes you wonder, doesn't it?"

"Now, yes. But angry ghosts weren't on my radar before you." Matt smiled at her. "Call me if you see him again." He hugged her and kissed her cheek.

"I will. Don't forget you left us without a car, and I don't want to be here all night."

"Have I ever forgotten you?" Matt asked.

"A few times." She tapped her finger on her forehead. "When you get involved in a case, you lose all sense of time." She chuckled at his raised eyebrows.

"I'll be here," he said as he walked to his car. He waved as he drove past her standing near the door.

Who was the man and what was he doing in the cemetery? Hopefully, he wasn't there because of Jessie. She seemed to attract strange people and the ghosts that came with them. The idea of ghosts still shook him. He might have to rethink his end-of-life beliefs.

He called in to the station to have Joe tell the officers on patrol to be on the lookout for the man. Matt didn't mention the ghosts but described what the man was wearing. With any luck, maybe one of his officers would see him around town and question him. Matt had enough on his plate at the moment without adding another element to the equation. Time would tell if the man was here for some nefarious reason. "Damn!" He tapped his fingers on the steering wheel. If Jessie saw him, there had to be a reason.

Matt arrived back at the station and found his day filled with more skirmishes around town. One fire would be put out by one of his officers only to have another one on the other side of town start up. He had a few of the instigators sitting in jail waiting for someone to bail them out. Throw in a few interesting phone calls, plus Kyle Simpson wanting to talk, and his afternoon was a busy one.

He still wasn't sold on the idea that Bristol was a

traveler from the past. He had to admit there were strange circumstances around Bristol's recovery, but he wasn't ready to embrace the theory yet. He had to come up with something that would prove it. The doctors' report said a few convincing facts and some unexpected ones that surprised them too, but the docs weren't in the room when Bristol's return to life actually happened. Matt needed to talk to the person who was sent to take his body to the hospital morgue. Jaxon agreed with him that the doctors were having a hard time explaining their findings. Boy, he could relate to not being able to back up some of the events of the past year with evidence, or even rationally explain them. Those doctors were wading into some of the strange world where he found himself.

"I'll be at your place by six with dinner. I'm picking up Peyton in a few." Jaxon walked into his office.

"I figured you would." Matt said.

"I talked to the doctors, and I'm sure you found out the same thing as I did. They're perplexed by what happened and are trying to explain the events of that night in the best way possible."

"There's the great dilemma, trying to explain the unexplainable." Matt stood, picking up the file on his desk as he did. "Jessie reminded me that I left them without a car, and I had better be on time. I guess we'd both better get on our way and talk later."

****

Jessie waved at Matt as she walked out the door. The man was right on time. He was nothing if not punctual, except for when he was late. She smiled to herself. It was the new girl's night to lock up at eight.

Soon, the store's extended hours would be over, and she would close at five again. The summer had been great for her business. At this rate she would be able to expand her store upstairs. Plans were in the works in her mind, at the bank, and on paper. Fall would be a great time to get started. She opened the car door, her face lighting up when she saw his handsome face.

"Hey, there." She slid into the front seat. "How was your day?"

"Interesting, but we can talk about that later." He signaled and moved into traffic. "I take it Bristol never showed up because I never got a call from you."

"As days go in my store, it was fairly uneventful. You know about the man in the cemetery, but he never came near the store. His visit there could have been legit," she told him.

"Do you believe the words coming out of your mouth?" Matt turned to glance at her.

"Not really, but as of the moment I don't care. I'm not sure what that says about me other than my mind needs to quit analyzing every little thing that I see or hear. There is enough going on without me adding unnecessarily to the case."

"Well, sweetheart, as much as I appreciate your concern, I like you seeing what the rest of us don't often see and adding your spin on the information." He glanced at her. "I need you there. Put your head back and rest for a minute. We'll be there before you know it."

She smiled. No argument, no sass. She simply leaned her head back and couldn't help herself—she actually did what he said.

Chapter 12

Matt couldn't believe she fell asleep almost as soon as she leaned her head back and closed her eyes. He knew she must still be having trouble with jet lag from her trip, and the dark smudges beneath her eyes reminded him how hard the last few days had been since her return. He still hadn't had time to talk to her about the trip. No shoptalk tonight until they spent some time together. He made his third tour around town to give her a little more time to rest before he had to awaken her. Matt finally pulled into his garage after Jaxon called to say he was on his way with their dinner.

"Hi, babe. Sorry to wake you, but Jaxon will be here with dinner." He touched her face, scooting her hair out of her eyes.

"I'm sorry. I wasn't very good company." She wiped the drool off her lips and cheek. "I hope I didn't snore or do something weird. I must have been quite a spectacle." She leaned forward in the seat and worked her fingers through her hair.

"You didn't make a sound." He smiled at her. "One minute we were talking and then you laid your head back, closed your eyes, and you were out in seconds. I figured you're still struggling with the time change. At least this time you obeyed me." He waited for her response.

"I wouldn't go there if I were you." She chuckled.

"How long was I out?" she asked.

"About an hour." He grinned at her.

"An hour!" She shook her head. "And what were you doing all that time?"

"Besides admiring your beauty, it gave me a chance to drive around the town a few times. At least for now, the cove is peaceful and quiet." He unlatched his seat belt. "Let's go in." He stepped out of the car and walked around to open her door.

"Thank you. I'm not sorry for falling asleep, and I appreciate you letting me. I feel a lot better."

She followed him through the door that he unlocked and held open. "I'll be going first for a while. I keep thinking about if I had I sent you in first like I usually do, I wouldn't have you with me tonight."

"I don't like the alternative much either." She frowned. "How about we make a pact to watch each other's backs and do our best not to get killed." She held out her hand to shake his.

"Works for me." He shook her hand with a silly grin on his face. "I like having you around."

****

After dinner, Jaxon and Peyton decided to go for a ride. Jessie was glad to have some time alone with Matt. They had had precious little since her return from Ireland. She placed the last dish in the dishwasher, wiped the counter, and filled her glass with tea.

"We made short work of that." Matt hung up the towel. "It helps that we didn't mess the kitchen up first by cooking."

"Things go faster when you're working with someone." She grabbed her glass and followed him into the living room.

"I've been dying to ask you if my bribe worked?" He sat beside her on the couch and slipped his arm around her shoulder. "No pressure, but I had high hopes that at the very least you missed me lots."

"I did, and the next long trip I take has to be with you. Maybe on our honeymoon, perhaps." She glanced at him.

"I wouldn't mind that at all." He placed his arm around her and pulled her to his side. "Tell me about your trip."

"We saw so many amazing places. I already told you about Kilkenny, which holds a special place in my heart. One of my other favorites was our time in Dublin, but I will share that with you another day." She proceeded to fill him in on her. She stopped talking when Peyton walked in an hour later. "I'll let you talk with Jaxon. I'm going to turn in early tonight." She leaned close and gave him a kiss goodnight on his cheek.

"Sweet dreams, sweetheart." Matt stood beside her and whispered in her ear, "Remember this is how I want to be kissed." He proceeded to show her.

"Matt, there are others watching." She started to walk away.

"Let's give them something to talk about." Matt waggled his brows and gave her one long delicious kiss. He nudged her toward the hall to the snickers he could hear in the background.

"Wait up, cous. I'm headed that way too." Peyton followed her down the hall. "Goodnight and only happy dreams. I hope you can sleep after that kiss." Peyton chuckled.

"I plan on it." She smiled at Peyton. "Don't tell

anyone, but sleep and nice dreams is what this girl desires most of all right now. Goodnight." Jessie entered her room and closed the door. It didn't take her long to fall asleep. She awakened a couple of times to the muffled sound of Matt and Jaxon talking. Hearing them brought comfort to her and she went right back to sleep.

****

"I don't think the girls have adjusted to the time change yet," Jaxon said. "Peyton yawned our whole ride."

"Jessie fell asleep in the car after I picked her up. I drove around town until you called, to let her sleep for a while." Matt muted the sound on the TV. "What more did you find out about the guy who attacked your field office?"

"Not only did he have some big plans, but there are a few more in the chat room where he spent a lot of time, conspiring to do the same. The whole thing has me wondering when did we good guys become the bad guys? Did I miss something? I've worked in law enforcement for a few years, and I've never seen anything like this in my lifetime. There have always been fringe groups, but nothing I can remember quite like this." Jaxon rested his head on the back of the couch. "Of course, I'm sure other generations could say the same thing. Such is human nature. We make our own trouble and don't learn from past generations' mistakes."

"I was thinking the same thing earlier. I know for a fact that there've been several heated times of unrest in our country over the years. I read about several today. It gave me hope. We've survived angry times before, but not before it caused our nation grief. The Vietnam War years, the Civil Rights Movement, and the assassination of a president to name a few. The sad part is the victims of the hostility. Innocents often get caught in the crossfire. We've had some rough years, but the country managed to stumble and progress through them. Hopefully, we will this time too." Matt frowned.

"What?" Jaxon looked at him.

"Jessie's dream is what. A rising tide with people caught in the waves is exactly how each of the times could be described. How else can you explain the dark awful things that humans were able to do to each other? Discontentment, feeding on anger, with a need to blame someone is a recipe for disaster. We are capable of heinous acts."

"You're right about that, and it's even more intense when you are living in those times where you can see the waves rising and not simply reading about them. It's a helpless sensation for me not to know if I can stop the force of the wave once it begins," Jaxon said.

"I heard from Tom that some of the guys in our office are helping with the mass shooting in Rocky Point." Matt leaned back in his recliner and lifted his legs.

"Yeah. The shooter is still on the loose. There aren't many leads yet. We'll need the public's eyes and ears. Our guys are putting in some long hours trying to track the suspect. He discarded his cellphone."

"I've heard a few details on the shooting." Matt glanced at Jaxon. "Didn't the suspect shoot several members of a family execution-style because he was asked to turn down his music?"

"There were five killed and five more injured."

Jaxon shook his head. "Such a damn shame and for what?"

"No rhyme nor reason. A bad day, blew a gasket, hell, who knows?"

"One of the agents described the crime scene as the worst he'd ever seen," Jaxon told him. "Three of the women were executed trying to protect the children. They shielded them with their own bodies. Thankfully, the children were spared. The police were called by several in the neighborhood about the loud music, but they arrived on the scene too late." Jaxon leaned forward, resting his head on his hand.

"Crimes like that one make no sense. So many lives are instantly ruined. I wish we could get people to take a step back and dial down the rhetoric. We all live on the same planet. You'd think we could find a way to get along." Matt shook his head. "Murder is a damn sad business."

"Don't I know it. I spent the first half of my career as a homicide detective. It was grueling and sad. Telling family members was the toughest part of the job. I got to know Elliot Dawson over his son's constant run-ins with the law. We became friends, and the night I had to make the drive to his house to tell him his only child was murdered was one of the hardest days of my life." Jaxon rubbed his temples. "I'd gladly give back the money if I could undo what happened to his son and his family. I don't believe he ever got over the loss, and eventually the devastation killed him."

"How could he? I've had to tell a few myself, and it's awful." Matt leaned his head back against the chair.

They talked well into the night about the different investigations they had open at the moment. From

Ashley, to the suspect who killed his wife, and Bobby Bristol, there was a lot to be considered. Along with the uptick of petty crimes around town, Matt and Jaxon would be busy.

Matt didn't want any more surprises. That was for damn sure. No amount of rising tension would distract him from the job he needed to do. His approach was always the same—to follow the evidence to its final end. It might be slow and methodical, but it had worked well for him. But he loved Jessie's approach and the light in her eyes when she put pieces of the puzzle together. When she was telling him the story of the last witch in Ireland who was accused of killing all four of her husbands, she had him seeing the place as if he were there. They had dined in Kyteler's Inn on the site of the woman's former home. Her details of their experience kept him entertained. Then she teased him with a true romantic story she wanted to share with him at some point. The way she looked at him when she teased the story gave him hope that they would be setting a wedding date soon. The spark between them couldn't be denied. Even in the midst of the hard times, there was always something good to keep him going. Matt shut off the TV, grinned to himself, and headed for bed.

Chapter 13

Matt drove Jessie to work again. She grumbled but was happy that he cared enough to make sure the store was safe for her to walk into. Jaxon was bringing Peyton later. Every time Jessie came through the doors into her store, a sense of happiness filled her. She loved her job, but she couldn't help but wonder what new experience awaited her today.

Turning on her computer, she got to work doing her morning routine while the processor warmed up. Some days it seemed slower than others. A lot like her she guessed. She waved at Molly who had a long line of customers waiting at the counter.

The morning was perfect for wistful thinking and daydreams. She sighed. Kilkenny would be a pretty site for a destination wedding. She couldn't imagine what that would cost. The brochure had said the vibrant city had become a popular venue for bachelor and bachelorette parties. Yeah, she could see that. Of course, Dublin was pretty great too. But it was the church across the street that called to her. She had never thought of a church wedding, but First Community Church was her first job when she arrived, and it brought her and Matt together in a strange roundabout way. "Thank you, Gina," she mused. Gina was the first ghost to greet her on her first day in town, and by no means the last.

"Stop wasting time, girl." She picked up the feather duster and swished it over the counter. She straightened the bookmarks, and then paused in front of her computer to check her emails. Number one among the unread emails that caught her eye was Jeremy's. He had helped her with research for articles too many times to count. Yep, she needed to get Jeremy to move to Blue Cove. She wanted to find a nice girl for him. He had been one of the best guy friends she had in New York. Matt wouldn't mind having him in town. He'd asked for Jeremy's help with research many times over the past year. Jeremy also worked great with Gary, Matt's tech guy. She could see him living here but wondered if he would like the small town. Someone who loved the action of New York and all that the city had to offer might hate the slow pace of Blue Cove. Still, it was worth a shot as far as she was concerned. Wasting time again, but she couldn't help herself—the morning was perfect for daydreaming.

Jessie walked to the front of the store like she did most mornings. She loved to keep her eye on the happenings across the street. Pastor John's car pulled into the church lot. Seeing him step out of the car brought a smile to her face. He always had an encouraging word when it came to her strange new life, and he would be perfect to officiate at the wedding.

"Goodness, you're way too distracted this morning," Jessie muttered. "It's time to get to get a move on." She heard the knock at the doors. Glancing at Joe's she rushed to open them for her cousin, whose hands were full.

"Good morning." Peyton came in with two cups of coffee in her hands. "I hope you slept as well as I did. I feel more like myself, finally."

"I did. It's amazing what a full night's sleep with no dreams to interrupt can do for a person." She sat next to Peyton. "This is just what I needed. Although, more sleep didn't get me out of my vacay mode. I've gotten precious little done this morning except for dreaming." Jessie chuckled.

"I know the feeling. I'm sure we'll get back into the swing of things soon. I have to. All teachers return to their rooms in a few weeks." Peyton took a sip of her coffee. "Although, a month of touring and seeing new sights will be hard to recover from. Especially the shopping trip in Paris. Have you worn your new dress yet?" Peyton asked.

"I'm saving that special number for the perfect moment." Jessie's eyes lit up thinking about the gorgeous dress.

"I'm doing the same."

"Seriously, it is one of the best purchases I've made in years. We're talking Paris fashion here, which I'll be making payments on the price tag for a while." Jessie sighed. "But I don't regret it for a minute."

"No regrets for me either. But hey, won't we look great while we pay our credit cards? I bought a few other items in that store, and so did you. Sadie told me she wanted to pay for both of our purchases, and we are to give her the bills. She wants them to be her treat since she got to go on a trip of a lifetime." Peyton gestured to stop Jessie's remark. "Don't shoot the messenger. You'll have to argue with her. I already have and to no avail." Peyton smiled at her. "You know how stubborn Grams can be when she gets an idea in her head. No one can talk her out of it, and we're just like her."

"True. I know stubborn. God only knows how many timeout chairs I've had to sit in over the years. I would still be if grownups could be sent there." Jessie laughed.

"Speaking of shopping, I heard about a new store opening up at Elm's Spring this weekend, and I think we should go. It's a home décor store and since some of your furniture got destroyed, I think it would be fun to go and check it out."

"Sounds like fun. The minute I tell Matt he'll say he has to drive us. But he can drop us off and go have coffee or something. He'd be a drag walking around the store. You know how intense our shopping outings can get." Jessie chuckled, remembering how many dresses she tried on in Paris before she found the one. "The mounting minutes would have Matt searching for the closest exit and trying to drag me with him before I finished my task."

"Finding the perfect item is a fine art that can't be rushed." Peyton laughed. "Oh, the hours we've spent combing through earrings at the jewelry counters and sales racks at the department store because there was a fifty-percent-off sale."

"Those were the days." Jessie rolled her eyes. "Speaking of markdowns, I have a stack of books to put on the small table over there for just such a purpose." Jessie pointed at the table with the sign on it. "The corners and covers are either bent or scratched from all the accidents with my books."

"I guess damage is bound to happen when books are all around you and people are always pulling them over when they fall."

"Add in the supernatural, you know—ghosts who like to toss them and a mad little leprechaun throwing them off the bottom shelf—and it spells damage." Jessie picked up a stack of books. "I guess I'd better get busy. It's almost time to open." She glanced at the clock. "I'm glad you still have a few weeks left before school starts. This summer has been fun hanging with you." Jessie arranged the books on the table and got ready to open for the day.

****

He didn't know what to think of this new world in which he found himself. He hadn't seen any of the last few days coming his way. Examining the gun that rested on the table, he couldn't imagine what he might have done with a weapon like this back in the day. Of course, it would have helped if it had come with some kind of instruction. Thankfully, the young man, his new persona, knew how to use the dang thing. His arm shook with every recoil. The bruises still lined his arm. He had no idea how to prevent more of the same unless he padded his sleeve. He pictured various possible ways he could manage to protect himself. Something for him to look into while he figured out how to enact his plan.

He found himself surrounded by amateurs at best when it came to travelers and humans. Mere infants that acted out of impulse with no real goal or purpose in mind, but he had a plan—one he had been perfecting for hundreds of years. His time had come. He could use a person's body, or influence their actions, and often did both. The only obstacle to completing his mission was that he couldn't always work around their strong wills.

****

Matt placed his badge back in his pocket. This morning had worked out perfectly. With the help of a family member's tip and an alert highway patrol officer, Matt's murder suspect, Casey Craven, was arrested without incident. At least now he could find a measure of justice for Ria. Two young lives destroyed, not to mention the family members impacted. It seemed like such a damn shame. He wished there were some way to foresee the potential for spousal murder. As in most cases, someone in the family had to have seen some warning sign they didn't want to believe. Those red flags tended to come out after the crime when the family tried to make sense out of the senseless. Hindsight was the best sight of all. Matt shook his head.

"Are you busy?" Jaxon knocked on his door. "I heard you made an arrest this morning."

"Yeah. Can't say I'm not happy about it. Still, it seems a shame that the young couple's lives have come to such a sad conclusion. I don't think most marriages start out on the premise of wanting to kill their spouse." Matt frowned. "Although, when a spouse is murdered on their honeymoon, you tend to wonder."

"Do you know how he killed her yet?" Jaxon sat in the chair in front of Matt's desk.

"Lewis, the coroner, faxed over a copy of the autopsy result this morning. She died of a chemical toxic mix. The lab is breaking it down as we speak. He strangled her after the fact to try to cover the needle marks. Craven has a degree in chemistry and worked with synthetic substances. He's a real peach of a guy."

"I wanted to tell you that there might have been another girl nabbed by your suspect. This time in Baycliff. The case has the same MO, and it appears that it could be Bristol. If true, our guy is a busy fella. I'm trying to get more info from our agent working with the authorities. I'll let you know when I get a return call."

"Have you talked to the locals there yet?" Matt asked.

"I've been working on the phone all morning. They're tightlipped about evidence right now. Agent Flynn from the field office in Rocky Pointe will be our best resource." Jaxon stood. "I don't want you to be caught off guard. Peyton and Jessie want to go to the new home décor store this weekend opening in Elm's Spring. Peyton mentioned that Jessie needed to replace some of her furniture. Her insurance adjuster is supposed to meet her at the cottage this week and will cut a check after he estimates the damage."

"I hope they don't think we'll let them drive there on their own and have a social outing." Matt shook his head. "No way is that going to happen right now, especially after what you just told me."

"Peyton told me that they expected one of us to take them, let them shop, and go have coffee. I told her we'd have to see." Jaxon walked toward the door.

"We can talk about their plan at dinner. I'd like to keep them under lock and key, but I don't want to limit them completely." Matt raked his hand through his hair. "They'd never agree to the plan anyway. The fact that they said we could take them is a step in the right direction."

"I thought the same thing, but I'm a bit of a pushover when Peyton seems to be acting reasonable." Jaxon chuckled and waved as he left.

Matt understood the feeling. Hell, he understood Jessie's desire to do as she pleased. He valued his freedom too. He couldn't protect her from everything even if he wanted to, and he did. What kind of life would that be? He'd be worn out, and she would resent his constant interference. He got it.

Chapter 14

Reba and Sadie showed up in the afternoon. Grams told them both in no uncertain terms that she wanted to pay for their shopping spree in Paris. She wouldn't take no for an answer. No matter how long they tried to convince her, she refused to budge.

"I know stubborn, girls. I learned to dig my heels in before you were a glimmer in your parents' eyes. You may as well give up and allow me to do this for you. I loved spending time with you both on our trip, I have the money, and I want you to enjoy it with me while I'm alive to watch you appreciate it. You'll still have your inheritance, but I'm all for easing the burden now. You wouldn't want to deprive me of that joy, would you?" She smiled and reached for their hands. "Let this old lady have her way."

"Old my foot. You outmaneuvered us. I'd call you cunning." Jessie hugged her. "How could we deny you the pleasure of spending your money the way you want?"

"Nicely done, Sadie." Reba chuckled. "I couldn't have done it better myself. Your use of guilt made a nice final touch." She leaned close and whispered in Sadie's ear, "With that bit of business taken care of, let's get down to what matters."

"And what would that be?" Jessie asked.

"You girls need to be careful. Especially you, dear

Jessie, at this time. There's a scheme in action that has its roots deep in the past of your family. The one at work will stop at nothing to set his plan in motion in our time, but ultimately it will fail. I can tell you with joy your wedding will go on but not before a few bumps that will hit way too close to home. That said, your future is but one part of this story. The upheaval you are sensing will not be solved in one case but will take many. Both of you girls, including your sister," Reba said glancing at Peyton, "will be caught in the crossfire many times over the next several months."

"Well, I didn't want to hear that. How about you, cous?" Jessie stood when another customer walked in. "I'm not surprised but can't say I'm overjoyed by the news."

Jessie was happy to escape the serious turn in the conversation. She knew in her heart that the rising tide of anger wouldn't be solved in a moment. The damage might take years to undo. She hoped not, but how did you rebuild the trust among people who once had been friends who let leaders, beliefs, or their politics separate them? A question only time and circumstances could answer. If history taught her anything, there was hope of the possibility that all the anger could be tamped down. It never really went away, but could fester under the radar. She didn't want to be in the center of the angry waves of her dream, and she most certainly didn't want to find herself there over the next several months. Nor did she want her family and friends to be there. Those waves seemed to bring endless rounds of chaos with them.

"Do you have this book?" The customer showed Jessie a piece of paper with a title written on it.

"If you don't mind a bent corner, I have that exact book on the sale table." She walked the lady over to the table and pointed to the title.

"Thank you. You have a couple of the books that I wanted. I can live with a bent corner or a scratch or two for a bargain." She smiled and snatched up the titles she wanted.

Jessie walked with the older woman to the counter to ring up her purchases. The shivers began at her neck and ran up and down Jessie's arms like spiders doing some odd dance. She glanced around to see the cause, but nothing appeared out of order. Still, they danced on as units of tiny unseen soldiers marching in unison up and down her spine. Something was amiss, but she had no idea what. The strange sensation was soon followed by the impression of being watched. That's when she noticed a male ghost hovering on the steps leading up to the attic, following her every move. Instinct told her he was there for some unknown purpose. But what? Who was he? In all of her sightings there had only been a few male ghosts. She could only wonder for a moment what it meant as she joined Peyton and the others at the table again.

"I need to run, girls. Sadie and I have another stop to make before our day is finished. I, for one, can't wait to see your Paris fashions." Reba stood. "The atmosphere has changed in here," she said. "I'm sure you've already noticed. Keep your eyes open."

Sadie hugged them both. "I want your receipts pronto. No grumbling. I want to do this for you."

"Yes, ma'am." Jessie saluted her.

"You little minx." Sadie playfully swatted Jessie on her backside. "Love you, girls."

"Love you too, Grams," both girls said together.

"What did Reba mean?" Peyton asked.

"We have an unfriendly looking ghost hanging out on the stairs leading to the attic. I have no idea why he's here, but I'm not sure I want to know either."

"Well, I hope he stays where he's at. I'm ready for this day to be done." Peyton squeezed Jessie's shoulder. "Audrey will be here before we know it, along with our rides. Reba's warning is more than enough for me to digest. I need to keep busy. Tell me what to do."

Jessie gave Peyton some busywork and she did the same. Even while working the rest of the day, she was aware of the ghostly eyes that tracked her every movement.

****

Matt's officers were kept busy most of the day. He couldn't remember a week when the number of officers dispatched all over the town was this high. From teen vandalism to a couple of domestic issues and fighting neighbors calls, the unrest had reached an almost fevered pitch.

After talking to the county sheriff and a police chief friend to see if they were experiencing anything similar, Matt was shocked that they too were seeing an uptick in crime in their areas. He expected times like this in the big cities, but the cove for the most part was peaceful— at least until Pastor Gina's murder at the church and Jessie's arrival last year.

At that moment, Blue Cove was filled with tourists, some of whom themselves were victims of crime. Not a good endorsement for vacationing in Blue Cove. Simple petty crime and thefts were up. Vandalism and assault were close behind in numbers. There was no trace of Ashley, and Frank couldn't be here until early next week. His schedule was packed. Worse yet, he had no idea when Bristol might show up again.

"Chief, do you have a minute?" Dylan knocked on his open door.

"Sure. What's up?" Matt motioned him in.

"Gary and Jaxon wanted us down in the tech room for a few minutes. They found something important that they thought you should see."

"Okay, let's go." Matt stood and followed Dylan down to Gary's office.

"Tell me what I'm looking at," Matt told Gary who pointed out several things he was finding in a few online chat rooms.

"There's a lot of talk about shootings. How to inflict the most casualties. I don't like the looks of this. They aren't saying when or where, but only that it's time to roll."

"What the hell is going on?" Dylan raked his hand through his hair. "It's like a freaking nightmare. How didn't we see this? Is this something new?"

"Not new, but it's been kept below the surface until the past few years. This stuff has been chatted about for years in secret meetings, but the internet has started connecting these people, which has emboldened them," Gary said.

"You see this?" Gary pointed to a patch on the sleeve of one of the men in the photo. Those letters refer to them being a part of death squad. That's a bit scary, don't you think?"

"It makes me wonder if anyone works anymore. How do they have time for all this junk?" Matt frowned.

"For some of these guys, this is their work. They raise funds on the fears of others and make quite a living."

"Thanks, Gary. You've given me more to think about." Matt put his hands on his hips.

"Me too, and I have enough already," Dylan said.

"The agency is monitoring the online chatter twenty-four seven, and believe me, it's enough to keep us all awake at nights," Jaxon mentioned to Matt as they walked back upstairs to his office.

"I remember those days. Tell me, Mr. FBI man, how are we going to combat this? We are outmanned and outgunned." Matt leaned his hip against his desk. "We've seen this historically on some level, but this is our time. What are we going to do?"

"That is the big question, isn't it. Authorities at every level are asking the same question and trying to push back against the idea that nothing can be done, and we need to move on. But each of these acts of violence imprint themselves on the psyche of this nation. At this rate, we'll all be suffering from PSTD, and not only the first responders."

"It used to be we could say it won't happen here, but that's no longer true. We need a plan." Matt smiled. "Now I sound like Jessie. I would like to hear Maxwell's take on this." Matt shook his head. "Damn, death squads. What's next?"

"I'm not sure we want to know." Jaxon sat in one of the chairs. "On a positive note, the FBI and our Allies Law Agencies took down a major online cybercrime group this past week. A global hacking scheme that held the computers of businesses hostage with ransomware. They forced them to pay huge sums of money to get their computers unlocked. We're talking a big deal."

"That's another one for the good guys." Matt gave him a thumbs-up.

Matt, Jaxon, and Dylan spent the afternoon in deep discussion. A teleconference call with Tom Maxwell backed up what they had learned in Gary's office earlier. By the time Matt and Jaxon left the station, they had a new file filled with notes and FBI warnings that Matt never thought he'd see in his lifetime. He couldn't wait to pick up Jessie, go home, and let his mind take a break. With any luck, her day was a good one with no issues or complications. What was the likelihood of that? He smiled. Still, he could hope. A nice peaceful night at home with his girl was exactly what he needed. A bit of chill time and a few stolen kisses. In his favor was the fact that Jaxon wanted the same thing. As soon as he pulled into the open space in front of her store, she opened the door with a smile on her face and waved as she came to the car. The tension of the day eased, and everything seemed right in his world for the moment.

Chapter 15

"Right on time." Jessie smiled when he opened the car door for her. "How was your day?" She slipped into the passenger seat and latched her seat belt.

"I'd call it interesting. How about yours?" he asked as he closed the door.

"Interesting about covers it." She laughed at him when he shook his head.

"Do you care to tell me the particulars of what made the day a standout?" His eyebrows rose.

"Only if you tell me. It can't all be one-sided, as you know." She touched his arm when she noticed his grim expression. "That bad, huh?"

"Let's say there's a lot of ugliness out there right now, and with it comes some bad actors. I've learned the hard way today that because of air travel and the internet, we live in a small world. What affects one side of the globe can change us all in a short time span."

"That's true. I tend to think of my little world and forget how close the global world is to our doorstep." Jessie exhaled a deep breath.

"We learned in our last case the dark web can connect people to some scary theories in a kind of strange brotherhood of sorts. That sense of camaraderie can embolden a lone wolf to act out." Matt frowned. "There is no way to plan or account for that kind of person. All you have to do is think about how we were caught off guard the other night."

Jessie shuddered. "How can I forget that awful moment, even if I'd like to?"

"Right now, I don't want you to. I've only told you a small part of what I learned today. It's on a need-to-know basis only for your peace of mind." He laid his hand on top of hers. "What made your day interesting?"

"You mean besides an unfriendly ghost hanging out in my store and a cryptic message from Reba? Nothing much." Jessie glanced at the window. She went on to describe the ghost and what Reba had shared with them earlier. "I shuddered at the thought of this awful atmosphere hanging around through several more cases. I understand but I don't like the idea at all."

"I hate to say it, but I think she's right on." Matt turned into the driveway, pushed the remote, and waited for the garage door to open. "I know one fact—we'll all need to be aware of our surroundings."

"We can't give in to the fear of what might happen, or we'll stop living." Jessie opened the car door when he came to a stop in the garage. "And yet, we can't go glibly through life with blinders to the changes happening in our world. Both can be true simultaneously."

"Exactly." Matt motioned her to stand behind him when he opened the door. "You wait here."

Jessie knew he meant well, but waiting until he checked out the house did nothing for her nerves. Matt seemed generally concerned, which made her wonder what he wasn't telling her. Maybe he was right that it was on a need-to-know basis. At this point, she didn't need or desire to know. Oh, who was she kidding? She wanted details. Facts made her think she was in control even if she wasn't.

Jessie could put a brave face on it, but truthfully Reba's words had shaken her earlier. Her nightly recurring dream told her the rising tide was real and life as she had known it was rapidly morphing into something unrecognizable to her. How could anyone think of marriage, and bringing children into a crazy world changing before their eyes? But that's exactly what she was contemplating. "Dig deep, girl, and plan. Your future happiness may depend on it," she muttered.

"All clear, sweetheart." He smiled at her. "I'm a bit jumpy after our Bristol encounter. I won't be like this forever. I promise."

"I know the feeling." She followed him into the house. "Have you been by my place to see how the repairs are coming?"

"Dylan told me earlier forensics is done, and the work is progressing on the damage. Although, I don't want you back in the place until Bristol is caught." He closed the door behind her.

"I understand. I won't fight you on that for now." She emphasized the words for now with a smile. "The thing is, the insurance company representative wants to meet me at the cottage to make sure everything is listed that got destroyed in the firefight."

"I can run you by tomorrow. We'll go when the workers are there."

"Did Jaxon tell you about us wanting to go to Elm's Spring to shop in the new home-décor store? This weekend is their grand opening, and everything is on sale."

"He told me and we're thinking about taking you girls. It might be nice to make a day of it together and take a break from here. Sound good?" He pulled her into his arms as she walked by him.

"Perfect." She leaned her head on his chest. His embrace made her almost forget the worries of the day.

Jessie and Peyton made dinner together as they talked about what items she wanted to replace first. Maybe this would be a good time to update her style a bit. Peyton could help her in that department. She liked comfortable and eclectic, which didn't seem to be on trend at the moment. She had never been trendy or with it, for that matter.

She glanced around Matt's place. He had good taste, and his kitchen was almost perfect with its granite, chrome, and the pop of aqua to soften the dark edginess. She loved it, but his living room could use a woman's touch. She was up to the challenge.

"Hey, cous. Where have you been? I've asked you several questions and you haven't answered one of them," Peyton said.

"Sorry, I wasn't paying attention. I've been overthinking things all day. I'll set the table, and you can tell the guys dinner will be ready in five minutes."

****

"Thanks for the awesome meal, ladies. I'll clean up." Matt collected their plates and carried them to the sink.

"I'll help." Jessie wet the sponge and began to clean the stove.

"Why don't you watch TV. I can take care of this." Matt slipped his arm around her waist.

"I have some nervous energy to work off before I can sleep." She continued to scrub the stove and work her way to the counter.

"You and me both." He playfully splashed water on her but wasn't prepared for the wet sponge that hit him on the head when he turned around.

"That's what you get." She laughed and got a face full of water from the faucet hose in his hand. "Boy, are you going to get it."

What started as playful flirting turned into a water war with a major clean-up when they were finished. Once the laughter subsided, he kissed her and handed her a mop while he dried the countertop and appliances.

"I guess we needed that." He chuckled.

"I need to dry off." She put the mop away. "I have some emails to answer anyway." She kissed his cheek and walked away.

He watched her saunter out of the kitchen. Uneasiness filled his gut when he could no longer see her. Their conversation earlier about the ghost in her store and Reba's message left him feeling unsettled. He'd been through cases with her before and had heard more than his share of strange warnings from Reba, but this time had a different feel to it. Nothing seemed wrong and yet everything did. He raked his hand through his hair. It was a damn mess, and he had no idea what crime would pop up next. Jessie's dream bothered him the most. Something or someone was reaching out to pull her in. Was it intentional or was she an innocent bystander? He had no idea, but he would do his best to find out and stop it.

He could tell the weight of it all was pressing down on her. Her small sanctuary had been invaded, some of her treasured belongings destroyed, and life was supposed to simply go on like nothing happened. Her vulnerability tugged at his heart, and at the same time, her strength blew him away. Love made him believe he could conquer every problem life threw at him. When she looked at him with those gorgeous blue eyes, he felt invincible but at the same time it left him exposed in the face of the possibility of losing her. *Get a grip, Matt. You'll keep her safe. You have to. You can't let yourself imagine any other possibility.*

Matt shut off the kitchen light and walked into the living room. Jaxon and Peyton were watching a TV show. "I'll see you in the morning. I want to check over the files I brought home." He walked down the hall toward his room. Pausing outside of Jessie's closed door, he wanted to see her, but he didn't want to bother her either. He made himself walk on, not wanting to disturb her with the strange mood he found himself in. Damn, he wished he knew how he could make it easier for her and take some of the pressure off her, but then again, he had enough for them both.

Chapter 16

After checking out her store this morning Matt had given Jessie a lackluster kiss on his way out the door. He seemed more than a little preoccupied as she watched him drive away. Of course, he was dealing with a lot, which had nothing to do with her, but at least he could have kissed her like he meant it.

Matt still didn't have a lead on Ashley or Bristol. He may have arrested the husband who had killed his wife and was building the case against him, but she could see why he was still concerned. On the upside, Matt told her this morning that the trip to Elm's Spring was a go. The thought of being able to replace some of her belongings lifted the heaviness of losing them. She waved at Molly working through a long line in the coffee shop. Joe's was hopping this morning.

She read the quick text from Matt telling her he would let her know when he was on his way to pick her up later. She wanted to go to the cottage, but at the same time she didn't want to. Her space had been invaded, and her nice cozy life there shattered. Would she ever be able to see the place again without hearing the sound of the gun, the smells, or the fear of that night?

"Good morning," Peyton said as she walked in the back door. "You went to bed early last night. I never saw you again after dinner."

"I was on an online chat with Jeremy, and once we started chatting, we had to spend time talking about our lives to catch up. He is my favorite guy friend after all. I was trying to find out if he met anyone yet. With some careful maneuvers and softball questions I got him to admit that he's still on the market. Any girl would be lucky to snatch him." Jessie smiled. "I can think of a few girls I could hook him up with if only he would move here."

"I won't ask you who." Peyton chuckled. "I don't want to get caught in the middle of your matchmaking scheme. Anything else interesting going on?"

"I'm not sure if you would call this attention-grabbing but I had to fill out some insurance forms that were emailed to me." She shrugged her shoulders. "Boring and sleep inducing. I dislike filling in detailed forms. On the bright side, Matt's going to take me by my place at lunchtime. I'm meeting with the insurance company's representative to document the loss of my property. I'm glad I got my renter's insurance policy. Katie's company will take care of the damage to the unit, but my belongings would have been a total loss without my policy."

"I got it too. Katie had encouraged me to when I moved in. Are you excited to go shopping on Saturday?" Peyton asked. "I'm ready to get out of town for a few hours. We always have fun when we shop."

"I am, but I'm still hesitant to do anything, which is unlike me. I've been out of whack since the other night."

"I can understand. I would be too." Peyton leaned her elbows on the counter.

"Well, I don't like the feeling. I need to get with

it." Jessie started her morning opening routine. Molly knocked on the doors and rushed through the door when Jessie opened them.

"Hey, have you had any strange things happening over here?" she asked.

"Strange how?" Jessie asked.

"Oh, you know, basic things like my pots and pans aren't in the same place where I left them along with the kitchen completely rearranged. Don't get me wrong. The place is spotless and some of the changes make sense, including moving the spices, but knowing I didn't clean or arrange the shelves makes the spotless kitchen seem a bit over-the-top for me. None of my help will take credit, or Kenny either." Molly paused tapping her finger to her forehead. "You know what? It reminds me of what happened when I had the unwanted ghostly visitor hanging out in my shop that one time." Molly's hands crossed protectively over her baby bump.

"It's been fairly quiet over here, but I'll keep an eye on your place to see if I can see any activity. We had a ghost hanging out on the stairs yesterday, and he's still there today. Besides being a tad menacing, he hasn't done anything but hover there and stare at us." Jessie shook her head.

"Doesn't that bother you? Just the thought of it totally creeps me out." Molly shook her head. "Even in my gothic punk days, I never envisioned real ghosts, much less saw them."

"Why you would have one rearranging your kitchen does make me wonder. I'll pop over in a while to check it out." Jessie squeezed Molly's hand. "I wouldn't mind one who likes to clean over here for a change of pace," Jessie said wistfully.

"Let me put it this way—if there's no ghost, then someone broke into the coffee shop last night and cleaned the kitchen without taking anything, which makes no sense to me. Still, I might need to change the locks." Molly turned to leave.

"Or maybe you should leave the locks alone in hopes that your unseen helper keeps cleaning for free." Jessie chuckled and waved when Molly glanced back at her.

"Not a bad idea."

"What do you think?" Peyton asked after Molly was gone.

"I have no idea. I'll go buy us some coffee and scones and see if anything pops into my mind." Jessie reached for her purse and walked into the coffee shop and got in line.

The longer she stood there, the more she could sense something was off in the coffee shop. She couldn't see anything out of the ordinary, but still the atmosphere told her there was a supernatural visitor on the premises. All she had to do was figure out what unseen visitor might like to tidy things up. Hmm. She placed her hand to her cheek. She needed to put some thought into this mystery.

When she got to the front of the line to order, she said to Molly, "I see what you mean. Something is definitely up, here, but I don't see anything odd right off. But just because I don't see the apparition doesn't necessarily mean she isn't here. I say she, because I can't imagine a male cleaning—unless of course they used to be a chef in their past life." She smiled at her own quip.

"At least I know I'm not off my rocker. Whoever they are they seem to know their way around a kitchen." Molly took her order and handed her two cups to fill with coffee. "Here you go." She handed Jessie a bag.

"Thanks." When Jessie reached for her bag, she noticed the shadowy figure float past in front of the open pass-through into the kitchen. She knew exactly who Molly's kitchen help was. The question was, would Molly want to know about her?

"Johanna, this is a new side to you. What are you doing here?" she muttered under her breath.

"Did you say something?" Molly asked.

"No, I'm just talking to myself. I'll see you later and let you know if I sense anything."

"Okay. I mean, I don't mind a ghost that cleans, but I've never heard of one." Molly shook her head. "What am I saying? Until you moved here, I never thought of ghosts at all," Molly whispered and waved at her as the next person in line walked up to the counter.

Jessie carried her purchases back to her shop. Another secret to be unraveled. What was Johanna doing at Joe's?

"Did you see anything?" Peyton asked her as soon as she closed the door.

"You could say I did." Jessie placed the coffee and bag on the table. She explained to Peyton about seeing Johanna there. "I know all these crazy things should surprise me, but nothing seems to anymore. I'm sure I still have room to be surprised, and I'm left wondering why this occurrence doesn't."

"Our ancestor, who looks like you, who died long ago, is cleaning the kitchen at the coffee shop. What's strange about that?" Peyton slapped her hand to her forehead.

"I have no idea." Jessie took a sip of her coffee and plopped down in the chair. "There has to be a reason for her appearance. One could try guessing, but I'm sure we'll know soon enough. I guess we'd better get ready to work. Who knows what else today will bring?"

"I can see our unfriendly guy is still hanging out in the same place. Doesn't it make you wonder who he is and why he is here at the same time Johanna is. Or is he around because she is?" Peyton mused.

"There's something to research. Did Johanna have an enemy or a protector?" Jessie passed the opened doors into Joe's and waved. She walked to the front of the store to turn the sign around on the front door. Some days she felt like she was flying blind when it came to this new life of theirs. Between the two of them, they should be able to figure out this new twist. They could write a book about their lives.

Customers trickled in, and whenever Jessie got an extra minute, she researched what she could find out about Johanna's life and the village where she lived. There wasn't a lot of information, but she knew the answer had to lie in the scene she had viewed with Johanna. Was the ghost one of the men who destroyed the village? She wished she knew his identity and what their appearance had to do with the events of the past few days. In her heart of hearts, she knew that it was somehow paramount to what was happening now. To consider the odds of that being true seemed farfetched even for her or Peyton.

****

Matt sent Jessie a text telling her they should have

lunch and then go to her place afterward. He knew she needed to meet the rep from the insurance company today. In general, he thought it might be good for her to see how the repairs were coming along. Dylan told him that Katie was making sure everything was done right. Matt smiled to himself. He could see Katie handling the situation perfectly. She wouldn't let them cut any corners. She was determined to keep the inn's five-star rating, which included those cottages.

He would be glad when Frank got there. Every day that went by made it that much harder to find Ashley. Damn, he wished he knew why Bristol showed up in his town, first as a victim and now as a criminal. Who shot the kid and dumped him? It was his job to figure that out. None of it made any sense. He tapped his pen on the desk.

From their last case, he had discovered the old police chief had left them a mess when it came to investigations, as he swept hush payments under the table. He had a couple of his officers working with the women entering file data to study more of his closed cases. Matt was sure they would find more junk to deal with before long. The timing seemed ripe for a crime spree, heaping more onto his workload. He wasn't happy about the thought, but the best he could do at the moment with the leads he had was wait for the next shoe to fall.

"Matt, do you have a minute?" Jaxon knocked on his open door with Dylan standing beside him.

"Sure. Sit." He gestured to the chairs in front of his desk. "What's up?"

"That's a loaded question." Dylan said. "What's not? Remember when we said we wished for our simple cases back—like writing tickets, settling arguments, and low-level juvenile vandalism? You know, the kind we dealt with before Jessie came to town? All I can say is we need to be careful what we ask for. It seems we have those days back on steroids. The calls are coming in at an all-time high. We've got guys having to work overtime to stay on top of them all."

"Add to that, the strange that seems to be normal now with the Reynolds girls here. I was thinking the time was ripe for a crime spree, a minute ago. But we have few leads to explain why it's happening at this point in time." Matt frowned.

"Maybe this will help." Jaxon pulled out a spreadsheet. "Jeremy and Gary have both been checking chat rooms and collaborated on these statistics. I matched them with the FBI monitors, and they are coming to some of the same conclusions. We are divided. That's easy enough to see on the surface, but that's nothing new."

"It doesn't take a damn rocket scientist to figure that out." Dylan chuckled.

"Not at all. We've gone down these roads before. What's different this time is the internet, the conspiracies that can travel the world in a matter of seconds, and the constant angry voices joined by large numbers wanting to take matters into their own hands." Jaxon pointed at a line on the sheet in front of them. "It's a breeding ground for a loner to find like-minded friends and feel emboldened. We have agents watching for signs among the chatter that show a credible threat and not just talk."

"Don't forget the death squads and militias." Dylan frowned. "What a mess."

"Which brings us back to our town. Somehow Jessie's dream, Bristol's miraculous recovery, and our missing girl fit into all of this, and we're about to find out how." Matt leaned his elbows on the desk.

"Damn." Dylan shook his head. "Do we want to know?"

"We have to. This is bigger than Blue Cove, and there's too much at stake to bury our heads in the sand no matter how much we might want to." Jaxon placed another copy of the spreadsheet on Matt's desk. "I had them make us each a copy." He handed one to Dylan. "We need to study it and ask questions. The answer lies where misinformation and hate connect to breed violence."

"What you said makes sense to me. It provokes plenty of questions," Matt said. "Misinformation coupled with isolationism may be at the heart of this angry movement. Let's study these sheets and we'll talk again." He stood. "After lunch, I'm taking Jessie by the cottage. She is meeting the adjuster from her insurance company and picking up a few more items."

"At least I can say she'll be pleased with how fast the work is going. Although I don't think Katie wants her back there anytime soon." Dylan stood. "Not until the guy who shot the place up is caught."

"If you're headed to Joe's for lunch, do you mind if I meet you there?" Jaxon asked him.

"Works for me. See you in a few." He walked down the hall and out to the parking lot. Kip waylaid him when he got to his car to tell him a story. It was no surprise to him that Jaxon beat him to Joe's.

****

Jessie smiled at Matt when he walked in the door.

She handed her customer the change and her bag. "Jaxon beat you and is having lunch with Peyton."

"I figured he might. Kip stopped me to tell me about his latest call. I'm telling you, Jess, it's getting weird in town."

"I'm not surprised." She gave him a gentle nudge. "Go get something to eat, and I'll be here when you get back."

"I'll bring you lunch. Anything in particular?"

"You choose, but I only want a half order of anything," she said.

"I'll be back in a few." He walked into Joe's.

Jessie saw him stop to talk to Jaxon and Peyton before he ordered. She went to sit in one of her cozy spots with two chairs and a small table. The perfect place to keep her eye on her ghost who seemed to stay in the same spot watching her. She found herself getting into a staring match with him throughout the day. She usually blinked first. Was it anger she saw on his face or was it possible he was simply doing his job? She wished she understood the reason for his unseemly vigil.

Matt returned with their lunch and placed the containers and two drinks on the table. "You told me to choose."

"Thank you. This looks great." Jessie opened the container to view one of Molly's great salad combinations. "What's not to like about fresh greens with grilled chicken, strawberries, and slivered almonds? Yum!" She licked her lips.

"I can't say that would be my first choice. I'm more of a smothered burrito kind of guy." He smiled, taking a whiff of the green chili covering his burrito.

"Molly has perfected this menu item, and you need to have at least a taste." He spooned up a bit and held it to her mouth.

"Hmm, that is tasty." She swallowed the flavorful morsel and then took a bite of her salad

"But I knew you would enjoy the salad. Why did you choose this table? We rarely sit here." Matt said.

"I wanted to keep my eye on the ghost who has been located in the same place the past few days and doesn't look happy about it. I don't think he's planning on going anywhere." She pointed to the stair area where the spirit hovered.

"Okay, that's more information than I wanted to know. I guess I should be used to conversations like this between us, but I can't say that I am there yet. I am growing, though." He took a bite of his burrito.

"Yes, you are." She patted his hand and reached for her iced tea. "I can still remember the first time I told you about seeing Gina's ghost. You didn't believe me in the beginning, if I recall." She smiled shaking her head. "Even after you told me I looked like I had seen a ghost." She laughed.

"You have to admit it was a stretch for my logical brain to accept. Still, I came around in time though, didn't I?" he asked.

"Yes, you did, and I've often wondered why. I'm not sure I would have believed me." She snorted and slapped her hand over her mouth. "Was it my attention to detail that eventually brought you around?"

"Nope, you were damn persistent and downright beautiful. I couldn't stop myself. I could overlook your ghosts if I got to be with you. I'm a simple man."

Jessie laughed outright. "I think we see those early

days differently. You pushed me away and didn't want me, a mere woman, messing with your investigation. And me being, well, me, I was bound to get in the middle once you told me not to, if only to irritate you." She closed the lid on her uneaten salad. "At least, until I met Gina's parents and saw her kids. At that point, it changed for me. I wanted to find justice for her."

"And that's what won me over. You cared," he told her. "And of course, you're easy on the eyes too." He waggled his brows.

She slapped his arm playfully. "You're such a guy."

"I never claimed to be anything else. I'm an easy-to-please guy that is totally smitten and in love with you. Even if I have to deal with the baggage that comes with you." He stood cleaning up his trash. "Are you ready?"

"I will be in a few." Jessie put her leftovers into the small fridge in the back room and walked back to the counter to check someone out. She reached for her purse and shoved her phone in.

As soon as Peyton returned from lunch to work, Jessie and Matt left for her cottage. She wanted to see her place and yet she didn't. Every item destroyed by gunfire would remind her of that awful moment. The chills raced down her arms. That night would be forever etched into her memory.

The lane back to the inn was lined with irises, reminding her once again why the Blue Iris Inn was a perfect name for the B&B. Jessie loved living near her best friend Katie for the past year, and when Sadie and Peyton moved to town, her life had gone from good to great. She wasn't about to let anyone take that joy from her, not even a creep with a powerful gun. She was determined not to let fear rule her life or emotions. Of course, that was easier said than done. She could talk the talk but living it might be a tad harder.

"You're quiet. Is everything all right?" Matt glanced at her when he pulled into a parking space.

"Thinking, is all." Jessie pursed her lips.

"About what?" he asked.

"Nothing important." She opened the door to get out.

"If it's important to you, it is to me also. You know, Jess, the only time you don't wait for me to open your car door is when you don't want to tell me what's going on." He pulled her into his arms before she walked ahead of him. "Tell me what's on your mind."

"I'm afraid but I don't want to be. I want to see my space and yet I don't. I've loved this place. It has been home for me. The whole shooting makes me angry. He's messed with my sense of security and well-being." She placed her hand over his mouth. "And before you say it, I know no place is ever really safe, but at least we want to believe our home is. I don't want to give that creep the power to take that from me."

"Then don't let him. Look around and see what you want the adjuster to see. He should be here soon. We'll work at finding Bobby Bristol and putting him behind bars or sending him back to where he belongs. Whatever needs to be done so you can come home. At least, until you call my place home."

"Look, Matt, I know how hard this all is for your mind to wrap itself around. It's the same for me too. I've managed to muddle through by trial and error."

"We've managed. We're in this together,

sweetheart, and don't you forget it. Ever since that day you first waltzed into my office, we've found a way to work together." He took her hand as they started down the path through the garden in full bloom. "The workers are here, and that's why I wanted you to come now. Dylan said a lot of work is already complete."

"Let's get it over with," she told him. "And just so you know, I didn't waltz into your life—I strutted." She stepped in front of him and showed him her strut.

"I get it." He laughed. "You and I need to talk. I'm anxious to know what you've decided. My hope is that while you're shopping, you'll think about the place we'll be sharing together at some point. I want you to put your touch on our place."

"You can count on it." She smiled. Her mind raced ahead with ideas to soften the masculine living room.

Matt held the door open, and she walked in first. She took the papers out of her purse and filled in the form listing the damage to her personal property. She would need a new sofa, desk, and décor pieces, to name a few. At least, the painting Grams had done survived with no damage. Bristol must have pointed the gun and shot randomly at everything in her living area. The damage to her belongings was extensive. There wasn't much worth saving. The tear escaped her eye and trickled down her cheek. Each item held a special memory, from her pillows that adorned her college dorm that had been tossed more times than she could count, to the sofa she had bought brand new for her apartment in New York. She wiped the tear away, but another one followed close behind the first. The hug she found herself wrapped in gave her the freedom to let them flow.

Chapter 17

There was nothing harder for Matt than to see Jessie cry. He would like to get hold of Bristol himself. With any luck, they would have him behind bars where he needed to be, soon. He followed her from room to room as the adjuster filled out the damage report and took pictures.

"I can see the repair is ongoing, but from what I can see you're very lucky to be alive." The man smiled at her. "I need to call this in to corporate, and I should have a check ready in a few minutes for you."

Matt waited with her when he went out to his car. "Lucky is one way to put it. Are you okay, sweetheart?" he asked.

"I know they're only things, and yet there are memories attached to some of them. I'm sure I'll be fine." She wiped the tears in her eyes. "This is my therapy."

"I know." He hugged her. "Do what you need to do to get through this." He ran his hand down her cheek. "Soon you'll replace them with many new memories. In the meanwhile, don't let him defeat you. Get mad and you be the one that defeats him."

****

When Matt dropped Jessie off at her store, she had a nice check in her purse to start the process to replace some of her belongings. In some ways it was not nearly enough to replace what she lost because of depreciation, but she would get a nice start. Shopping for a few new items would be fun and therapeutic. Peyton would see to that.

She waved at her cousin who was waiting on a customer. Jessie made a beeline for her computer. She wanted to know why Johanna was in Molly's store and who the dude was hanging out above the stairs. How would she ever begin to connect the two since she had no idea what his name was or even if he lived in Kilkenny during Johanna's lifetime? He must have. There was no way they both would suddenly show up at the same time if they weren't connected somehow.

Between the normal customer interruptions, she hadn't learned much more about her unearthly visitors when her time at work ended. She would do more research later tonight. What would be nicer was if Johanna were to explain her presence herself.

Jessie turned the business over for the last three hours of the day to Audrey when she came in for the short evening shift. She couldn't believe it was almost the middle of July. Their trip had taken a good part of the summer. Peyton would be back working at the school before long. She kept watch out the window for Matt's car and went out the door as soon as he pulled up.

"Did you hear anything about Ashley?" she asked when she scooted into the front seat.

"No. But there's another abduction in Baycliff that sounds eerily similar to Ashley's," he told her.

"That's not good. Two missing girls. If their descriptions are similar, then someone may be up to his old tricks." Jessie scrunched her face in thought. She went on to tell him about Johanna's presence in the coffee shop. "I can't believe she rearranged the kitchen. Molly knew something was up. The thing is, I believe both ghosts are connected and here for a reason. Now all I have to do is figure out why."

"While you're working on that angle, I'll be working it from mine. Two ghosts hanging out anywhere are two too many for me." He chuckled. "But knowing you the way I do, I'm sure I will find out soon enough why they are here." He glanced at her. "On a more serious note, your dream is beginning to make sense to me. I'm seeing the effects of the rising tide and hearing more evidence of it from other authorities."

"I find the whole prospect fascinating and yet scary at the same time. Grams was telling us about the turmoil of the sixties, and I remember getting a small taste of it while I was there. The anti-war protests had some kids fleeing to Canada to escape the draft. And Peyton saw the unrest through our great-great grandmother's eyes during the Spanish Flu era. There was division then too. I guess as long as there are people there are bound to be troubles."

"Doesn't it make you wonder why various times are more charged than others?" Matt pulled into his driveway. "The world seems smaller at the moment than I can remember as a kid."

"Of course, everything is amplified with the internet and a twenty-four-hour news cycle. Look how fast chatter can travel around the world with the click of a button." She glanced at him.

"True. Imagine if the Spanish Flu hit in our generation with air travel. We are certainly more global." Matt unlatched his seat belt.

"It's a small world after all sounds cliché but is actually true." Jessie smiled and hummed the song to make her point.

"Jaxon gave us a lesson on Artificial Intelligence today too. Tech has made amazing discoveries, such as cancer detection using technology. In the wrong hands, talk about scary. I'm not sure how we're going to control that cat since we let it out of the bag. Even the creators want controls put on the use of AI, but I think we might be too late to manage it already."

"I've been hearing about the capabilities of artificial intelligence, along with the downsides. I have to admit that I only recently started to pay attention. My dad always used to say that computers would take over the world and we would no longer think for ourselves. That was his excuse to me every time I asked for one and he didn't want to spend the money." Jessie chuckled. "He has a big fancy one now, though."

"Funny, my grandpops used to say something similar. Maybe they were smarter than we gave them credit for." Matt turned in his seat to look at her. "At least, after what I heard earlier, that's my position at the moment. People's creative skills, intellectual property, and images could be used and not compensated for. There are real ethical issues being raised."

"I hear you. Leave it to us to take something that could be useful and turn it into a problem for our planet's existence We humans seem to get ourselves into trouble more often than we should." Jessie reached for his hand. "You have a front row seat to that show. I'm not telling you anything new."

"Do you want to go out to dinner? I'm not in the mood to cook. I'll text Jaxon and let him know."

"Sounds good to me. I hope you have somewhere in mind." She leaned her head back against the neck rest.

"I know the perfect place." He sent the text and then backed out of the driveway.

They drove a few miles out of Blue Cove. Off the highway, in a grove of trees, a small restaurant that touted itself as perfect for family dining stood. Once inside the door, they were greeted by an elderly woman and a clean comfortable atmosphere. Not to mention, something smelled divine.

"Good evening, folks. I have a nice quiet table that's perfect for you." She grabbed two menus and motioned for them to follow her. "Marcie will be right with you."

"Look at the view." Jessie pointed at the trees and wildflowers outside the window. "I have driven past this area many times but don't remember seeing this placed tucked back here." She picked up the menu and thanked the young woman who placed a glass of water in front of her.

"Jaxon told me about this place. He said the food was great." Matt slipped on his glasses to read the menu. "No more serious talk; it's not good for the digestion."

"I can live with that." Jessie peered over the top of her menu at him.

After they placed their order with Marcie, they talked about family, growing up, and she told him more about her trip. Matt had some funny stories he shared. His mother must have been a saint raising the three boys. They did some pretty wild things. They made Jessie's life seem fairly routine and even a tad boring.

She laughed often and found herself totally relaxed for the first time since the night of shooting. Marcie's sweet mannerisms and smile topped off the evening on a high note. A recent graduate from high school, she was working to add to her college funds. Matt gave her a generous tip, which made him awesome in Jessie's eyes. As far as she was concerned, the evening was perfect and much too short before the drive back to the cove ensued and reality pressed itself back to the forefront.

Bobby Bristol was still waiting to be caught, Ashley needed to be found, and nothing had changed to ease the tension of Jessie's dream, and yet for a moment the tension had eased. Matt had a way of taking her mind away from present circumstances if only for an instant. He was a good man. The last remaining questions were answered during their conversation. Any hesitancy she had felt seemed to melt away as the evening progressed. His large tip was the icing on the cake. The drive home and their kiss goodnight sealed the deal in her mind. There was no way she would let him get away. Matt was a keeper.

Chapter 18

Matt stretched out on his bed and folded his arms beneath his head. He smiled. He could sense Jessie's resistance fading. Yeah, he would be calling to tell his family about the wedding date soon. Evan, his big brother, would be happy. Evan had called him earlier to tell him he was going to pop the question to Destiny, Peyton's friend. And Chad, his best friend growing up, was going to ask Jessie's friend Sally to marry him. It seemed like the perfect time for him to step in the water. Maybe that wasn't the best analogy because of Jessie's dream.

Was there really any perfect time? People have been marrying and raising families in the midst of hardship since the dawn of time. At some point, needing things to be perfect had crept into his thinking. Of course, there was no such thing. There was no ideal, convenient time when everything was exactly right, although tonight came pretty close for him. He could see many nights around a dinner table, learning all he could about the woman he loved. Yep, it was damn near perfect, and he would be content to live with a bit of mystery. Well, maybe when it came to Jessie there might be a lot of mystery involved.

He closed his eyes and drifted off to sleep. The sound of a door creaking awakened him at some point. He jumped out of bed and reached for his gun. He opened the door quietly and met Jaxon in the hall with his gun drawn.

"You take the front door and I'll take the one from the garage into the kitchen," Matt whispered, and Jaxon nodded.

Matt crept toward the kitchen in time to see the dark shape coming into the door. "Stop, and drop your weapon." Matt didn't think twice when he saw the gun pointed in his direction—he fired a shot. The guy groaned and escaped through the door. He pursued and followed through the side door, but there was no sign of the intruder. The motion lights gave proof that the man had been hit. Matt followed the blood trail all the way to the street where the droplets disappeared, along with the man.

"I heard a shot. Are you okay?" Jaxon asked as he came outside.

"I'm fine, but our intruder might not be." Matt pointed at the blood drops. "How in the hell did he get away so fast?" He rubbed his temple. "I didn't hear a car, which means he has to still be close by. I'm calling for backup. I'm not exactly dressed to run through the neighborhood." He stood on the sidewalk wearing only his boxers, tee, and no shoes. "And neither are you." He pointed at Jaxon. They walked back through the garage into the house.

****

Jessie sat up, pushing her hair out of her eyes. "Was that a gunshot?" She strained to listen for another sound. All was quiet. Swinging her legs over the side of the bed, she reached for her robe when she heard Matt talking to Jaxon in the hall. Jessie put her ear to the door to listen and then opened it when she heard Matt's voice again.

"I thought I heard a shot." She pulled her robe around her. Matt looked handsome standing there in his jeans, tee shirt, and his hair tousled.

"You did. We had an intruder. I shot him but he managed to escape." Matt walked over to her.

"Was it Bobby?" She shivered.

"I don't know. I never saw him up close. I have called in backup and they're driving through the neighborhood. I shot at him only after I saw his raised gun. He came in through the side garage door into the kitchen. I'm usually better about locking up."

"I thought you did when we got home." She took a few steps into the hall when Peyton opened her door.

"I thought I had too. I may have been distracted by our kiss." He frowned. "I have to keep focused on the job. This guy means business."

"I'm sure I heard gunfire," Peyton said as she stepped out into the hall.

"You did." Jessie nodded and went on to fill her in on the details as the guys talked. "They don't know who it was, but Matt wounded him."

"That's a bit scary, don't you think?" Peyton grabbed Jessie's hand. "He came here. Could it be the same guy who shot your place up?"

"I have no concrete evidence." She smiled. She was starting to sound like Matt. "At this point, I am only speculating but I have a theory, of course." Jessie followed Matt into the living room. The more she listened to Matt and Jaxon talk the more she understood that she had to figure out why Johanna was here. She was an important key. And while she was researching, it wouldn't hurt to know who the spirit in her store was and if Bristol was Skylar in another form or someone unknown to her. Something big was up, but what?

She sat on the sofa and listened to Matt giving orders on the phone. She felt a bit like watching a tennis match—her head moved back and forth between Matt and Jaxon as they paced the room like a woman possessed. Matt reached one side of the room when Kip raced through the front door followed by an officer she hadn't met yet. They conversed with Jaxon and Matt and told him before they left that two officers would be stationed outside of the house to keep watch. It made her feel better, but in her heart she knew that this would come down to her and the suspect, whoever he was. The last time, with Garett Massey, he hadn't played fair. Through some strange wizardry, the officers couldn't move from the spot where they stood, and she had to break Massey's power herself. She still remembered their shock when the man simply disappeared when they went to cuff him. Would it be the same with Bristol? Probably. Nothing seemed to be normal when she was involved. She should know soon enough. Matt wouldn't be happy, but he'd get used to the idea in time or via circumstance. Usually there wasn't a choice.

"I guess you heard most of the conversation." Matt glanced at her. "They found no trace of him." He frowned. "I know what you're going to say."

"Is that right?" Her brows rose as she tilted her head.

"You were going to remind me that most of our investigations have elements in them that aren't logical, or something profoundly similar. I don't have to like the process, but I have to learn to live with the unexplainable."

"Well, I wouldn't have put it quite that way, but we'll go with your statement. Yours sounds more professional. I would have said something more like, we've been there, done that, and now live with it." She chuckled.

He grinned. "Sometimes you don't make any sense. You can joke when most women would be crying."

"I'm learning to adjust to my new life. Laughter is a must for my survival. That, and tears, of course. Besides, you heard the door squeak, and I only woke up after the gunshot. You're way ahead of me when it comes to knowing what's going on in the visible world."

"Is that right?"

She nodded. "You'll keep me safe."

"I'll do my best." He kissed her. "Get some sleep. I doubt he'll be back tonight." Matt nudged her gently toward the hallway before he turned her into his arms and kissed her again.

****

He stuffed a rag into his shirt to stop the flow of blood from his wound. Grazed by a damn bullet and he had no idea why this fella tried to get into that house. Controlling some people's personality foibles wasn't always easy. He had to leave the hospital in the city so fast that he never got his host's name, but the guy must have a real death wish. Why else would he go into the cop's house for another shootout. He seemed to jump into things with no real plan of action. Wouldn't you know it was just his dumb luck to jump into the body of a loose cannon. The only reason the cop and the woman were still alive was because he forced the young man to his will. He needed her alive to see his plan through. Damn, this was harder this time.

The mission he was given was too important to act on impulse, but this body's thoughts and alpha male tendencies weren't making it easy. He could repair the mess to his arm, but he couldn't remember the last time he had trouble with a host. At least for the moment, he needed to get the man's anger under control. His host's youthful craving might come in handy later on, but not yet. "Don't do anything stupid, or you'll get yourself killed, and I'll find myself looking for someone else." He grimaced when he pressed down harder on the wound.

****

Matt had no idea how the suspect got away. His gut churned at his next thought. What if the guy had made it farther into the house without being detected? As much as he hated to give in, he would call the alarm company in the morning. He didn't need another shootout to be his wake-up call.

Matt leaned back in his recliner, not wanting to return to his bedroom. Lucky two times—he couldn't count on a third. He needed to remain alert. Taking each element of the investigation that he knew at this point, he tried to logically work his way through each one. Jessie's dream, he could understand and had data to back it up. What happened to Kyle and Ashley was a bit harder to analyze because of Bristol. He was an unknown factor. He threw the whole investigation into the unexplainable with being both a victim and now a suspect. A young man who had died from his injury but was here alive and shooting up Jessie's place. Matt tried to find out all the information he could from Bobby's mother. Her heart was broken as she told Matt about his father and later his stepfather's abuse. Bobby ran with the wrong crowd, and nothing she said would deter him. Damn, what a mess. She didn't know half of it. Beyond the question of how it was even possible, was what could he do about him?

Chapter 19

Jessie waved at Matt as he drove away. He had checked out her store, walking right past the mean-looking spirit hovering over the stairs. Of course, Matt couldn't see the dude like she could. His location did make her wonder if there was something he was guarding upstairs or if something bad had happened there long ago. Fanciful thinking on her part, but she couldn't help dredging up scenarios. She had to admit she was glad that Matt was being protective of her.

She hadn't told Matt that she had the dream again. Each time the water rushed toward her, it was harder to fight the waves threatening to overtake her. Last night's dream was more detailed and vivid. She had awakened in a cold sweat with the strangest feeling of impending danger. After her nightmare and the intruder, sleep eluded her. She needed a break. Jessie was happy tomorrow was their shopping day. Matt was dragging his feet about it but said he'd take them. Jaxon was coming too.

Jessie went through her morning routine to open. The simple repetitive act along with Peyton's arrival had a calming effect on her. After she turned the open sign around, Reba waved as she stepped out of her car, which had the opposite impact. Her friend only showed up when she had something to say, and Jessie didn't always want to hear the message.

"Good morning, my dears." Reba walked in the door that Jessie held open for her. "It's a glorious day out there."

"What brings you out so early this morning?" Peyton asked.

"I'm on a mission but not without a bit of tea and a lovely scone. We will need nourishment to fortify us today, I should think." She placed her sweater on the back of the chair. "I will return in a few. In the meantime, you need to figure out why that spirit's aura is that of a warrior. We need to do something about him."

"Can't wait to hear the rest of what she has to say." Jessie smiled at Peyton. "I wonder what her mission is that requires nourishment."

"We're about to find out." Peyton turned to watch Reba come in, with Molly carrying the cups of tea and scones on a tray.

"Join me, my dears." Reba sat in a chair at the table in the middle of the store. "We have much to discuss. I want details and you need answers." She patted the chair beside her.

Jessie took a sip of the tea that Reba handed her when she sat down. "I'm not sure we have any details to give you. We seem to be flying dark on this one, with plenty of pieces but few answers."

"Well then, let's put some of the pieces together and make sense out of them." Reba handed them each a napkin and a scone.

"Where do we start?" Peyton asked.

"Let's start with the supernatural activity in your store and in the coffee shop. Who are they and why are they here?" Reba glanced over her cup of tea at Jessie.

"It's true there is a ghost in the coffee shop. Jessie can tell you more about that." Peyton scrunched her face. "As you are aware, we have one here also. We see our unfriendly ghost's grumpy face every day."

"What about Joe's?" Reba asked looking at Jessie.

"When Molly told me her kitchen was being rearranged and wondered if we were having any trouble, I went to check it out. This time her kitchen had been cleaned, which she knew she hadn't done and neither had any of her help. The shelves were arranged in an orderly and more efficient manner. A nice problem to have but still a mystery. I'm sorry if I never mentioned this to you." Jessie sipped her tea and went on to explain. "I could sense a presence there but didn't see anything at first."

"I did too, and that's why I asked." Reba dabbed at her mouth with her napkin.

"It turns out it's Johanna, but I have no idea why she's there," Jessie said.

"At least Johanna is biding her time in a good way, unlike him." Peyton pointed at the stairs.

"She's here because she has a piece of the puzzle," Reba said with confidence. "But as for the one hanging out with you, I have no idea why he's here. Although, I think Johanna might." Reba took a sip of her tea. "He perplexes me. He's a restless one, and out of his element, which has me wondering."

"You and me both. It is possible that he's attached to one of our investigations, but truthfully, I have no idea." Jessie took a bite of her scone.

"Let's start with that premise," Reba stated.

"It could be one of the people who was jumped into and dumped along the way, and he's not happy about it. Maybe he's waiting for the person to come into the store." Peyton jumped up. "That's sounds fantastical even to me."

"But feasible and something to think about," Jessie added. "Or maybe he's from Johanna's time as you suggested." Jessie pointed at Reba.

"That's possible, but who is he? Any idea?" Peyton frowned.

"No." Jessie shook her head.

"You will know soon enough, but I like the way your minds work when you work together. I have a caution for both of you. Be careful. Someone is watching for the opportunity to do harm to you both. He's from the past but also your present and will seek you out in an unlikely place. You'll be fine in the long run. As he sees it, he's on an important mission. One that I'm sure we wouldn't agree with. He's definitely here to stir up trouble." Reba sipped her tea. "We are living in complex times with this one because though the immediate issues may be solved, there are crimes that will stretch into cases in the future."

"Which would make sense after some of what Matt talked to me about last night after the intruder." Jessie pursed her lips.

"Intruder? What intruder?" Reba raised her voice several notches. "I didn't hear the word intruder in our conversation up to now."

Jessie told her about the break-in at Matt's house. "Matt shot at him and wounded him, but he still got away."

"That changes everything, doesn't it?" Reba glanced at both of them. "Our guy isn't afraid, is he? Which reminds me—we need to do something about that spirit. He's bringing the atmosphere down in your store. Go about your business, and I'll remain and have a chat with the fella and try to find out his purpose for hanging around."

To the casual observer, Reba looked peaceful and deeply involved in the magazine in front of her, but Jessie knew there was something more going on. The turmoil swirling through her store let her know that Reba was dealing with the ghost who seemed to be getting more agitated as the day progressed.

The store was busy, but Jessie kept abreast of the situation happening around her. At one point, the angry spirit zipped overhead, sending shivers running down her arms, and when he flew back around, she thought he came at her like a kamikaze pilot who lifted only before a direct hit. She wanted to swat at him, but didn't want to be seen by one of her customers as beating the air.

She shook her head. Her life was the thing of novels, and no one would believe her if she told them. Pure fiction, but real enough for her.

"What do you think Reba is up to? She's been sitting there for over an hour," Peyton asked softly.

"She's dealing with our local ghoul." Jessie kept her eye on the ghost flying around the room.

"I don't think he's happy about whatever she's doing because the atmosphere in here is charged."

"I know. He's been zipping around the store for a while now. I'm not sure why, but he seems to be getting more agitated with each turn around the store." Jessie ducked automatically as he flew by again. "Frankly, I'm getting tired of it all. It's time for a little chat with Reba. Watch the register for me, please." Jessie walked toward the table when the spirit flew past her and out the door as a new customer walked in. "Okay, my sweet friend, start talking."

"My, he is a stubborn one. I knew the minute I zeroed in on him he wasn't from around here." Reba patted the chair. "He's gone for the moment, but he'll be back. It's his duty, he told me in no uncertain terms, to stand guard, and he wouldn't leave until his task was finished. We had better get used to him. He refused to tell me what he was here to do but only that he came from far away and long ago."

"What is that supposed to mean?" Jessie frowned. "I don't need him here."

"He seemed to think you do even though he wasn't pleased. He would rather be at home in Kilkenny doing whatever he does there. Don't you find it a tad amazing that there's a whole world invisible to most but still real whether we see it or not? I find the whole idea invigorating and quite incredible."

"Others might call it farfetched," Jessie said with a touch of sarcasm.

"But not us, dear girl. We know better because we've been privileged to see that world, haven't we?" Reba patted her hand.

"I'm not sure about the privilege part, but we've definitely seen some strange things."

"Listen to me. It's your dream that brought both Johanna and him here. They're connected in some way. He wasn't a talkative fella and quite stingy with the details. Mostly he became unsettled with each question I put to him. A bit rough around the edges, he wasn't a pleasant fella at all. Which means he wasn't a nice man to be around in life either, or maybe that's how they all were. Women rarely questioned a man then."

"Doesn't it make you wonder who he was in life?" Jessie glanced at Reba.

"I'm always curious, dear girl. I'll leave you to find the details about our mystery spirit's life, but I know one detail for sure—his life ended abruptly, and he's been angry ever since." Reba stood. "I need to go, but remember this—you'll get more information by being sweet to him even though he's a grouch."

"I have no idea how to get information out of a ghost that can't even talk." Jessie followed her to the door.

Reba turned around and looked her in the eye. "Come, dear girl, you're inventive enough." She pointed at her. "Remember singing the song you learned in Sunday School to get rid of the darkness that threatened to overtake you in your case in Palm Springs. You'll figure out how to talk with your twitchy visitor. Don't underestimate yourself. It's the only way you'll grow. I'll leave you to figure it out." Reba walked through the door Jessie held open. "Be on guard. Everything is moving into overdrive. I don't want anything to happen to you or your dear cousin."

"I don't want anything to happen to us either," Jessie mumbled under her breath. She waved goodbye to Reba as she drove away.

The ghost had better not return for a while because she was feeling a bit unsettled herself, and she might not be nice to her unwanted guest, whoever he was. Although she could understand why he might be upset. An unfinished life was not a happy ending for anyone.

Chapter 20

The two cousins' happy chatter in the back seat made Matt smile. He loved seeing his girl relax and enjoy herself. After Jessie told him about her conversation with Reba, he was glad she could find any pleasure in life. Their conversation last night was another episode of mind-blowing circumstances that he found hard to wrap his head around.

She might find the details a bit intimidating at first but always found a way to work through them. Not him. He'd simply put them on the backburner of his mind and try not to think about them until Jessie brought them up in a way that he could logically deal with them or simply leave them in the category of the unexplainable. Both he and Jaxon had a few of those oddities that they left out of reports.

"There's a coffee shop near the place where the girls want to shop. We'll be close enough if they need us but far enough away where they don't feel like we're hovering." Jaxon glanced at the two women chattering away in the back seat.

"Good. I've been a tad uneasy about this whole business today." Matt got into the turn lane when he saw the sign to Elm's Spring.

"Me too, but I chalked it up to everything going on. I'm overprotective when it comes to Peyton, or at least she tells me I am, all the time." He grinned.

"I know I am, but after the last few days, I've earned the right to be. I'm not going to apologize for being safe. I'd rather be safe than sorry, as the saying goes. I'll let you in on a secret—I think Jessie likes it all the while she's telling me she doesn't." Matt chuckled. "I'm afraid it's too late for me to change my ways."

"I hear you. Besides, right now it's a bit strange and not the time to ease up. Because of their unique abilities, they have a target on their back."

Matt pulled up in front of the crowded store. "Here you are, ladies. I'll be back to pick you up in an hour and a half unless you text me to come earlier."

"If anything, she might tell you to come later. We know how to shop." Peyton smiled as she closed the door.

Jessie leaned through Matt's open window and kissed him. "See you in a few and thanks for bringing us." She started to walk away and then turned. "I love you."

"I love you too."

Matt watched her walk into the store, not liking what he detected. Jessie was troubled. Did that mean her instinct was telling her something was up? "Let's get our coffee to go and come back to shop with them. If my guess is right, my girl is having second thoughts about being here today."

"I'm down with that. I wasn't sure it was a good idea from the beginning, but they seemed excited to go. Peyton has been talking about it for days."

"Jessie has been too. That's why her mood this morning threw me a curve." Matt pulled into the line at the coffee shop and placed their order. As soon as they paid the cashier and got their drinks, he got a text alert on his phone.

****

Jessie took a shopping cart when they got into the store and instead of starting at the front and working her way to the back, she started toward the back with Peyton walking quickly at her side. With Reba's warning to be on guard ringing in her ear she did something completely out of character for her.

"Something is wrong." Peyton made the statement and picked up her pace.

"I know. I had doubts about coming, and I should have listened to the warning in my head." Jessie stopped near the display of picture frames. "What should we do? I don't want to go out the front. Is there a back exit?"

"I have no idea." Peyton glanced around the building.

They had reached the back when they heard what sounded like gunfire erupting in the distance but seemed to get closer. People began screaming and running in all directions. A store clerk rushed by them with keys in his hand and motioned at them to follow him. He inserted the key and held the door open into a back storage area.

Several people ran in behind them. He told them to silence their phones and put a finger to his lips, telling them to be quiet. The young man locked and barricaded the door when the sound of gunfire appeared to get closer to their location. Jessie sat on the floor with her back against the wall as the sound of rapid shots and screams could be heard outside the door. She texted Matt the words "active shooter" and held tight to

Peyton wondering if this was how their lives would end. They huddled together while the safety of their world seemed to shatter around them.

She had no gun with her, no vest to protect her, and besides, she had seen what the power of that gun could do. Powerless to help those who she knew might be dying outside the confines of the room she huddled in, tears began to roll down her cheeks.

****

The moment Matt read her text his world began to crash around him. He had to get to her. What had he been thinking to let her come today? Bristol was still out there. The sound of sirens pushed him into action. "We need to get back to the store."

"I know. Peyton texted me too. Damn, I hope we're not too late." Jaxon stared out the passenger window.

Matt pulled into the parking lot as the swat team was racing into the building. Matt parked the car and jumped out and ran toward the doors where an officer stopped both him and Jaxon. They showed him their badges. There were several sprays of gunfire and then silence.

"Can we help you in any way?" Jaxon asked.

"This was supposed to be a great moment for our town. Now this. Damn." The young officer shook his head. "This isn't supposed to happen in our town."

As more police arrived, the perimeter of the store was sealed off. Matt had seen two victims lying in the parking lot along with several car windows shot out in his quick jaunt to the door.

Only his training kept him from rushing through the doors in search of Jessie. The silence was getting to him. *"Shooter is neutralized, I repeat, the shooter is neutralized,"* came over the officer's radio. The medics rushed by them, and slowly the police worked their way through the store. Matt and Jaxon were allowed to help in the process.

Once inside the door Matt couldn't believe what he saw. The new store looked like a war zone. There were a couple of victims right inside the door who were beyond help. Medics were tending to the wounded where they found them. Matt had counted at least ten victims, and he hadn't made it around the store yet. Some were employees—he knew from their name badges—and a few must be customers. Hell, what a mess.

Matt gulped, holding his breath each time he passed a victim lying in a pool of blood. Relief and guilt mingled together in him each time he saw it wasn't Jessie or Peyton. Where were they?

"Matt, I need you to come take a look at the shooter," Jaxon told him when he answered his phone.

"Where are you?" Matt asked.

"Midway down aisle nine."

When Matt found Jaxon, he was squatting with another officer beside a young man dressed in black wearing a vest and carrying several rounds of ammo. When he got a look at the face of the man, Matt knew him. Bobby Bristol was a victim again. Was he dead or did he jump?

"We meet again," Matt said under his breath. The young man had been a victim twice. Matt still hadn't found the shooter who dumped him outside of Blue Cove. And this time another used his body to commit this heinous crime. Why? What was he after?

****

When the gunfire stopped, it seemed like an eternity before someone knocked on the door. The officer on the other side of the door told the young clerk who he was and to open up. The occupants were then given instructions as they were led out of the store. Jessie wanted to believe that she was strong and had changed in the past year. Somehow, she was tougher and could hold her own, but what she saw as they walked up the aisle and out the front door made her physically sick. She knew the destruction, the smell, but she wasn't prepared for the human toll, nor the spirits so suddenly ripped from their earthly bodies. Once outside they were asked to give a statement. They were released to leave after they gave their names and phone numbers to another officer.

Jessie texted Matt to tell him where they were outside. They found a small retaining wall where they could sit and wait. Jessie put her arm around Peyton's shoulder, and they cried together until there were no more tears.

"At least, now I understand why we went to the back of the store first. I would never have done that normally. Peyton, we could be dead. I can't believe what I saw in there." She gulped to hold back the sob rising in her throat.

"I know. I doubt we'll ever be able to forget the scene." Peyton dabbed her eyes with a tissue.

"People were there only to shop, a normal action and not one you'd think they'd have to worry about someone shooting them. Why? I don't get it anymore. How can a person, without remorse, take innocent peoples' lives? I've heard about mass shootings on the news, but to see it up close and personal changes everything." She swiped at the tears running down her cheeks.

"I know, and seeing all those spirits wandering through the store makes me think the victims registered the shock and the suddenness." Peyton shivered rubbing her arms.

"There's Matt." Jessie stood and waved at him and Jaxon. Within seconds she was scooped up into his arms in a huge hug. Safe and loved were the emotions that ran through her mind. She shuddered and every muscle in her body quivered as the shock started to settle in.

"Where were you?" Matt asked as soon as they were all in the car.

She explained about going first to the back of the store and the young store clerk who saved several lives by hiding them in the storage room. "I didn't get his name. We owe him our lives. I want to thank him, but I don't ever want to go back in that store again."

Once in the car, Jessie laid her head back against the seat. She didn't want to close her eyes or see the images of bodies, blood, and ghosts. She could see the waves of her dreams swallowing more victims and getting closer to her. She had escaped twice, but how many more times could she?

Chapter 21

Matt was itching to ask them both questions. But they needed time to process their horrific morning and get over the shock. If that was even possible. He wanted to tell Jess the shooter's ID. A big trouble spot for him. Instinct told him Bristol was there because Jessie and Peyton were. Matt wasn't sure what that knowledge would do to her. She would bear the guilt of what happened. Plus, he didn't think for a minute that it ended today with the death of Bobby Bristol.

The ride home was quiet. He could see the moisture glistening in her overly bright eyes every time he looked in the rearview mirror. He made a pledge not to lecture her about paying attention to her premonitions. She was uneasy when he dropped her off. He had seen it in her actions. Hell, what could he say? He was struggling with his own guilt for not going with his instinct. What could he say to her that he shouldn't say to himself! The first minutes in that store were sheer torture for him, not knowing if she was one of the injured or, worse yet, fatalities.

Jaxon turned around and glanced in the backseat. "Are you okay, sweetheart?" he asked Peyton.

"As strange as this may sound, I'm counting my lucky stars that I'm still alive. If we hadn't gone to the back of the store first, and if that young man hadn't opened the door to the storage room, this day could have ended differently. Call it fate, luck, or providence, I'm grateful to be here." Peyton leaned forward and squeezed Jaxon's shoulders. "I'm sure I haven't processed everything yet, but I'm grateful."

"I was thinking the same thing." Jessie wiped at another tear rolling down her cheek. "I will do my best not to dismiss people who have lost someone in a shooting. What bothers me the most is all the people might have died or were injured because the shooter knew we were in the store." Jessie's voice quivered. "I was uneasy this morning, but I had no idea why. I didn't see any of this coming, only Reba's last warning played in my mind repeatedly—to pay attention and to be careful."

"As Reba always tells us, we only know what we know. We can't manufacture premonitions. If we did, that would be us and nothing more. For some reason we didn't foresee this one." Peyton reached for Jessie's hand. "You can't blame yourself for not knowing."

"I might not have seen what would happen, but I did sense something wasn't right." She saw Matt looking at her in the mirror. "I know you have questions and probably a lecture too. Give it your best shot." She gave him a weak smile.

"You're right about the questions. I could tell earlier something was bothering you, but I'd have to lecture myself because I knew in my gut something wasn't right." He glanced at her in the mirror. "Why did you go to the back of the aisle first?" he asked.

"I have no idea. I grabbed a cart and went at once toward the back. I was looking for a back door. I started to have that smothering feeling that I have in my dream. It wasn't long before we heard the first gunshots. Far away at first, like they were fired outside. Then the spray of bullets and screams grew louder. That's when I knew the shooter was inside." Jessie reached into her purse for a tissue. "The cries for help, the moans, and someone pleading for their life are etched into my mind."

"When we walked out, we passed by bodies that were shredded. The police were beginning to cover them and process the scene but what I saw, I don't know how I'll ever unsee." Peyton took the tissue Jessie handed her. "The young man who opened the storage room saved many lives, and I'm sure there will be many more heroic stories. As well, sad human stories will be told that will break our heart all over again."

"I know Bristol was the shooter. Did he make it?" She met Matt's eyes in the rearview mirror.

"No, he was neutralized." He frowned. "But I don't think it's over."

"If we hear of a missing person who should have been in the store we'll know if he jumped into someone else, as crazy as that may sound." Jessie closed her eyes. "I'm not sure why he's here, but I don't think he was meant to do that. I'm not even sure if we were really the targets. Something doesn't feel right about all this."

Matt watched her. "I'm not sure how to interpret that."

"I'm not sure either." She gulped.

Matt frowned. Hate groups had shifted their tactics over the years. They had gone from parades and militias to wearing suits and ties. They had joined legitimate organizations and started recruiting from within to change the culture more to their liking. According to the new information coming across the wire, the greatest threat to the country was homegrown.

Jessie's and Peyton's abilities were needed more now than ever. They couldn't see everything, but they could see enough to point law enforcement in the right direction. They were an amazing asset. Were there more like them out there somewhere?

"We're home." Matt gently awakened Jessie. "Looks like for a while, sweetheart, you'll be doing your shopping online. I'm sorry the day turned out the way it did." He hugged her and she shuddered in his arms. "We'll get through this together, sweetheart. I've seen a few murder scenes, but this one was tough for me to see. I can't imagine how you are processing what you saw, but we can help each other." He moved his hands up and down her back until she relaxed in his arms. "Promise me, if you are sensing anything off, no matter how small, that you'll tell me. I didn't want to leave you this morning. We ordered coffee and were headed back to the store to be with you when your text arrived. I shouldn't have left feeling the way I did. I know better."

She pulled back in his arms to look at his face. "You aren't to blame."

"No, and neither are you. Each day we make choices and never know how they will affect our life. We do the best that we can."

****

Again, Matt proved himself to be a keeper, and she was tired of dragging her feet. It might be nice to dream about a wedding instead of a murder. She was more than ready to give in to the luxury and dreams of a life with someone who loved her. First, she had to get through this, and then she would be ready to move on.

Matt and Jaxon had shooed them to their rooms with the promise of making dinner. Jessie stretched out on her bed and rolled over on her side. How did today fit into the broader picture? Because Bristol died in the attack, they now had no idea who he had become. Seeing all the spirits suddenly ripped from their bodies made her think of the ghost in her store. Shock and anger described the look permanently etched on his face. Had he met his demise in a similarly devastating manner? She might need to have a chat with him at some point.

Was Johanna here to encourage her to make a difference in her time? Anything was possible. Who killed Bobby before he jumped? If Bristol was dead, where was Ashley? Her thoughts went around in circles as one question brought up another and then another. Jessie was positive that this case might only be the tip of the iceberg regarding what was happening at the cove and around the world. What that meant for the future, she had no idea. All she could do was figure out how her piece fit and in what way she could affect those she rubbed up against in life.

Her eyes closed and blissfully, for a moment, she saw nothing. No victims lying on the ground, no waves clawing their way toward her, and no spirits displaced from their homes in an abrupt manner, only silence and a sense that in this brief moment all was well.

Chapter 22

Matt's voice reached through the fog in her head. "Jess, dinner is ready."

"I'm awake," she said. Her voice sounded groggy. She sat up, swinging her legs over the side of the bed. "How long did I sleep?" She pushed her hair out of her eyes.

"A while." Matt stood at the foot of the bed and waited for her. "I wasn't sure if you were awake enough to make it on your own." He linked his arm through hers.

"I'm not old, Matt." She pinched his arm and chuckled.

"No, but you were sound asleep." He led her to the table and pulled out the chair for her. "I was concerned you might walk into a wall or something."

She smiled and patted his cheek. "Thank you. I might have."

Matt watched and listened to their chatter and answers to his questions at dinner. He searched for a key in their conversation to how Jessie was sorting through all the events in her mind. He knew her well enough to know she had arranged the pieces she already knew and was finding ways to connect them into a bigger picture.

He loved that about her. No matter how tough her situation became, she found a way to plow through and find answers to make sense of what she was seeing. Those connections gave him, with his logical brain, a way to move forward and process an investigation that made no sense to him at all.

Her dream, he could understand, but Bristol's story was another matter. Even though he had to work around the Skylar/Massey issue in one of their cases, he never expected to have to face the idea of a traveler jumping into another body for a second time. But here he was again.

"I've tried to put all the pieces I know together in some kind of order. I might have a theory about why the ghost in my store looks perturbed," Jessie said. She explained seeing the newly displaced spirits' expressions and how the same might have happened to the fellow in her store.

"That's a real possibility." Peyton's face lit up. "He's not recent, though. Right?"

"I may be wrong, but I think he's from Johanna's time." Jessie took a bite of the salad in front of her.

"Is it possible he's one of Dame Alice Kyteler's husbands?" Peyton asked.

"Well. that would certainly put a new twist on things. Anything is possible, I guess. I'll have to think about your idea for a while. It has merit." Jessie sipped her iced tea. "You guys know how to make a good meal. Thank you."

"I want you to tell me from the beginning everything that happened from the time you walked into the store," Matt told her.

"Again?" She frowned.

"Yes. You know how this works, sweetheart. Details are important. Maybe this time you'll remember seeing something or someone that you didn't mention before." Matt opened his small note pad and reached for his pen.

"You too, Peyton," Jaxon said. "We need all the details that we can get."

"Actually, Jess, tell me why you were hesitant to go in the store to begin with."

"I guess the concern has been brewing for a few days. First, my dream has me unsettled, the night Bristol shot at us freaked me out, and the intruder the other night didn't help either. Add the ghosts and Reba's warning to be on guard, and I think I've been on edge. I wish I could have seen it coming, but I had no clue Bristol would go on a shooting rampage. It doesn't add up. It's like he was being driven. I can't image why, if it is Skylar. Why would he shoot all those innocent people? None of this makes sense. For that matter, why would he try to kill me?"

"Hmm," Peyton said. "You're right. Didn't he try to keep you at the commune when you traveled back to the sixties?"

"Yes," Jessie said. "He was a manipulator and controlled the girls. He didn't mean to kill Kimberly and was haunted by her death. He didn't know about Hope. The twins were separated at birth and met secretly over the years. Imagine his surprise when he saw her. Skylar was more of a make-love-not-war kind of guy."

"There's a term I haven't heard in a while." Matt smiled at her. "Let's say for now that Skylar would be more of a red herring in a mystery. A possibility to take the light off another but not the real culprit."

"It seems we need to learn more about Bristol and

the other man. The traveler or whoever jumped into Bristol has to be someone with an angry past and a violent nature." Jessie frowned. "This presents a whole new set of problems."

"Hell." Matt rubbed his temple. "How are we supposed to investigate the unknown?"

"We have to go back and research the man who died at the same time as Bobby and jumped into his body. There's an answer there with him somewhere. I wonder what Madison can tell us."

"I talked to the doctor in charge at the time. He said they found something strange in his bloodwork. It didn't match that of the man's other medical records or Bobby's. He couldn't account for the reason." Jaxon told them more about the conversation he'd had.

"We need to get Jeremy involved. He might be able to trace the history of the man, which might tell us more about him." Jessie stood, picked up her plate, and carried it to the sink.

Matt could tell the awful events of the day were beginning to catch up with her. "Are you okay?" He studied her movements back and forth across the kitchen.

"I have to do something to make the awfulness go away." She carried another dish from the table to the counter.

"You know, sweetheart, you didn't need to clean up. I would have taken care of it."

"I know, but I wanted to. I need to keep busy." She hung the towel up to dry. "I needed to keep my hands busy. I find mundane routine a perfect distraction. Rinse, load, and repeat, and do it all again. Over and over."

"It's a temporary fix, Jess." He wrapped his arms around her waist, pulling her back against his chest.

"I know, but any time away from reliving what I saw is time well spent even if it's only a short reprieve."

"In that case, let's watch a mindless comedy and chill." He took her by the hand and led her to the sofa.

He glanced at her several times during the course of the movie. Matt could tell she was barely hanging on to her emotions. Her wet glistening eyes were a dead giveaway. She didn't give up the pretense of watching until the credits rolled. She gave him a peck on the cheek and whispered good night in his ear. She was gutsy. He'd give her that. Things were tough enough without adding all the supernatural she dealt with. Whoever said women were the weaker ones had got it all wrong. Damn, she was one strong woman.

Stretched out on his bed, Matt went over their earlier conversation. Both Jessie and Peyton remembered a few more details as they went over their story a second time. Jessie was right about finding every piece of information they could on the man who jumped into Bristol. Bobby had either lived a short and violent life or had experienced violence twice. He would be the one charged with the mass murder today either way. A double nightmare for his family. What made the whole event even stranger was the real Bobby died in the hospital after being left for dead at the side of the road. He didn't kill anyone today, or did he? If not him, then who?

That would never go into his report, of course. Bobby would go down as having recovered and walked out of the hospital, only to commit several violent crimes. Matt wondered about the background of the man who was the real murderer, or was it Bristol? He had no idea how any of this worked.

After a quick text to Jeremy and Gary, he started thinking about the track with Frank and Carlene on Monday, the first day Frank was able to get to town. With any luck, they would find Ashley alive and well.

Chapter 23

Monday rolled in after a quiet Sunday. Jessie was thankful to get back to work. There were moments yesterday when the restlessness made her want to jump out of her skin. She knew she needed to talk to someone and would make an appointment today. Her cousin said the same thing before they went their separate ways this morning.

Peyton had a teachers' meeting at the school. Her cousin was eager and excited to get back to her students and the job she loved most. Jessie promised to go see her classroom once the school year began. Peyton invested a lot of time in her store and visiting her freshly restored classroom was the least she could do. Peyton living in Blue Cove meant everything to her. They often helped each other navigate the new terrain of their lives.

Jessie went through her morning routine to open a bit more distractedly today but managed to get the job done. Her ghost hovered in the same spot where he had been for days before Reba's chat with him. His disposition hadn't changed in the least bit. Next, she wanted to check out the coffee shop before her day began—a perfect reason to go see Molly, purchase her favorite morning treat, and see if Johanna was still rearranging Molly's kitchen.

Her question was answered the moment she walked

into Joe's. Johanna stood at the front of the store, staring out the window. Jessie moved toward her and went to sit in the chair beside where she stood.

"Do you want your usual?" Molly asked her.

"Yes, please." She stayed in the chair, not moving. Something important was happening, and Jessie didn't want to miss it. Johanna turned to her.

"It's time. I'll be waiting for you." She turned and walked away.

Jessie watched her until Johanna slipped through the closed doors into her store. She talked to Molly, paid for her order, and went into her store, closing the doors behind her. The store wouldn't open for another thirty minutes.

She placed her items on the counter and went to stand by Johanna. Mr. Grumpy Ghost flew near her head and zipped back and forth around them. "What time is it?" she asked.

"Time for you to know." Johanna waved the ghost off and sent him back to his place near the stairs. "He won't harm you. He goes where I go to watch over me, and now he must watch over you."

"I don't understand. Why must he watch over me? Will he remain in my store forever?" Jessie shuddered at the thought.

"We"—she pointed at Jessie and herself—"are different, as I'm sure you know by now. You and your cousins were born into a line of women who have been given special gifts. Passed down from one generation to the next one. Some embraced their gifts and some, to their regret, over time pushed their abilities away. You understand but a small part of yours. Knowing the ancestral line from where you came is important, and with that knowledge comes power and responsibility. I didn't know the full extent of my ability until I had suffered much loss. I don't intend for you to do the same. I kept writings of the discoveries I made in my lifetime. Many in our family line did as well. I have come to pass this special treasure on to you. We are from different times and languages, but you will find the translations that have been added over time by other women in our line. You are here for this time, and the beliefs and magic of your ancestors flows in your veins." Johanna pulled out a scroll with many others rolled inside. She handed them to Jessie.

When Jessie's hand touched the parchment, a tingling warmth shot through her hand and up her arm. The voices began to speak into her mind, generations of wisdom, from her sisters in time. She couldn't wait to see what secrets their writings held.

"Did they all have premonitions and see ghosts?" Jessie asked.

"No. Some read minds and others the auras around a person. Some were healers with herbs, while others' hands were gifted to remove disease. But each gift was meant for the good of others and never to be used for their own reward. Those who abused that rule found themselves on the dark side abusing the ones they were meant to help." Johanna touched Jessie's arm. "That rule still applies to this day."

Finally, she might understand herself and how she came to have this gift of sight. Once Johanna reassured her the ghost would remain only as long as he was needed, Jessie relaxed. She wouldn't waste any more time worrying about him. Johanna also told her she would learn more about him as time went on. Was what just happened a dream, a vision, or something more? The parchments in her hand told her that the visitation had to be somewhat real. Johanna's last words went deep into her heart. Only for the good of others.

Jessie opened all the doors, and the normal part of her day began. The morning saw plenty of customers but no one she could share about her morning with. Glances at the clock, text-message checks, and the endless waiting for her phone to ring filled her time. Matt promised to call if the tracker turned up Ashley's whereabouts.

"Hey, cous. I'm here and in one piece." Peyton chuckled. "It was nice to drive my own car today, but don't tell Matt." She grinned and rushed into the back room to make sure the door was locked. "I got out of the meeting earlier than I thought. I'm not a fan of meetings. What's new?"

"I've had quite a morning." Jessie handed the customer her bag. "I'll tell you later." Another customer stepped up to the counter with a stack of books.

"I've heard some great reviews on the book from several of my customers." Jessie lifted the book in her hand before placing it in the bag. "I have put it on my to-read list."

"My friend told me to grab a copy. She said it was a must read. During the warm, humid summer days I find reading my go to activity." The lady smiled at her. "It must be nice to work among all these lovely books."

"It is. Between the books and my customers, I have the best job ever." Jessie handed the woman her change. "Have a nice day." The woman had such a lovely smile.

"You won't believe what I'm going to show you."

Jessie looked around to make sure the store was empty. She pulled the parchment scrolls from their hiding spot and placed them on the counter. "I don't want anyone to see them." She lowered her voice to a whisper. "They are priceless."

"Oh my gosh, Jess, these are ancient. Where did you get them?" Peyton watched as Jessie slowly unrolled the biggest scroll containing the rest.

"Johanna gave them to me." Jessie explained her earlier visit and what she had shared with her. "We are a part of a long line of female ancestors who have the gift of sight and various other gifts. She told me it was important to know who we are and the gift we have. She also told me a little bit about our unfriendly ghost. He's here to help out, but I don't know how or why yet."

"I guess we'll find out in time. Look at this amazing writing. The penmanship is exquisite."

"We will study them together." Jessie carefully rolled and stashed the scrolls carefully back in their hiding place when she saw a car pull in the space in front of the store. "Tonight." She smiled and went to wait on a customer who walked in.

****

Matt drove Frank out to the place where Kyle and Ashley were attacked, and Ashley was abducted. While Frank unloaded Carlene from the crate and put her on track line, Matt got the scent item out of his trunk.

"It's been a few days. I hope she'll be able to pick up the scent." Matt handed over the bag with Ashley's sweater.

Frank knelt in front of Carlene and held the item in front of her nose. "Let's find her, girl." Carlene sniffed the air and began to move down a path deeper into a wooded area. "Do you know where this trail leads?"

"Through the woods which run along the outskirts of the whole town. Beyond them is the highway," Matt explained, showing Frank a map of the town on his phone. "This is a popular recreational area. People love the area to hike or run in the summer. In the winter, the area is filled with cross-country skiers and the occasional snowshoer."

"Do you know if there any abandoned houses or outbuildings in the area?" Frank asked.

"Yes, there are. Why?" Matt walked beside Frank as Carlene pulled him forward.

"Then maybe we'll get lucky and find her alive. He might have stashed her somewhere until he could return to get her."

They passed several outbuildings, but Carlene kept moving forward. After what seemed like a few miles from the point of origin, Carlene started moving at a faster pace. Both Frank and Matt found it hard to keep pace with her.

"Frank, hold her back." Matt pointed at a fenced area straight in front of them. "There might be someone guarding the area." He pulled out his gun and motioned to Frank to try to keep the dog quiet. "I want to check for a guard." He doubled back and went off to the right to approach the complex from another angle. The closer he got, the more cold prickles ran down his neck. He hunched low, moving closer, listening for any sound. It reminded him a bit of the cult compound they raided in one of their other cases. Not the same by any means or even in the same area, but well-fortified in appearance. He wanted to make sure that there wasn't a sharpshooter standing guard before Carlene went near the place. The menacing growl was the first sign that his instincts had been right. The large German shepherd growled, pacing back and forth at the fence baring his teeth. Matt waited. No one came in response to the dog's incessant barking. Maybe he was the only one on guard duty.

Carlene nudged Matt's hand. "I tried to hold her back, but she's bent on getting in there, which leads me to believe Ashley is in there somewhere. What are we going to do about that fella? He doesn't look too friendly." Frank pointed at the shepherd snarling in their direction.

"I'm sure he's not happy to see us. We are going to need help," Matt told him.

"We can't harm the dog." Frank glanced at the animal running along the fence.

"Nope, not going to happen." Matt called for Animal Control backup and gave them their location. "We'll do this by the book." He was happy to see Jaxon and some of his team. He could use more help.

When the guard dog was safely in a crate, Carlene started into the fenced area, passing by several small outbuildings to one slightly bigger in the middle of the property. She sat at the door and waited for Frank.

Matt and Jaxon, in vests and with guns drawn, went into the building first to make sure the area was clear. Carlene raced in with them and was the first one to spot the two girls. Matt followed the direction the hound went to find them tied to a post and shackled. The tape over the mouths wasn't a good sign. Neither was the fact they were hardly moving. How long had they been like this without food or water? They needed medical care fast, but they were still alive. Chalk another one up for Carlene. Matt took a deep breath and released the tension in his body. Dylan led the team who got to work checking out the rest of the buildings and looking for evidence. At least Matt knew if Bobby had jumped into another body, he hadn't made it back here yet.

Chapter 24

Damn, damn, damn. They had discovered the place. How? He was hoping to let the girls go before they were found. Bristol had been impossible to control. He had devised an awful plan for the girls. Not that he hadn't done bad things in his time. That was the problem with jumping—you often got more than you bargained for.

What happened to the guard dog? Peering through a pair of black-rimmed glasses, he observed the activity of the police while hidden out of view among the trees. The guy who wore these babies had some serious eye issues. He took the glasses off, taking a closer look at them. Hey, they were part of his new home until he could find something better. He definitely needed a better model.

The minute that damn cop ran into the store and shot the bullet that ripped through the main artery in his thigh, he knew his new persona was a goner. Lucky for him, the man's body lying nearby wasn't in bad shape as dead bodies go. Making a quick decision before it was too late, he jumped. Dead men can't jump. He still needed a body to work through from time to time.

No doubt about it—he liked the body of the young kid better but not his wild impulsive nature. At least wearing this body disguise, no one would guess that he could be guilty of any crime. Yeah, he was Mr. Nice

Guy for the moment. He could influence a lot of trouble hidden in this unsuspecting fellow. He looked down at his plaid sports shirt covering his chest, smoothing his hand over the cotton material. Under normal circumstances he wouldn't be caught dead in a getup like this, much less alive. At least he would be able to blend into the crowd as another senior with poor taste. He touched the top of his head. The gray hair was a nice touch, though. The old guy had a headful. He raked his hand through the thick mane. He had been bald a few times over the years and had been called chrome dome on more than one occasion. Hell, moving through that store wielding that powerful gun in his hand like a movie villain had been the thrill of all his lifetimes, but not a part of his plan. Killing the girl was not a part of his plan at the moment.

****

Jessie received a text from Matt telling her he'd be there soon. Dinner with Frank was on for the evening, and he had a lot to tell her about. She smiled to herself. She had a lot to tell him too.

Johanna had pulled back the curtain to let her see a bit more of her heritage, with the promise that the writings would explain more about how to use the abilities in her life. Time would tell.

The whole experience would be another mind-altering episode for Matt in the continuing series of her life. The man did ask her to marry him knowing the truth. Was he brave or what? Although, there seemed to be no end to the chapters that would continuously be added to the mystery of her life, and soon, theirs together. If she were smart, she would set the date, walk the aisle, and remind him daily that he was the one who wanted her and the baggage that came with her. Give him no time to reconsider was a new mantra to live by.

Jaxon arrived for Peyton first. "I'll see you at dinner. I guess we're going out with you guys too. I want to get a closer look at those scrolls. I wonder if great-great-grandma Katherine is in there too. I know Grams's mom wanted nothing to do with the magic, but Sadie dabbled a bit, and I know Katherine did too."

"It seems that our Irish ancestors understood the gift much better than we, their American counterparts, do." Jessie walked with Peyton to the door. "I don't know about you, but I'm determined to learn." Jessie waved at her cousin as she got into the car to leave.

When Audrey arrived a few minutes later, Jessie had finished tallying her sales for the day. Glancing at the clock, she noted Matt would be there in a few minutes. She took the scrolls out from their hiding place and covered them with her sweater. She didn't want to answer any questions about their existence with someone who wouldn't understand. At the moment, she considered them a gift to her from the past.

"I've finished calculating today's sales, Audrey. All you'll need to do is add the evening numbers, and I'll post them tomorrow morning." Jessie smiled at her. "You know the routine. You're an old pro by now."

"Enjoy your evening. We only have a few more weeks of summer hours, and then it will be fall before we know it. To tell you the truth, I will miss the summer. It seems to have gone way too fast." Audrey pointed out the window. "Looks like Matt is here."

"You're right. The summer went fast. Of course, I was gone for a month of it. Have a nice evening." Jessie waved as she went out the door.

"Hey, sweetheart." Matt opened the car door for her.

"Thank you." She slipped into the passenger seat. "Where are we going?"

"We had a long day and are all tired. Frank suggested we order in, and I thought it sounded good. Frank can let Carlene out of her crate and be close by. I don't mind chilling and putting my feet up. I hope you don't mind." He glanced at her before pulling out into traffic.

"Sounds like a perfect evening to me. I have something I wanted to check out on my computer tonight." She toyed with the seat belt that pulled tight when he stopped. "Did Carlene do her job?"

"She did. She led us to Ashley and the other girl from Baycliff. I haven't had a chance to question them yet. They were both in bad shape. I don't know how long they had gone without water or food. Their mouths were taped shut." Matt went on to explain where and how they found the girls.

"You mean he tied them up and left them there? What a colossal jerk."

"My sentiment exactly." He grinned at her. "That and a few other choice words to describe him not fit for your sweet ears."

"I highly doubt that." She chuckled. "I can think of a few of my own although I'm sure they wouldn't hold a candle to yours. After the year I've experienced living in Blue Cove, it's safe to say there is little that can still shock me. Or at least, to be exact, your colorful expressive language wouldn't." With pursed lips she turned to look at him. "Do you think the girls will be all right?"

"The prognosis seems good if they respond well to the treatment. The nurse told me she would call as soon as they are strong enough to be questioned. What?" He took a quick glance at her when he stopped at the light. "I know that expression."

"Do they have protection around the clock?" she asked.

"Yes. Does that put you at ease?" He turned the corner toward home.

"A wee bit."

"But?" He pulled into the driveway and stopped the car.

"Depending on who are guy is now, he could look like anyone. A doctor, a nurse, I think anybody could be our suspect. How will the officer know who to be on guard against?"

"Besides a no-visitors-allowed rule, Jeremy is researching any missing person from the shooting at the store. He said they have one, and he's waiting for an updated photo to send on to us."

"I hope Jeremy sends the picture to us before the guy figures out where the girls are." She opened the car door.

"You can't go in before I check out the house. We're the first ones here."

"I know." She sighed. "I hope you don't get tired of watching out for me."

"Who, me?" He took his Glock out of the holster. "Never, sweetheart." He chucked her chin and moved toward the door.

Jessie waited for him to signal all clear. He seemed to be taking more time than usual. Worst-case scenarios started to rush through her mind. She found herself closing the distance between the car and the door in short order. Her hand extended for the doorknob.

"Where do you think you're going?" Matt walked in through the open garage door.

"To make sure you were okay." She jumped at the sound of his voice, pulling her hand back from the door handle.

"What did you plan on doing if I needed help? Hit the guy with your sweater or purse?" He reached her in a few big steps. "The reason I check first is that I don't want anything to happen to you."

"I don't particularly want anything to happen to you either." She reached for his outstretched hand. "I'm getting used to having you around."

"That's nice to hear. Sorry that I worried you. I decided to go out the front and check the outside while I was at it. I had forgotten Frank and Carlene were inside keeping watch." He laced his fingers through hers. "We can go inside, and you can tell me what you are trying to hide under your sweater."

"You can't know what I'm doing with this sweater." She rolled her eyes at him.

"I sort of can." He grinned at her. "First of all, call it instinct. I can always tell when something is up with you. Next, you didn't have the sweater when I dropped you off this morning, and it's almost ninety with high humidity at the moment. You're definitely not cold. I could see something sticking out every time you shifted the sweater. Besides all that, it's your total distraction that lets me know your mind is somewhere else." He opened the door into the house for her. "Fess up, sweetheart. You know I have my ways of getting you to talk." He closed the garage door.

He was right, of course. But she couldn't let his ego have a total win. "You might think you know, but I'm about to rock your logical mind." She gave him a playful smile, swatted his arm, and strutted past him.

Chapter 25

To say Jessie rocked Matt's logical mind might be an understatement. When she pulled out the scrolls and told him how she came to acquire them, it stopped him in his tracks. He wasn't sure how her story was plausible, but he knew Jess, and it had to be true. The writings were amazing even if he couldn't understand their meanings. Some things were clear even to him, like a cistern being the water supply for the family, and when Johanna mentioned her abode. Jessie was delighted when she understood or connected with one of the writers. Her sisters in time, she had called them.

He was out of his league, and he wasn't afraid to say it. Some of the parchments were written in ancient languages. She couldn't read them, but that didn't stop her from poring over each entry with care. When she told him she could hear them, well, that was over the top. She had to be as surprised by that turn of events as he was. At the moment, he could understand her reasoning for not letting many people see them. There was no easy way to explain how they came to be in her possession. Someone would pay a lot of money to get their hands on them legally or illegally. But Jessie wasn't sure if they were hers to keep or only on loan for a season. Maybe Peyton and she would add their thoughts to the scrolls and someday pass them on.

Matt couldn't believe he could even somewhat

believe how she had come to be in possession of the parchments. Flexible and open were words that came to mind. He lived a fairly uncomplicated life until Jessie came into it. At least he found some consolation in the fact she was as shocked as he was by the events of the past year.

"This must seem strange to you." She patted his hand. "It would be more shocking to me if I hadn't gone to Ireland and had a small introduction into my ancestral line." She chuckled. "There were more than a few odd members in my family line."

"It does make me wonder who might show up in mine. You know how this works for me, sweetheart. I leave the unusual to you and you tell me how it works, and I use it to logically work through my investigation." He helped her gather the scrolls. The others were arriving.

"I can't promise you more relatives won't be coming or aren't already here. I'm learning to accept this part of me. I find the link to others rather comforting. Peyton and I aren't the only ones. You should find it that way too. Think about it—you're not the only man attached to a woman who isn't normal. Others have gone before you."

He had loved watching her face light up when she could understand more of what was in the writings. Spending this time alone together was enlightening for him. Even he was amazed by the drawings of herbs used for healing—they seemed quite detailed. He traced them, using his phone to take photographs of them. Some of the names had changed, but many still grew in the Kilkenny area. He followed her movement when she scooped up the scrolls and left the room.

Why now? What did any of this have to do with what was happening right now? If he knew Jess, she would put the pieces together in her mind.

"The food should be here soon," he told Frank as he walked in the door with Carlene.

"I'll get the plates. You grab the utensils, Jaxon." Peyton opened the cupboard and grabbed the dishes. "Where's my cousin?"

"In her room. She'll be right out." Matt went to the door when the bell rang.

"Jess, dinner is here. Come get it hot," Matt called to her.

"I'll be right there," she called back.

Matt had ordered spaghetti and lasagna family style with garlic bread and plenty of salad. As soon as their plates were filled, they settled into a friendly dinner conversation. Matt and Jaxon talked about how Carlene found the girls. Jaxon had a positive update from the hospital. Both girls were sleeping but were improving and would be ready for questioning in the morning. Another text came during dinner from Jeremy, showing the missing person from the store shooting.

"Did Jeremy send you a photo?" Matt asked.

"Yes. He could be more dangerous than Bobby." Jessie showed Peyton the photo on her phone.

"What makes you think so? I mean, the man is an older gentleman." Matt shook his head.

"That's why. Who would suspect a kind older gentleman. He's beloved, according to all the descriptions of the man. Of course, we know the man or entity who is using his body may not be such a nice guy."

Sometimes Matt could swear Jessie had police

training the way her mind put facts together. She was right. Howard Digby could pass through security with that face. No visitors allowed had been a good idea. He sent the photo to Kenny and told him to send it out to the others. Between his smiling eyes behind his horn-rimmed glasses and his gray hair, he looked like any grandfather walking down the street.

After Jessie helped Matt clean up, she kissed his cheek. "I want to spend some time with the parchments. I'll be out to say goodnight to everyone later."

"Okay, sweetheart." He kissed her for real. No small peck on the cheek. "Come back for another later."

"You can count on it." She sauntered past him to her room.

****

Jessie sat on her bed with her computer close by as she unrolled the first scroll. Excitement and anticipation filled her. Her destiny awaited her discovery in some mystical way. Ever since she was young, she had had a strong feeling that she was different. Obstinate, yes, but there was more to the story. Places flashed through her mind, along with people during the day, and at night she had strange dreams. Not always, but now and then they would take her by surprise, even as a youngster. She never told anyone about them because she didn't understand why they happened to her. They scared her and left her feeling alone. Now, of course, they made more sense. She still wasn't sure how she fit in. She didn't think she was a healer, but she wasn't sure. There were travelers, those who were destined to challenge the darkness in their times. In her heart she knew this was her moment to find out. Would she pass this down some day to a daughter if she had one? Would Peyton or Madison? What impact would their abilities make on the world?

What she wanted most was to help Matt make Blue Cove, her little part of the world, a better place to live. They had worked well together to date but not without some close calls. The nature of his job, she guessed. Johanna had many as well. She ran her hand carefully over the parchment as the strange warmth sensation worked its way through her fingertips, up her arms, and throughout her body. Sighing, she listened to the voices of her sisters waiting to be heard.

"Jess, have you figured out the world's problems?" Peyton knocked on her door.

"I could use your help. Come in," Jessie told her.

"I see why you wanted to be alone. I've been thinking about these all day and how our family might fit in the picture."

"Did you come to any conclusion? Peyton, these are amazing. I can't understand the writing for the most part. I've had to look up countless words. Like this one." She pointed at the word *bratt*. "It means a cloak or covering cloth. Or this one, *brogan*, which means a shoe or boot. This writer is giving us details about what she wore. I guess that much hasn't changed." She smiled.

"The artwork is amazing." Peyton pointed at the drawing of a beautiful flower.

"Some of these are healing herbs and plants. I know nothing about their properties, only what I can make out through the internet. Still, it fascinates me. It almost feels like I'm coming home."

"I understand. When I slipped into our great-great grandma's life and times, I began to understand we were part of something bigger than us. Now, this only makes it seem more real."

"It's a journey of discovery, as Reba told us. I won't share it with everyone. This is for us. How we use the gift in our corner of the world will be up to us." Jessie grabbed Peyton's hand. "Johanna's only warning was it has to be used for others and not for our personal gain."

"Makes sense to me. Greed is on the dark side. We've seen that often enough."

"Johanna, like Kathrine, lived what seemed on the surface a normal life. She married, had children, and still managed to impact her village."

"And we will too, dear cousin. We will too." Peyton walked toward the door. "I think I'll spend some time with my prince now, and you should do the same. We can't neglect our guys."

Jessie rewrapped the parchments. Peyton was right, of course. Matt had promised her another kiss if she came back. She wanted to collect. Boy, did she.

She fanned her face as she thought about it later. Stretched out on her bed, she replayed the evening in her mind. She might have shocked Matt with her playful flirting, but he seemed happy with the results. As she rolled onto her side, she smiled, closed her eyes, and went to sleep dreaming of her handsome guy.

Chapter 26

After he dropped Jessie off and did his morning check, Matt drove toward the hospital to talk to Ashley. Jess had surprised him big-time last night. He loved her playful side, which she rarely showed to him. But when she did, it made for a memorable evening. The way his mind worked overtime, he couldn't help wondering why. Not that there had to be a reason, but if the last week had taught him anything, she had something going on in that pretty little head of hers. Eventually, she would tell him as much as she could so as not to blow his mind.

There was no doubt about it—there was an atmosphere of a coming storm, a rising tide, or whatever you wanted to call the present climate in town and the country. All the calls had him concerned that his small department couldn't handle the sheer volume. Maybe Ashley could shed some light on the reason she was abducted. But now the suspect looked different. How long he would remain in a body that might restrain his activity was anybody's guess. Matt arrived at the hospital and met Jaxon in the parking lot. Once inside, they rode the elevator up to the fourth floor.

"Chief Parker, wait a minute," the head nurse called out as he walked past the nurses' station. "We had a visitor a little earlier that I thought you might like to know about."

Matt stopped. "Who was it?"

"He never gave us his name. I've never seen him around here before, but he wanted to see the two girls. He told us he was Ashley's family doctor and her parents wanted him to check in on her. The thing was, when I asked for his credentials or an order from her attending physician, which is hospital policy, he left without a response when I turned to answer the ringing phone."

Jaxon pulled up the suspect's photo on his phone. "Is this the man?"

"Yes, that's him. Should I have let him see the girls?" she asked.

"No, he's a possible suspect. You did the right thing," Matt told her.

"He seemed like such a nice older gentleman." She shook her head. "I wanted to believe him. He was polite but when he couldn't produce the documents, I thought I might need to call security."

"You responded perfectly, Linda." Jaxon read her name tag.

"You can't always tell by someone's looks what's in their minds." Matt thanked her and continued on to the girls' room. Jessie had been right about his new persona being a good disguise for his motives.

Matt and Jaxon left the hospital forty minutes later with a better understanding of the individual they were dealing with. Both girls were afraid of their abductor. Bobby Bristol was intimidating. Howard Digby looked like someone's sweet grandpa, and neither girl had seen him before. Both Bobby and Howard were one and the same with whoever the traveler was. Or, as Jessie reminded Matt, maybe they were the same and maybe they weren't. Another troubling idea to think about.

"It gets a bit confusing, doesn't it?" Jaxon opened his car door. "How can I tell my boss that the young man who abducted them at gunpoint now looks like someone's grandfather who actually might be someone from the past—or not."

Matt slapped his hand to his forehead. "I was thinking the same thing, and the fact I could entertain the possibility makes me wonder about myself." He shook his head.

"I hear you. We'll find the way to write a report on the investigation once we solve it." Jaxon opened his car door. "I'll catch up with you this afternoon. I have to head to Hanover for a meeting."

"Sounds good." Matt walked to his car, going over the details of the interview in his head. Their captor had taped the girls' mouths after feeding them one meal and tied them to the steel posts in the center of the room. Basically, he left them there to die while he went on his shooting spree a few days later. Bottled water was found in the building where they were discovered, but they had no way to get to it.

Ashely remembered hearing Bristol say that they would soon be joined by others, and he had big plans for them. He never told them any concrete details about those plans but only that they would never forget what he did to them. Matt couldn't see how, unless killing them was being merciful. Nothing about their abductions or what they were told made any sense to him unless it fit into the rising tide that Jessie kept talking about. Human trafficking came to mind, which meant money for Bristol. Matt shook his head. Of course, at some point Bristol would be back for the girls even if he were in a different form. Was he looking to change bodies again? Would the new man remember the girls or his plans for the girls? By now, he must know they moved the girls and were on to him. Now all Matt had to do was figure out what the delusional man was up to, because he was still out there in one form or another.

He pulled out his phone. "Hey, Jess, can you get away for an hour at lunch? I need to run something by you."

"Sure enough. Peyton can cover for me, or Tiffany, the new girl. I'll see you when you get here. I have a customer and I need to run."

"See you later." Matt disconnected the call.

****

The nurse wouldn't let him see the girls, which meant his photo was probably out there. No visitors allowed without the doctor's approval, she yapped firmly at him. All he had wanted to do was make sure they were okay. That kid's incoherent plans messed up everything. He had been one royal mistake, and this guy wasn't much better. Nicer but not better. He had to get rid of this body soon because he would never fulfill his destiny with his form. Howard Digby, the ID in his wallet said. Images of his wife and grandchildren had interrupted his thoughts more than once. He should have been more careful many years ago, and then he wouldn't have needed to travel through time jumping in and out of bodies. What a mess. But soon there would be no more jumping. He'd be free to operate without restraints. He had to find the treasure that belonged to him. It was his ticket to freedom and power.

****

As soon as Jessie checked out her customer, Reba rushed through the door. "Good morning, sweet lady." Jessie waved at her.

"Hello, my dear. A lovely day is off and running." Reba sat in her favorite chair. "We will talk as we can. Your store is going to get busy. I saw the tourist bus parked down the road, and you know what that means. They'll be headed to Joe's for coffee and then they'll wander into your store. It's the natural thing to do." She smiled at Jessie. "Go about your business. I'll be thinking about what I need to tell you."

"Sounds good." Jessie waited on several customers. When the last one was checked out, she went to sit by Reba. "Sorry it took so long."

"Not to worry, dear. I enjoy people watching, living and dead. Your store has had plenty of activity today. That fellow guarding the stairs doesn't appear to be going anywhere or look any happier."

"No. I figure he's here until he's not." Jessie chuckled and glanced at the menacing-looking ghost. "He's behaving himself even if he's a bit grumpy looking."

"The reason I came today is I've been thinking about your dream. Are you still having the same one?"

"Yes, with a few details added here and there." Jessie pursed her lips. "I told you about the people being swept out in the waves, and about the waves reaching out to grab me like claws. What I didn't tell you is that the waves covered our town, the country, and the world." Jessie shook her head. "That part of the dream was a bit shocking to me and, if I'm honest, scary too because I have no idea how to interpret the meaning."

"That's always tricky. Did you learn anything from Johanna?" Reba asked.

"I'm learning about the many strong women in my family line. Each of them seemed to have a specialty from which they operated. Some were considered healers in their days and grew special herbs that they learned to combine for different ailments. I've only begun to understand a few of the writings."

"Where do you fit in?" Reba studied her face.

"I'm not sure, but I hope to find out. That's what this time must be all about. Along with the fact I've figured out that I don't want to do this alone."

"I'm glad you're coming to terms with your need to be loved and supported. Matt is the answer," Reba said nodding her head. "But what is remarkable for me is both you and Peyton are at the cove at this time. Something is gathering steam to need you both in the same town. Add to that the possibility of Madison being gifted—well, that seems a bit much. She's involved, even if she doesn't know her gift yet. Why the three of you? I admit I'm stumped, and the question has been rumbling around in my brain for several days. I hope you'll be able to enlighten me. I'd like to put this troublesome thought to bed."

"To be truthful, I never thought of a reason why. I've been so happy to have Peyton to bounce things off of that I never considered the why. Maybe I should." Jessie glanced at the clock. Matt would be here for lunch soon.

"You need to, my dear, if for no other reason than to let this old lady have some sleep." Reba patted Jessie's hand. "You girls are important to me. Both of you being in Blue Cove is more than a coincidence—

it's fate, destiny, providence, or whatever you want to call it. I want to know why." Reba stood. "I need to be on my way. Come here, girl, and let me hug you. We need answers."

"Answers would be nice." Jessie walked into Reba's waiting arms. She exhaled a deep breath. Reba's arms were a safe place.

"We'll have them before you know it." Reba released Jessie. "I'll be back soon. I'm meeting Lawrence for lunch, and I believe you're meeting your handsome guy too." Reba walked arm in arm with Jessie to the door.

"Matt said he wanted to talk." She held the door open for Reba.

"I'm sure he does, but frankly, my dear girl, he can't get enough of you. It's time to put that dear man out of his misery and marry him." Reba laughed and waved.

"My exact thoughts," Jessie said under her breath and waved as Reba pulled away from the curb.

Jessie got to work putting out a few new titles. She couldn't wait to let Katie know their favorite author had a new book out. She loved the normal moments she spent with her best friend, chatting about anything but ghosts and murders. At least now they could talk about a new book. If she were honest, she missed those carefree days with Katie talking about fashions, the latest movie, or gossip. She sighed. Oh well. *That was then, and this is now. It's all good.* She waved at Tiffany, her summer part-time hire. She was headed to college in the fall and wanted to earn some money before she left. Hiring her proved to be a win-win for both of them.

Tiffany took the stack of books in Jessie's hand. "I'll put these on the shelf for you."

"Thank you." She smiled glancing at the clock. With Matt coming soon, Tiffany could fill in for a few minutes on her own until Peyton arrived. Moments like this, alone with her simple thoughts, made life feel normal. Except for the frowning ghost standing guard on the stairs, she could almost believe she was an average bookshop owner. *I wonder why he picked that particular spot to stand guard. There must be a reason.* She tapped her fingers on the counter and then went to Tiffany and filled her in on the schedule for the day.

Chapter 27

After they ordered at the counter, Matt pulled the chair out for Jessie. "What's new?"

"That's a loaded question to ask me." She chuckled. "You never know what kind of answer you'll get."

"True. Maybe I should simply say surprise me if you can." He smiled. "Then wait until you do. Because I know you will."

"Did Ashley have any new information?" Jessie thanked the young woman who delivered their lunch to the table.

"She remembered a few details about when she was abducted. Bristol scared both of the girls. He was rough and demanding." Matt took a sip of his tea and explained what the girls told him about what Bristol said. "I wonder if he had any reason other than being on a rampage."

"As strange as this may sound, I remember the girls at the commune believed Skylar was their savior in some way." Jessie placed her napkin on her lap. "I'm not sure you can make sense of anything a narcissist might say, or maybe he simply found himself acting on impulse from some outside influence. We'll understand this better soon, or maybe not."

"What makes you think that?" Matt's forehead furrowed in thought.

"Reba came into my store earlier." She gazed into his eyes.

"Of course, she did." Matt frowned.

"Anyway, she asked me a question that has got me thinking," Jessie told him.

"She usually does." Matt took a bite of his sandwich.

Jessie slapped his hand. "I'm serious. She asked why there are two of us with the gift in town and possibly three at this time. Why now?"

"Damn, you're right. That's something to think about." He took another bite of his sandwich. "I never thought about the why, but I will."

"That's what I said. I'm sure there has to be a reason. At least, Reba seems to think it isn't a coincidence. She's rarely wrong."

"You're right, and now I'm concerned. Just because we rescued the two girls doesn't mean this is over, does it? There's more, and you know how I don't like surprises." Matt's frown deepened.

"It depends on the surprise for me. Don't frown. As Reba always tells me, you'll get wrinkles." Jessie smiled at him.

"Reba is a smart woman. I wish she could tell us what is happening," Matt grumbled.

"As my friend would say, she only can tell me what she knows, but I believe all of this fits together in some way. My dreams, Johanna's visit, and the parchments are all important. The girls, the shooting, and the traveler fit into the overall picture, along with the attacks on us and even the ghost in my store. I can't wait to find out how." She ate a strawberry from her salad. "Even the fact there are two of us in this small town has to be for a reason. I hope your logical mind can figure out why." She paused and frowned.

"That's unlikely. I will make sense of it all after you tell me what's going on. Something tells me your mind is working on a new angle now. Lay it on me." He leaned back in his chair and folded his arms.

"I'm not there yet, but I'll tell you when I make sense of the ideas coming and going in my head. Right now, they are disjointed theories at best." She sipped her tea.

They spent the rest of their lunch going over the details they knew. Matt had more to think about when he left her at the store. Jaxon had sent him another FBI notice hot off the press warning about an uptick of chatter calling for action against government agencies and leaders. People were doxing public figures by posting their addresses, phone numbers, and family members online with a goal to shame or harass them. Some had already received death threats. Jaxon said today they had picked up a suspect outside a former president's house with a cache of weapons and high-capacity magazines in his car. The neighbors called the police because the man paced in front of the former-president's house and his actions seemed suspicious. He was taken into custody, and they discovered his inflammatory statements online.

Social media emboldened and made strange heroes out of people willing to kill to make their political statements. Matt raked his hand through his hair. Could times get any stranger? They probably could, but he'd hate to think of the ramifications of it. He was having a hard enough time with all that was going on at the moment in Blue Cove. Who would show up next? Ah hell, he didn't want to know. His hands fisted at his side.

****

Jessie spent any of her free time during the afternoon between customers talking to her cousin and watching her grumpy ghost standing guard on the stairs. She wished she could figure him out. He was important, but she had no idea why. Unless, of course, the traveler was somehow known to him. If they were even looking at a traveler. For now, she would accept that the ghost was there because Johanna said she needed him. Jessie would understand soon enough, which was the same thing she always said when she didn't know. For a change it would be nice to offer Matt more than one of her weak platitudes or theories at best.

What was the purpose of a gift if you could only see a small fragment of what was happening? Frustrated with what she couldn't see and not wanting to see what she could. Maybe she needed a therapist. She chuckled. Oh, yeah, she already was seeing one, but not for this area of her life. Who would believe her anyway?

"You seemed pleased with something," Peyton said.

"It's this wayward mind of mine. I wish I could simply shut off my silly musings." Jessie scrunched her face.

"How well I know. We are more alike than we realize." Peyton touched Jessie's tapping fingers to stop them.

"True. I can't make heads or tails of all my thoughts right now. I'm sure they'll make more sense in time or, if Reba is correct, this might only be the beginning of a long and strange period of time."

"Time will tell. At least, at this moment things are calm. I mean besides our strange visitor, who doesn't seem in a hurry to do much but look stern. I'm not afraid of him anymore. I don't believe that anger is directed at us, which is one point in his favor." She knocked on the wood bookshelf. "You can't be too careful when you're born in the chime hour." Peyton laughed.

"Cover all of your bases or something like that." Jessie gestured with a wave of her hand.

The rest of the day, they were kept busy with customers and the ever-fun mystery-book club. During a lull in the action, Jessie sensed someone was watching the store. At several points it was so strong that she walked to the front of the store to look out the window but saw no one. "I'll be back. I need to get a few books from the back room," she told Peyton.

****

His sole reason for being in this insignificant part of the world rested inside the walls of that building. He glanced at Idle Time Bookstore. He was wasting hours trying to make right some of the crazy mistakes from the days spent in Bristol's body and dealing with the mistakes from his erratic behavior. Not that he was a saint. Thousands would stand in line to get a shot at him. Still, there were rules and some actions that even in his depraved condition he wouldn't stoop to. You didn't kidnap young girls for no good reason or kill people on a whim. The loss of life was only allowable in the advancement of a greater good. Call it a lesson learned along the way.

Howard Digby's missing-person photo was everywhere. Last night he had seen the man's face, the one he now shared, on the news, and this morning the same face stared back at him from his computer. He couldn't hang out in good old Digby's body much longer. He was starting to feel at home in the old guy's form. If he stayed much longer, the man's kind thoughts and good heart could corrupt him. But at least he wanted to find a way to return him to his family. It might be a shock to see the living version of old Howard after fearing his demise, but the circumstances warranted it. He had made the decision and that was that. Maybe he was getting soft.

He glanced again at the store. The suddenness of the ray of light that penetrated his shield of darkness sent shivers racing down his back. He knew the feeling—he had experienced it before. There seemed to be a strong energy that emanated from the building. Battles weren't fought the same way anymore. How he longed for the days of old.

Chapter 28

Jessie bent down to open a box of books stored in the back room when the sound of metal clanging against metal startled her. Afraid to investigate, she peeked over her shoulder with care and found herself in Kilkenny in the middle of a fierce battle. Standing alone on a small knoll, she saw the scene as it unfolded before her. The clash of swords reverberated through the air, along with the smell of sweat and blood. Grunts and groans from men in agony shook her, and she covered her ears to stop the sounds of those pleading for their life. Men were dying, along with anyone else who got in the way. Black smoke darkened the day's sky, making it appear almost night. One by one, houses were set ablaze by torches thrown by men racing through the village on horseback. Amid the screams of fleeing women and children, the rancid odor of smoke stung her nostrils and lungs as she wept and gasped for air. She rubbed her eyes when out of the mist and smoke of the battle she saw him. A warrior seated on a huge black stallion charged forward with a thunderous yell, wielding a sword over his head, preparing to swing it down. He wore a knee-length hauberk of chain mail, carried a kite-shaped shield, and wore a conical helmet with an iron nasal plate to protect his face. Even from the distance where she stood, she could see the fire in his eyes. There was no doubt he was the leader and responsible for the destruction his men were executing. Impressive, mesmerizing, and scary—she couldn't take her eyes off him.

His sword arced downward as he made his way through the fighting men. Almost inhuman in strength, his shoulders were broad, and his strong thighs gripped his horse's flanks as he fought through the battle calling out commands. Driven by an unearthly force, he pushed forward wielding his sword through the air, knocking one man after another to the ground with the sheer power of his brute strength. Jessie shivered. Frozen in place, a suffocating dread settled around her heart as she witnessed death spreading across the land. As a dark storm without warning, he led his men, destroying all in their way. Men, women, and children fell prey to his knights' invasion.

Jessie followed the progress of the horse carrying the raging warrior to where Johanna stood still and alone, blocking his way with her hand raised high. She didn't move as the man came within striking distance of her and stopped suddenly with a roar. Pulling up on the reins, his horse reared in the air. His flaying hooves came down within inches of striking her. Jessie held her breath.

"Woman, you dare to defy me," the man bellowed. His hand tightened around his sword.

"Aye." She looked him in the eyes. "You are in our land to conquer and kill, but I'm here to stop you. You've won. You need not kill another soul."

"Do you not understand that I can kill you with one swipe of my sword?" He lifted his sword over his head, swinging it in a downward motion coming to within inches of her face. The sword whistled as it danced, slicing through the air and making an eerie musical song in the hand of its composer.

"Aye, you can. But you can never destroy the light that shines in me or the kindness my people will show you if you stop this madness." She placed her hands defiantly on her hips and never took her eyes off the man.

Jessie watched as one woman after another came to stand behind their sister. Their bravery matched the men on the battlefield. The man mumbled something under his breath, turned his horse around, and made his way back to the battle. Suddenly the scene changed, and Jessie saw the knights living side by side among those in the village. How long had it taken for peace to prevail? Johanna had done her part.

"Every people and generation must choose what is important to them, because someone will challenge and try to take away what you love and force you to bend your knee to them. Stand against the oppressor in whatever form they take. Light always wins over darkness, and kindness will bring anger to its knees. Only love can beat back hatred. True peace only happens when love wins the day," an ancient-sounding voice spoke to her.

"Hey, Jess, are you okay back there?" Peyton called.

"I'll be right there." Jessie wiped a tear from her cheek. "Wow," she said under her breath. She carried the books and placed them on the counter. She would be thinking about what she saw for a while. She reached for a pencil to jot down the words she heard before she forgot them all.

****

After making plans for another track in the morning before Frank left town, Matt texted Jessie several times without any response. That was not like her. Reason told him she would call if there was an issue, but it didn't stop him from wanting to rush over to check on her. Would his instinct to protect her ever lessen? He sure hoped so.

"Hey, Matt, you got a minute?" Jaxon knocked on his open door.

"Yeah. What's up?"

"Frank told me you are going to try a track to find Howard Digby tomorrow. Do you think Carlene will be able to find him?"

"She is capable, but this is a strange situation. We're guessing at best that it'll work." Matt tapped his pen on the pad. "I'm not sure what we're dealing with or even how long Howard will be the one were searching for, but we can't sit around and do nothing. I'm not sure where the guy will strike next." Matt handed Jaxon the latest picture of Howard Digby that Jeremy had emailed this morning. "I hope he's alive and that we can somehow return him to his beautiful family." He pointed at the photo.

"I hear you. Is that even possible?" Jaxon leaned his hip against the wall.

"I have no idea." Matt shook his head.

"Well, call me curious, but I'm wondering what this case is about. I know we have the two kidnapped girls, but Bristol seemed to be acting alone and on impulse when it comes to them. We have Howard, but other than trying to get into see them we have no other sightings of him. Is it possible they're a diversion?"

"I've been thinking the same thing. Crime is up in

town, but at the moment, it is a pain but nothing like Jessie described in her dream. There has to be more. We aren't seeing the bigger picture. I'm sure there's something we're missing. What that is, I wish to hell I knew."

"Peyton texted me a while ago and said Jessie has been acting strange all morning. She was sure to add that it was odd even for her cousin." Jaxon chuckled.

"I was wondering why she hasn't answered any of my texts. I think it's time I paid her a visit. We might be about to find out more." Matt stood. "Do you want to come with me? You might want to hear what she has to say."

"If a visit will help us find a way forward through this, I'm game." Jaxon followed Matt out to the car. "I feel like I'm flying blind, looking for anything that will explain this case. I'm nothing if not methodical, and this whole investigation is driving me nuts." He latched his seat belt. "None of it fits together at the moment."

"I'm right there with you." Matt started the car. "I can't believe I'm about to say this, but we are going to have to think outside of the box again. I thought maybe this time might be simple, but instinct tells me I'm not going to like what I'm about to hear." He pulled out of the parking lot and headed toward Jessie's store.

****

Jessie handed the customer his bag when she saw Matt's cruiser pull into the open space in front of her store. It was too early for him to pick her up, and she wondered why he was there.

"Did you get any of my texts?" he asked when he walked in.

"Sorry." She took a quick look at her phone. "I

guess I've been a bit preoccupied most of the day."

"Ever since you went into the back room to get that stack of books, you've been in a different world. I mentioned to Jaxon you were acting odd." Peyton went to stand by Jaxon. "Thanks for coming," she whispered, leaning close to him.

"Would you care to explain what is going on to me? It's not like you to not answer my texts." Matt reached for her hand. "Before you start, let me ask—do you think it's important somehow to the case?"

"I'll explain, but I'm sure you'll find it hard to believe. As for whether what happened to me is in some way connected to Blue Cove and the traveler, I would say probably, but I don't know how or why."

"Fair enough. Let's hear it." Matt pulled out a chair for her and sat beside her.

Jessie retold the events from earlier. "His strength was amazing, but Johanna, backed up by the women of the village, stopped him in his tracks. Then this voice spoke to me." Jessie leaned into Matt's side. She read what she could remember that was said to her. "You see, this is obviously a test of some kind for our generation. Has the warrior come in spirit through every generation? I don't know. But we have to decide how we can best stop the invasion of our time."

"Wow, cous. No wonder you were acting odd today. I would be too. That's a lot to think about." Peyton squeezed Jaxon's hand in hers.

"Leaving out the whole battle and what you saw, I can at least relate to standing up against the rising tide in our time." Matt frowned. "How do you handle this stuff?" He shook his head.

"Reba told us at one point that we would be on a

journey discovering ourselves. She was right as usual. I understand more about this ancestral gift each day, and I'm learning I can live a somewhat normal life. To me that's a win-win. The question will always be, can the people who want to share our lives be able to handle that this is who we are?" Jessie turned when the bell rang at the door. "I find what I'm discovering quite fascinating." Jessie went to help the customer who came in.

When Matt walked past her, he leaned close to her and said, "Just so you know, I can handle this side of you. I find this side of you intriguing." His breath tickled her ear. "See you later, sweetheart." Matt squeezed her shoulder.

That man. Jessie smiled. His touch always reassured her that he was unwavering in his love, and boy, was she glad. It would probably be tested many times in the days ahead.

Chapter 29

"Did Jessie's description about the battle for Kilkenny hit you the way it did me?" Jaxon asked.

"If you mean, did she see the battlefield? My answer would be yes. Does it fit into our case scenario? Probably, even if at the moment I can't see how." Matt did a U-turn and headed back toward the station. A white car sped by them in a blur. He swore an expletive under his breath, turned on his siren, and gave chase. He called for backup as he followed the car racing down Main Street headed toward the freeway. Matt clocked his speed at over eighty mph. Even when Matt backed off hoping to slow the driver down, the white car never braked. There was nothing Matt could do when the car barreled through the red light and hit the small car that was already in the middle of the intersection.

Matt stopped the cruiser and jumped out with Jaxon close behind. Calling dispatch for an ambulance, he raced toward the crash. His first impression was no one could have survived the tangled wreckage. On closer inspection, the crash appeared even more horrific. There were two people who looked to be in serious condition and one who surprised Matt and Jaxon both. Another bizarre fact to add to a growing list of the strange and unexplainable events of the last few weeks.

"What happened?" The face of Howard Digby stared wide-eyed at them. "The last thing I remember was being shot at. How did I get here?" He shook his head.

"A mystery we intend to investigate as soon as we get you checked out." Matt put his hand out to restrain Digby when he tried to move. "You need these folks to look you over before you move. We'll figure this out together." Matt motioned to Jaxon to follow him. They walked a short distance away to talk when the medics reached the car.

"Was that weird or what?" Jaxon frowned. "Is he the suspect, or is he Mr. Digby back from the dead?"

"You've got me. We might need help to figure this out. The guy in the white car kept saying his gas pedal was stuck. He's in a bad way."

"What about the driver of the car Howard was in? Will he make it?" Jaxon glanced at the medics loading the patient into the ambulance. "This one has all the earmarks of another odd twist in the case, don't you think?"

"Yes. Especially the fact that Digby is alive. It doesn't make any sense. It's usually about a jump and the previous victim doesn't usually survive. I wonder why now. I can't wait to question Digby and see what Jessie thinks. Speaking of her, I need to call her." He reached for the phone in his pocket.

Matt spent the next several minutes telling Jessie what he knew. "I want you to talk to Howard. His part in this makes no sense," he told her. "He's being checked out now, and at some point, his family will be notified that he's alive."

"Will you charge him? I doubt he's responsible for

anything that has happened. He might be as confused by what happened as we are."

Matt frowned. "I guess that will depend on the interview. At least at the moment, Carlene won't need to do that track to search for him in the morning."

"She may still need to find the next guy our suspect has jumped into. All this makes me wonder. I guess I really don't know how any of this works, but I have a feeling because Howard is alive, we might find out more this time."

"Can you leave the store for a while?" Matt asked her.

"Peyton is here, and she can take over."

"I'll swing by and pick you up now. We need to get to the hospital before Howard disappears like other travelers have."

"I'll be ready, and I mean for anything. See you soon."

****

Maybe ready for anything was too strong of a statement. Jessie shook her head as she went over in her mind the conversation they had with Digby. The last memory he had was of being shot and close to death. He told them about the fear when he saw the gunman, the excruciating pain when the bullet's impact lifted him off the ground, and then feeling nothing as darkness surrounded him. The next memory he had was of him in some hospital looking for two girls he had never met. He had no idea how he got there or why. Stranger still, he had a constant voice in his head, and he found himself in places where he couldn't remember how, or much less why, he was there. Several times in their conversation he wondered aloud if it was possible that he had dementia. The voice speaking in his head was at constant war with his own thoughts. The last statement he heard from whoever belonged to the voice was that he needed to shake the old dude and send him home to his family. He had made up his mind for him to live.

Howard was as confused by the whole conversation taking place in his mind as Jessie was. Bewilderment seemed to be the word he used most, and even more after he talked about the accident he had survived earlier. None of it jibed. He was sure he was dying when he was shot. Now all he wanted to do was see his wife and grandkids.

Was it possible that the traveler had to deal with and try to control the personality of the person they jump into? Jessie had never considered the idea before. How could she find out and know for sure? None of it seemed possible, much less real. Matt hoped she could give him a possible answer.

One thing she was sure of—Digby was not responsible for any criminal activity. If anything, he kept the person from doing more by the sheer goodness inside of him. Bobby Bristol, on the other hand, might have gone off the rails and wasn't easy to control. All clues to consider. Talk about a learning curve. Digby and Bristol presented a major challenge to how she had reasoned this out in the past.

"You've been quiet since you got back, cous. What's going on?" Peyton asked as soon as she checked out the last customer.

Jessie told her what she had learned. "Digby's story changes a lot in my thinking on the subject. Not that I know much." Jessie leaned against the counter.

"Do you think it's possible that the traveler must contend with their host's personality?"

"I never thought about the details before. Just the fact they could travel or jump from one person to another was more than I wanted to understand. But now that you mention it, the whole idea of the host's personality staying with them makes sense. Or is it possible that it only happens in certain cases? I mean, how many times can one nearly die and jump to another before their time runs out?"

"Also a valid question along with the fact that we're having such a strange conversation." Jessie pushed away when the bell at the front door rang. She glanced at the grumpy ghost standing guard. "Boy, I wish you could talk," she whispered. "Or maybe not," she responded to his frown.

"Can I help you?" Jessie approached her next customer, a pretty young girl with shoulder length red hair.

"I wish." She turned at the sound of Jessie's voice. "Do you have a place where I can hang this? I doubt that it will help, but I can't stand doing nothing but wait." Her pretty green eyes were framed by long dark lashes and mascara smudges from recent tears.

"I'd be happy to tack this to my community board." Jessie found herself staring at the photo of a smiling Howard Digby.

"Thank you. I'd appreciate any help. We have no idea where he is, and the police told us he had been shot. We haven't been able to track which hospital he was taken to." The young girl swiped at the tears in her eyes.

"If you'll wait a minute, I might be able to get you

more help." She went to the counter, pulled out her phone, and texted Matt.

His response was short and sweet. —*I'll be right there.*—

"Are you related to him?" Jessie asked.

"He's my grandfather. My grandma is sick with worry. I wish I could do more. Their anniversary is coming up, and I would like to find some answers for her."

"I have someone coming who can help. My name is Jessie." She gave the girl a hug. "I know this must have been a hard time for your family."

"We think Grandpa must have gone to the store that morning to buy an anniversary gift. Grandma had been talking about a painting she had seen advertised for their grand opening. We heard about the shooting, and then he was gone. We have no more details than that." She sat on one of the chairs near where Jessie stood. "I'm Ariel, their youngest granddaughter. I'm too bullheaded to believe he's gone for good. Each time I get the chance, I go to the next town on my list to put up these posters. I hope you don't mind."

"Being stubborn sometimes pays off in a good way." She waved at Matt when he walked in. "Chief Parker, this is Ariel, Howard Digby's granddaughter. She's looking for answers."

"She's come to the right place. If you'll come with me, I think we can answer a few of your questions."

Jessie watched them drive away with a smile on her face. At least this story would have a happy ending even if they had no idea how it was possible.

Chapter 30

Matt would remember this moment for the rest of his life. Howard's eyes lit up when he saw Ariel walk into his hospital room. Matt wished he could have captured the moment for them.

Ariel ran to his bedside, crying as she went. "We had no idea where you went," she told him over again several times. "You have to call Grandma. She's been heartsick." She made the call while she rattled off questions to which Howard had no answers.

Matt managed to snap a couple of photos on his phone and arranged with Ariel to text them to her before he left the room. He stood in the hall while Howard talked to his wife. He would be free to go home to his family as soon as the hospital released him in the morning. One thing Matt knew was Howard had no part in a crime spree—if anything, he might have prevented more from happening by being the man that he was. The fact that he was allowed to live was a big deal. How the traveler arranged it was a mystery for the time being, but not for long.

"I can't thank you enough for bringing me here." Ariel came out to the hall. "He doesn't seem to remember how he got here anymore than we can understand how it's possible. I'm not going to fret about it. I would like answers, of course, and maybe he'll remember in time. But for now, all our family is on their way, and we are grateful to have him back, however it happened. I'll always think of it as the Digby miracle." She smiled at Matt.

"I think that's the perfect way to look at the situation. He survived a shooter and walked away from a serious car accident. I would call that a miracle too. I'll leave you two to talk and enjoy the gift you were given." Matt smiled at Linda, the head nurse, and seeing the perplexed look on her face, he stopped to explain Howard's presence. From a suspect to an injured person in the hospital could only be explained without sharing the whole truth. Linda saw it as the beginning stages of dementia and he neither confirmed nor denied her prognosis.

Matt checked in on Ashley and the other girl whose families were in and out of their rooms most of the day. They were finally able to breathe a sigh of relief. Both girls had improved physically but would need counseling to get through the mental anguish of the trauma. He scheduled one more interview with them in the morning, after they were released from the hospital and before they went home. Next, he checked in on the other two crash victims, and the news for them wasn't as good. Both men were sleeping, and Matt would have to wait until morning to talk with them.

His day had been a long one. Rarely did a day that had this many twists end on a high note. He was ready for home and to pick up Jessie.

****

Jessie glanced at the clock. She walked to the front of the store to look out the window then would head back to the counter a few minutes later. It seemed like forever since Matt had left with Ariel to see her grandfather. What was happening? Oh, to be a fly on the wall to see the reunion. It wouldn't answer any of her pressing questions, but it would be a special moment. Every one of the moments you can get in life were important. At least that was the way she thought about it. You couldn't have too many of them, in her estimation.

She glanced at the clock again and began to total the sales for her part of the day. Audrey would add the rest before she closed later. She had to keep busy. The hour was ticking by way too slowly only because she wanted to hear what happened. Today was pretty amazing, all things considered. Howard Digby's return was nothing short of a miracle. There wasn't a hint of anyone else in him. The fact that the voices in his head were gone was a good sign.

With her totals added, she was happy when Audrey walked in the door. Peyton came in from Joe's with a box of goodies for dessert tonight, and the three of them spent the next thirty minutes talking until Matt arrived.

The first thing when she got in the car she asked, "How did it go with Ariel and her grandfather?"

"Like you'd imagine." He smiled at her. "I'll remember this day for a long time."

"I thought it would." Jessie sighed. "It had to be. I have no idea how he survived both traumatic events, but he's alive and that's a marvel."

"Why him? In our other cases it seemed one died, and one lived. What's different this time?" Matt signaled his move into traffic.

"I don't know but I hope to find out soon. You know me—I think everything is somehow connected. I could be way off on this one, but I don't think so." She turned to look out the passenger window.

"Let's start with the premise that they are related. Begin at the beginning with your trip and let's work our way through each detail. I'll give you time to think about the subject and we'll talk at dinner. That way the others can jump in." Matt moved into the turn lane.

"I can do that." Jessie smiled at him.

"Subject change." He glanced at her. "We haven't had much personal time to talk about us lately. You still have to tell me Sadie's story."

Jessie smiled, thinking about their night in Dublin. "I'm looking forward to telling you about that time. My grandpa Max was awesome. Sadie misses him every day. Although—" Jessie paused, her finger tapping on the armrest. "—she was almost swept off her feet in Dublin by an older gentleman. Grams blushed like a schoolgirl." Jessie chuckled.

"Sounds fun."

"Matt, we had the best time. I'll always treasure that time we had together with her. Sadie loved every minute of the trip and so did we."

"Where does that leave us?" he asked.

"I had already made up my mind before you surprised me with the tickets to Ireland. The trip confirmed to me that I had made the right decision. We're perfect together." She placed her hand on his arm. "I don't know how you can live with all my baggage and still love me, but the fact that you can tells me you're the perfect man for me."

"Good to know. I think I've handled my charming self rather well." He waggled his eyebrows.

"Not bad, although there were a few times that left me wondering." She laughed. "In my dream, Johanna told me the man who could accept all that I am was the one for me. I'm not sure many men could deal with their wife seeing ghosts and the like. You're a keeper, in my book."

"Let's set a date." Matt opened the garage door and pulled his car in.

"Sounds good." She would have said more but Peyton rushed out of the house and opened the car door.

"I'm glad you're here." She leaned closer to Jessie as she got out of the car. "I want to take another look at those scrolls. I've been thinking about them all day. Jaxon is making dinner, and now would be a perfect time to get started. I already set the table." She took Jessie's hand.

"We'll finish our discussion later." Jessie playfully fluttered her lashes at Matt as she was pulled past him.

"I'll hold you to that promise." He smiled at her.

Once inside the room with Peyton, she pulled out the parchments. She kept in mind what Matt wanted her to think about. Every time she touched the parchment, the sense of connection to something greater than herself reached out and grabbed her.

"Do you feel the same way I do?" Peyton asked.

"What do you mean?"

"Not alone. There are many more like us. I've researched a few of the names that I've seen on the writings, and do you know what?" Peyton asked. "I could have been one of them. The premonitions and the way I traveled back in time were my first manifestations as a grown-up. But I've started having memories from my childhood. I remember I could see the auras as colors around my parents and knew when to take my sister to our hiding place. I didn't understand what I was seeing at the time, but now I can. Those colors saved us more than once."

"I hear you. Our trip to Ireland was not only to see a beautiful country but to also learn more about who we are and our connection to our history." Jessie squeezed Peyton's hand. "There is a reason for us to have these gifts and to be alive at this time."

Side by side, Jessie and Peyton studied the next scroll in the grouping. Jessie could hear the voices of her ancestors speaking their meaning to her thoughts. She got excited with each new element she learned. Contentment grew with each new revelation of who she was and could become.

Chapter 31

"Jess, dinner is ready." Matt knocked on the door.

"We'll be right out," she answered. She reached for Peyton's hand. "Let's go." She smiled. "Our destiny is waiting." Jessie snorted.

"Speaking of Destiny, my best friend, you do realize that her relationship with Evan is getting hot. I bet he asks her to marry him soon. That means my best friend might be your sister-in-law."

"I heard that. I think Sally, my high school friend, might be getting engaged to Matt's best friend growing up, Chad. Pretty awesome if you ask me. Before you know it, we'll all be old married ladies."

"Hmm, I'm not too sure I like the sound of that. Especially the old part." Peyton laughed.

"We have Katie to thank for all of this. She's the reason I moved here, and then one by one, the rest of you followed. She wouldn't be happy to hear that she's to blame for us finding this new part of our lives. She doesn't even want to talk about it. She pretends this side of me doesn't exist." They walked down the hall arm in arm toward the kitchen.

"There's a unique spin on our situation. We can't pretend it doesn't exist, although I've tried, because it's who we are," Peyton said.

"True, as we are finding out. It doesn't simply go away when you wish it."

"I'm famished," Peyton said they reached the kitchen. "Boy, does something smell good."

****

Matt studied Jessie as she walked into the room. Her eyes sparkled, a blush tinged her cheeks, and she looked more beautiful than ever to him. Something was up. He couldn't wait to hear what. Peyton seemed to be equally excited.

"I wanted to have a discussion with everyone tonight. You're included in this one, Frank," Matt said as soon as everyone was seated and their meal was on the table. "Carlene won't be needed to track Digby, but before you go home, I may still have another track for you. Can you hang in another day?"

"I can stay for one more day and then I need to get home." Frank spooned mashed potatoes on his plate. "Jaxon, this is a feast." He passed the platter of chicken to Peyton.

"Jessie believes that all of the elements of what is happening are somehow tied together. I wanted us to discuss this with all of you and get your opinions. I'm not sure if we have a full picture of the investigation yet. I hope Ashley will remember more when I stop by to see her tomorrow." He took a bite of his salad. "Jess, why don't you start with the trip to Ireland?"

Jessie told them about their trip which included the dream. "I don't think we've seen the full manifestation of the dream yet. Only bits and pieces."

They discussed back and forth all through dinner. Matt found himself getting frustrated. They seemed to be getting nowhere fast. This wasn't one of his best ideas. He needed to talk to Jessie. She kept taking a backseat to the others. He was sure she had more going on inside her head to tie all of the moving parts together than she was saying. He got up from the table to carry his plate to the sink.

"Is it all right if I go outside? I know even though Bobby is no longer a threat, there's still another one out there who might be." Jessie placed her plate in the sink.

"We can go out together. There's a bench in the garden calling our names." Matt took her hand. "We're going out for some air," he told the group still discussing the case.

"Thank you. I needed this." Jessie sat on the bench. "I love this spot. The view is beautiful."

"I agree. It's one of my favorite spots to come when I need to think." He laced his fingers through hers while the silence of the evening settled around them. "What's up?"

"What do you mean?" Jessie glanced at him.

"You seemed to fade into the background in there and I want to know why?"

"I realized anything I would say is pure speculation at this point. There are many things I'm not sure of. The key is, I don't believe we've seen the worse yet. What Bristol did was horrific. I believe it was his actions and not the one using him. It's strange. I never thought that the traveler would have to contend with the personality of the host, but with Bristol and Digby, it's true. I have no idea why, but I'm sure of it."

"What do you think it means?" Matt asked, squeezing her hand.

"This is bigger than one simple crime or action. I almost see it as a bid to take over the minds of many and destroy our world as we know it. A bid from some unseen force or idea to pit neighbors against neighbors and nations against nations. Though it will still be fought and won one person or crime at a time, tyrants and the bullies will crawl out from their hiding places, and it will be an all-out war for the minds and affections of the masses."

"I'm not sure how that can be accomplished." Matt frowned.

"It will come from every corner of the world and internet as a constant barrage of misinformation. I would like to stick my head in the sand and go on with my life, but everyone will have to decide at some point. It will be forced upon us." Jessie shivered. "Sorry. It sounds overly dramatic even to me." She shook her head.

"Other generations have faced equally disturbing things. I guess we shouldn't be surprised if we have to also." He wrapped his arm around her shoulders. "We can't do much about it tonight." Content to sit with his arm around her, he didn't want to think of any other possibility but a happy life with her. But all the daily FBI warnings told him she was closer to the truth than she realized. Damn, not a happy thought.

"Tell me about your grandparents' story. I could use some good news." Matt squeezed her shoulder for encouragement." He sat quietly by her side and waited. Her voice was what he wanted to hear most.

****

"The sixties were a time of turmoil. Not much different than today, I guess. Different issues but turbulent no less. The period was marked by the assassination of a president, the Viet Nam War, and Civil Rights Movement. The time was filled with anti-war protests and women's rallies, marches and sit-ins. It was time of change for women, and Grams caught the fever, even if her mother hadn't. Her family, as defined by Grams, was straight, churchgoing, and normal. Although Sadie thought of herself as a wild child and wanted to join in the movement of her time. It's the secret we share because of my trip back in time to the sixties." She leaned her head back against his arm.

"Go on." He stroked her hair. "How did she meet your grandpa?"

"Grandpa Max, on the other hand, was a part of the sixties' counterculture known as the hippie movement. They brought the revolution of peace, drugs, and free love across the country. They trekked by the thousands into San Francisco to Haight-Ashbury. Maybe a better description is they flooded into the area and took over. The Haight was the center of their countercultural revolution. Max made his way there after graduation, via art school in New York City." She closed her eyes and smiled. "It's hard to think of your grandparents any differently than you know them. He was the first in his small town to turn onto the drug culture and grow his hair long,"

"I guess we all have to wrestle with finding ourselves before we settle down." Matt grinned. "Who hasn't sowed a few wild oats in their youth?"

"Gramps said they were trying to escape middle-class society which they saw as materialistic and repressive. When life and the drug scene in the city got too crazy, he built a tree house in the redwoods until the authorities ran them out and tore down their structures. He eventually made his way to a commune in New Mexico."

"Wow, he sounds like a character." Matt chuckled.

"Grams said we didn't know the half. She learned something new every time he told another story."

"How did they get together?"

"They met at a war protest where Bob Dylan and Joan Baez were singing. Actually, it was the one I went to. How crazy is that?"

"It's right up there." He smiled, twisting her hair around his fingers.

"Grams said it was love at first sight. Sure, he had long hair and a shaggy beard, but his eyes told her everything she needed to know about him. The next time she saw him, his friend brought him to the church her family attended one Sunday morning. She didn't recognize the clean-shaven, short-haired, handsome young man, except for his eyes. He asked her out on a date, much to her parents' chagrin. Three weeks later, he asked her to marry him, and three months and five days later, they were married in that church. The kicker was, they were married for over fifty years. They were completely different in every way but had fun and loved each other until Grandpa passed away. I swear, when she told us their story, it was filled with the love she still felt for him."

"You have a good heritage. I'm glad the universe saw fit to send you my way."

"Hearing their story and seeing Johanna's made me realize there are no perfect conditions, but people can make choices to keep their relationships alive in spite of the hardships that come their way."

"Nothing is ever simple, but that's why we need each other." His hand stroked her cheek.

"You already know I come with baggage. I'm stubborn, and I will fight you if I think I'm right." She turned to face him. "You like your own way too, and we will fight often, but I'm convinced we are better together than alone."

"You've got that right, babe. There's not a question in my mind. As soon as this is over..." He paused when she put a finger to his lips.

"This is just beginning. There will be many problems to solve in our lives. If I learned anything while in Ireland, there is no perfect time. I only know that I don't want to do life alone anymore." She snuggled into his side and leaned her head against his chest.

"Nor do I. We have some decisions to make." He held her in his arms.

Jessie had no idea how long they remained there, only that it was right. The peace she had in this moment wouldn't last, and she wanted to drink in every minute.

Chapter 32

The dream started like all the others, only it was Johanna who stood looking out to sea and not herself as the waves lapped the shoreline. Patches of bright blue sky peeked through the clouds as the mist parted above her head; the lush green landscape surrounded her motionless figure on three sides; and as if on cue, the sun's rays broke through and shone on her, making her appear ethereal. Stoic, still, and strong, she never moved from her position. Jessie was drawn to her. One by one, women lined up beside and behind her as the sea became tumultuous and the waves grew higher. Swelling, they rose to the height where the women stood, swirling around their feet, only to recede and begin the process again. Johanna never flinched nor did the women around her. No matter the churning of the sea nor the height of the wave, the water could not pull them from the place in line where they stood. Line after line, woman after woman, until soon the faces came into her view. And there, near the back of the line, her face stared back at her. Peyton stood beside her, their arms linked together. The face on Peyton's left side was blurred, but the face on Jessie's right belonged to Reba. Johanna raised her hand, and each of the women followed her action. Their show of strength turned the waters back until the waves were tamed and lapped the shore once again.

Jessie sat up and turned on her light. She wanted to write down the details. Again, she was reminded there were those in each generation that fought to hold back the darkness in their time with the gifts they had been given. Was the person with the blurred face next to Peyton her sister, Madison? If so, they would find out soon enough. She saw Sadie's arm latched through the arm of whoever the person was.

Jessie decided to make an early start to her day and got moving. After her shower and morning routine, she picked out her outfit for the day. Hopefully, she would be back in her cottage soon. She wanted more clothing options.

"Good morning, cousin." Peyton smiled at Jessie when she walked into the kitchen. "I see you're up early too."

"I awakened early and figured I might as well get my day going." Jessie leaned against the counter.

"Same here. I couldn't get those scrolls and all the women that wrote in them over the years out of my mind." Peyton took a sip from her cup. "There's hot water in the kettle on the stove if you want hot tea. For some reason, tea and toast sounded like the perfect way to start my day."

"Works for me." Jessie placed a tea bag in her cup and poured in the hot water. She placed a slice of bread into the toaster while her tea steeped.

"You gals are up early," Frank said as he walked out with Carlene. "I understand her—she needs to go out—but why are you two up so early?"

"One of those nights." Jessie smiled at him as she buttered her toast.

"What kept you up?" Peyton asked.

"I went to sleep fine, but my dream had me writing down details after I woke up." Jessie went on to explain her dream.

"That's awesome. If Reba was there, do you think Madison might be the other one that Sadie held onto?"

"Could be. We will know in time. Remember how Sadie and I wondered about you? The answer came to us when you found out about it yourself."

"True. I have to admit when I saw EJ's ghost at the hotel after I saw him first as a murder victim floating in the pool was a bit of shock for me." Peyton smiled. "It did let me meet my hunky detective, though."

"There's always a silver lining." Jessie chuckled. "I wonder who Madison would meet if she manifested this gift. In the end, the man must accept even the weird parts of her."

"Not as easy as it sounds, I'm sure. In that regard, we were lucky." Peyton took a bite of her toast.

"I'm not sure if it was luck or arranged." Jessie finished the last sip of her tea.

"Oh, good, you're up. I need to get to the station for a meeting. Do you mind going to work earlier?" Matt asked.

"I don't mind but I would rather drive myself. That way you wouldn't have to bother." Jessie glanced at his face and waited for his reaction.

"I hope to accommodate you soon. If I knew the guy went the way of Bristol and Digby, you'd be free to go home. I don't think he has. I wish I knew what he was up to, though, and how you're connected. One fact I know from past cases is that you probably are."

"Of course you're right. But you can't blame a girl for trying." Jessie stood. "I'll get my purse and be ready to leave in a few minutes."

"Me too." Peyton followed her cousin down the hall.

There was one part of her dream that she was still trying to understand. If it were true, it made more sense than how she had viewed details up until now. Didn't Reba tell her they would grow into their gift? Maybe with growth understanding also grew.

****

It gave Matt the creeps every time he checked out the attic in Jessie's store. Maybe it was the fact that he had to pass the stairs knowing, according to Jessie, that a ghost stood guard there. A grumpy looking fellow, as she often like to describe him. The thought of a ghost never concerned him before. No, it was instinct that told him there was more to it. But what? Every time he went up there, he checked for electronics or any sign of someone being up there recently. There was nothing visible. Gary had given him a small tool to detect for listening devices. Nothing could be detected but something felt off up there. He didn't want to worry her with his unfounded concern until he had a concrete reason for his unease. The attic seemed secure, but he would almost bet that it wasn't.

He went into the conference room to get ready for his meeting. The files Joe handed him documented the criminal activity and threats in town and the surrounding jurisdictions near the cove. There was enough information in each of the files to keep his officers on their toes for a while. He had asked Frank to attend, hoping that he could add a fresh perspective. The meeting lasted several hours. Assignments for the week were handed out, and Gary filled them in on the online chatter they should be concerned about. Matt explained the thought he had after leaving Jessie's store at the end of their discussion.

"Maybe we need to go over the attic more thoroughly," Gary suggested.

"Doesn't she want to expand the store upstairs?" Jaxon asked.

"Yes," Matt said. "Why?"

"We could use that as cover to check out the attic without alerting them to a problem if there isn't a need for it." Jaxon stood. "At this point with all that's going on, we need to run down every lead or cause for concern that we can. If it's nothing, all the better—that eliminates one more cause for concern."

"Works for me. I planned on going there this afternoon. You volunteered to come along." Matt grinned at him.

"I figured as much."

"Frank, you want to come along? Maybe Carlene will find something we can't. You too, Gary."

"Won't they think it strange if all of us show up unplanned?" Gray gathered his files.

"I'll be up front with her. Jessie would figure it out anyway. When it comes to an investigation, she is way ahead of me."

Joe knocked on the door. "Matt, the hospital called. They want you over there pronto It seems they have a bit of an issue."

"Let's roll." Matt pointed at Jaxon. He was no Jessie, but he knew he wasn't going to like what they were about to hear.

****

He was getting better at the exchange action as

time went on. Of course, he'd had multiple years to perfect the tradeoff. Finding a host was never an issue, but learning to control their personality could create major problems for him. A victim often had a mind of their own and a free will, which made his choices harder to enact. The real man he was had died years ago. He still missed the guy. All that was left of him was his essence, but he had done a lot over the centuries using willing people in his plans. Once in a while, he needed a body to walk around in. Bristol had been a mistake. A big one. His crazy attack at the girl's home and the slaughter of innocent people was the wrong way to go about it. He had done that a few times, only to fail.

To control, one had to be strong and subtle. Speak the true part out loud while shielding a hidden agenda, he reminded himself. Howard was too kind and passive. Okay, a bit old. At least, thanks to him, he would live out his life with his family. Hell, maybe he was getting soft. Years could do that to anyone. Somewhere between Bristol and Digby was the one he needed to do the task before him. Being a villain was no piece of cake. Having no body wasn't much fun either unless, of course, he had the power to move masses. He needed to get his hands on the treasure.

Bristol did fit into the anger he was trying to generate, but he moved too quickly before he wanted his presence known. There had to be a method and order to the madness he created. He didn't want to create a single event but a movement of anger and discontent.

Chapter 33

Matt glanced at Jaxon as they rode the elevator down. "I should have seen that coming, but it still surprises me."

"I know. Ashley filled in a few details she had forgotten. That was good and will beef up the report. With Bristol dead, it doesn't matter much. He's the one who abducted the girls." Jaxon walked out the doors when they opened.

"True, and we couldn't explain the rest anyway. Howard seemed unclear on what happened to him. His strong memories are of being shot, and when he thought he was dying, and of the accident. He had no idea how he survived either, and neither do I." Matt unlocked the car doors. "I still can't figure out how Miller walked out of the hospital undetected after being in the accident."

"We seem to have another mess. I'd like to know how any of this is possible. Then again, maybe I don't want details." Jaxon stood by the car.

"I'll get Gary and Jeremy to work on finding out everything about Gordon Miller and Fred Hinkley. Fred is still under sedation. Linda said she would call if there was any change."

"Was he the driver of the white car or the car Howard was in?" Jaxon opened the car door.

"Gordon Miller was in the car with Howard. He is

the guy who walked out of the hospital without being released, and he's the one we need to be concerned about. He had significant injuries." Matt latched his seat belt. He shook his head. "Another unexplainable mess."

"I swear I don't get any of this and wouldn't believe it for a minute if I hadn't lived through a few weird incidents already. I have a couple of questions for Jessie and Peyton though." Jaxon frowned.

"You and me both." Matt pulled out of the hospital parking lot. "Looks like the attic might need to wait until tomorrow if I can convince Frank to stay on another day."

"I'll let Kenny know. He can alert the others."

****

Jessie thought Matt stayed upstairs longer each time he went up there. Maybe it was her imagination, but he seemed to be carrying the weight of the world on his shoulders this morning. She wanted to help him, and she was hopeful that what she had learned would ease some of his cares. Who was she kidding? His rational brain would be messed with once again.

Matt had nothing to prove to her, but he had shown his patience and love to her repeatedly. She hoped he could summon that tolerance one more time. *Be honest, Jessie, he had better have great stamina for the challenges he will face marrying you.* Yes, there was weird baggage that came with her, but it didn't end there, and he already knew it. Stubborn was her middle name.

He was stubborn too. They might have a donnybrook or two in their marriage, but the makeup would be awesome. She sighed, closing her eyes.

"Hello, dear girl." Reba walked into the store from

the coffee shop. "I only have a few minutes. Lawerence is meeting me for a late lunch. Molly has some tasty new things on her menu."

"Reba, you never need a reason for stopping by, but something tells me you have one." Jessie smiled at her.

"Of course, I do. I'm a woman on a mission or, as my husband likes to say, I have a bee in my bonnet." Reba patted Jessie's hand. "Things are about to get interesting for you. Not to say they haven't been already, but I mean in a whole new way. You"—she squeezed Jessie's hand—"have seen a lot already. Remember I told you grow into the gift when you both are about to be bombarded with understanding?"

"I'm not sure I like your word choice." Peyton chuckled.

"I only can say what I see."

Jessie told her about the dream and seeing Reba's face among the women. "You were there right beside me."

Reba wiped a tear from her eye. "You, dear child, have made my day. To be counted among all those great sisters is indeed an honor." She sniffed. "I see Lawrence waiting. "We'll talk more later. Maybe this chat was for me as much as you. Love you, girls."

"Right back at you, my friend." Jessie waved at Lawrence.

Peyton glanced at her phone. "Jaxon texted me that he is on his way here with Matt. He said they wanted to talk to us. I wondered what they want."

"We're about to find out." Jessie pointed out the window where Matt was getting out of the car.

"We need to talk," he said, kissing her on the

246

cheek. "We'll be right back." Matt rushed past her into Joe's.

Jessie studied the man she loved as he stood at the counter. Something troubled him. His forehead was furrowed, and his hands were fisted at his side. The smile he gave Molly didn't quite reach his eyes. Unlike the charming carefree man she first met, she couldn't help but wonder if she might be the reason for the tension written on his face. More than he realized. Too many things had happened since the first time she walked into his office to spar with him and then to fall in love with him over time.

Jessie smiled at him when he came back with Jaxon following close behind. "I take it you were too busy to eat until now."

"Yes, we had a busy morning." He took a bite of the sandwich as he sat. "I'll cut to the chase. Our visitor has jumped again, and I have Jeremy and Gary looking into Gordon Miller's background and anything they can find on the man. This makes twice that no one died when he jumped. Why do you suppose that is?" Matt stretched out his legs and sat back in the chair.

"I have a theory on that." Jessie sat beside him. "I read an article about a young woman who received a heart transplant. Before she got the heart, she wasn't a nice person at all. She received the heart of a young man who was known and loved by many. She recalled how when she awakened and once past all the pain, it was like she had someone new walking inside her. She became more like the one whose heart beat in her chest. It got me thinking."

"Enlighten us. I can kind of see where you're going." Matt's forehead lines deepened.

"A traveler, in order to live in a new time, must jump and become that person. But the essence or a spirit can simply find a host to live in or influence. The world is filled with magical beliefs. Pookas, fairies, and leprechauns we have heard of in stories and experienced firsthand. Others believe in good and bad spirits. I think, and this is simply my idea for now, we are dealing with the essence or spirit who challenges each generation with something they must overcome and press against. For Johanna, she faced a real warrior who was determined to destroy her people. For another, it was famine and hunger who stole their lands and crops."

"And you think that is what we are dealing with?" Matt asked.

"Yes," she told him. "The problem with this means of traveling is sometimes the human they look to control can do more or less damage and be hard to control. Bobby was wild and filled with anger and hard to control. Howard was too passive, and he stemmed his anger. Like the man's heart changed the girl when she received it. The one we are dealing with must persuade many on a path to divide them from others. This may be hard to fight against. The world is a smaller place thanks to air travel and the internet."

"I have one problem with the theory. He said he was returning like he promised in the note." Matt raked his hand through his hair.

"I remember that. Maybe it wasn't me he was after as much as something he thinks I have or possess. Maybe he was looking for something, and that's why we're still alive. Just an idea, but it's still a theory in progress."

"How can you fight a spirit or an essence?" Matt's hand fisted.

"I was going to ask the same question," Jaxon said.

Jessie told him about the dream. "I saw Peyton and Reba standing in that group of women along with me. I have to believe there is a way to turn the tide. Maybe not today or tomorrow but with time. There are many ways you can fight." She smiled. "It doesn't always have to be out front. Remember when you picked up that stick on the makeshift altar in the Palm Springs' case and you knew not to touch it again? I sang a Sunday school song from when I was kid to stop the darkness that threatened to overtake me. Grams and Katie sat beside me on the floor and sang along."

"Who could forget that? Picking up that stick knocked me to the ground. That was an eye-opening moment for me. Not everything you deal with has a nice tidy explanation." Matt leaned forward in the chair. "Guns that wouldn't shoot, police who were frozen in place, and a suspect that died saving you. That was one strange case."

"We've had a year full of them." She reached for his hand. "We've come a long way."

"Do you remember when we were talking about the sixties the other night?" His thumb stroked her hand.

"Yes." She tried to pull her hand away, but he held it tight.

"Those were a turbulent ten years, but as you reminded me, there were strange things then too for which there were few explanations. Now, with the whole world traveling more and the internet, the world seems smaller and moving faster." He frowned. "I'm not saying they had it easier. The riots of that time period were tough on everyone. It's only that hate seems to travel faster now and is more emboldened because it has found a place globally where it can communicate."

"Still, we only deal with what is happening in front of us. Collect evidence, deal with the crimes that we are alerted to, and arrest suspects based on that evidence. It's our job." Jaxon tapped his fingers on the table as he spoke.

"As I'm constantly reminded, we have to be ahead of the game. Criminals are coming up with new scams all the time, and we can't police in the same old ways because we are used to them. The FBI taught me that. Gary reminds me every day about online chatter that we need to stay abreast of. Our world is changing and so must our methods." Matt smiled. "I'll go on the record as saying I still am a logical thinker, and I'll let these two deal with the stranger aspects." Matt took a sip of his tea. "Do you have any other questions, Mr. FBI man?"

"Explain to me again the difference between a traveler and a spirit?"

Jessie explained her theory again. "But it's only one idea."

"I'm going play the devil's advocate here and ask, then why did Bristol live and walk out of the hospital, but the other guy died?" Jaxon brows furrowed.

"Good question, man." Matt nodded at him.

"I don't know, unless the traveler wanted it that way." Jessie shrugged. "This is uncharted waters for me too."

"None of this is logical anyway. I guess it doesn't

matter what the theory is." Jaxon stood.

"I'll be by later to do some measurements upstairs. If you want to expand to a second floor, we need to see if it will work." Matt picked up his trash, gave her a quick kiss, and followed Jaxon out the door.

Matt was up to something. She smiled. Maybe a surprise. She would let him keep his secret for now, but she would get it out of him eventually.

Chapter 34

An hour before Jessie's day was over, Matt came back like he promised, but with Frank, Carlene, and Gary too. Okay, now Jessie knew something was up for sure.

"Excuse me." She grabbed Matt's hand before he reached the stairs where Carlene stood at the bottom growling. "I know you're not here to measure anything. Gary and Carlene aren't needed for that. What are you up to?"

"I'm acting on a hunch. It might be nothing, but I'll tell you after I'm done." He petted Carlene's head. "Frank, what's up with her?"

"Dogs can sense what we don't. Any guesses, Jessie?"

"I'd say the spirit on the stairway might have something to do with it. As far as anything else, I have no idea," she spoke softly into Frank's ear, then walked away to wait on a customer. A new idea popped into her head. She would have to research this one. It made as much sense as anything else they had discussed the past few days.

She went about her usual routine until Audrey and Heather showed up. Matt was still upstairs. As she totaled her sales for the day, Kip came in, followed by Dylan. They made their way up to the attic. What was going on up there? It couldn't be good if it took five of them and a dog to take care of whatever it was.

Matt sent her text. —*Hey, Jess, when you get a chance come up here, please.*—

—*Okay.*— she wrote back to him. "Peyton, could you watch the store for minute? Matt wants me upstairs."

"Sure thing. It's quiet anyway. I've been wondering what's happening up there. I can't wait to hear."

Jessie headed up the stairs. Excitement mingled with dread filled her with each step that took her closer to the top. "Knock it off, girl. He's checked it out every day and there's been nothing up there." she whispered quietly. "What's going on?" she asked when she saw them standing there.

"Every time I checked this area out something troubled me. This morning was stronger than ever. I've looked for listening devices and anything that I could see on the surface but never found anything. I asked Frank and Gary to come to help me this time."

"Did you find anything?"

"No listening devices." Matt shook his head. "This whole area was cleared after you bought the building."

"What are you saying? Did you find more bugs?" she asked.

"No, but we found something, and I hope you can tell us what we're looking at. I know we never saw this here before." Matt took her to the area and pointed at an item nestled in the insulation. "I didn't want anyone to touch it."

The hand-carved, ornate wooden box had a unique Celtic symbol etched into the top. She had seen the symbol before in the scrolls. She took her phone out of her pocket and searched on the internet for its meaning. Her hand shook as she lifted the box from its resting place.

"Should you touch that?" Kip asked.

"Yes, I believe it's meant for me to see." She pointed at the top of the box. "This is an ancient symbol for a Celtic Warrior." She ran her hand along the top of the box. A warm sensation ran up her arm and throughout her body. "It's beautiful." Her voice shook with emotion.

"Are you going to open it, or maybe a better question is, should you?" Matt asked.

"There's something almost mystical about it. I'm not sure what to do. I will leave it where we found it and think about what I should do. I think that maybe it is one of the reasons the ghost is guarding the stairs. Could it be why we are being visited again? Is the traveler looking for it too? Something to think about." She placed the beautiful box back in the spot where they had found it. Her hand still tingled with a warm presence from touching the box.

"I want a promise from you, and these guys are my witness." He reached for her hand and pulled back the minute he touched it. "What was that?" His brows rose.

"It came from the box." She smiled sheepishly at him. "Didn't you want them to witness some promise?"

"Yes, and after that little episode, it seems more important now." He lifted her chin. "I want you to promise that you or Peyton won't open the box unless one of us is with you. Your combined track records of disappearing leave us with no other choice."

"I promise, but if it's going to happen, you being there won't stop me." She chuckled to herself when she saw his expression.

"The hell it won't." Matt scrunched his face.

"Believe what you want." She stroked his cheek which felt like granite until he relaxed.

"I'll be sure to tell you when I'm ready to open this beauty." She pointed at the ornate small chest and placed some loose insulation over the contours to hide it. A true treasure for safekeeping watched over by a spirit from the past. Who knows? Maybe he was the original owner. Jessie smiled to herself. Her imagination could take flight to strange places in a moment's time given the freedom.

"I may not trust the contents, but I do trust you." He gave her a quick hug. "We're not done up here, but you are free to go. We'll be ready to leave soon." He turned to watch Carlene. "And yes, I know. You're riding with me," he told her.

****

Matt heard her mumble something as she turned to walk down the stairs. Idiot was definitely used in the sentence. He laughed to himself. She always took the bait. He had no idea what stopped her from opening the box until he got the zing from touching her hand. Erring on the side of caution might be a good idea. Slow down, think it through, and then open for a view of the contents.

How the box got here was a mystery he wanted solved. Who put it there to be found and who was looking for it were both questions that needed answered. The sooner the better. Her life could be in jeopardy if someone knew the contents and was searching for the small chest.

"Matt, you might want to have a look at this,"

Frank called out to him. "I wonder how many of these artifacts are hidden up here."

Nestled behind a wooden beam was a sheathed dagger. Matt would love to get a closer look at it. Even from where he stopped, he could see the emerald in the handle. The mystery seemed to be growing when Frank discovered another find. An ancient Celtic Cross. Matt was stumped. Hidden in plain sight to be found. Why?

"Has this chest been up here all along?" Kip reached for the latch and was knocked to the ground. "Dang, what was that?"

"No one touch anything!" Matt reached his hand down to help Kip up.

"Hell, another bizarre twist." Jaxon frowned. "What's next? A sword or javelin?"

"All I know is that I didn't see any of this here yesterday, this morning, or when we first came up the stairs. But I did have a strange sensation that something wasn't right. I have no idea how any of this got here or why." Matt leaned against the wall near the chest.

"I can't wait to hear Jessie's take on this. It's sure to be a mind-bending doozey." Gary gathered his equipment.

"The items appear to be ancient, which means either someone robbed them and planted them here or we have another odd twist to figure out." Matt shook his head. "I find it strange that none of these items were here when we first came up the stairs to look around, don't you?" Matt looked at the guys gathered around him.

"Matt, let's make another pass and make sure we have found everything," Gary said.

"These were meant to be found the way they are

placed. Another element to add to the mystery. It's almost like a game of Clue. At first you don't see it, look again and then you do." Jaxon smiled. "This could get interesting."

****

Jessie kept glancing at the stairs. She could hear them moving around as the floorboards creaked, and the sound of their muffled voices. What could possibly be keeping them? She was ready to go home. Her stomach growled. Any food sounded good right at the moment too; she was hungry. She glanced at the clock. It was almost six. No wonder her stomach was growling, and she had skipped lunch today too.

Why hadn't she opened the box? Even now she tried to avoid the subject. *Face it, Jessie, you were scared.* All this was getting a bit too mystical for her. She prided herself on believing she was in control. At the moment, this part of her life seemed fantastical. To be honest, the past year left her wondering if she was drifting out of reality. If her parents knew what was going on, they would have her in therapy and away from Blue Cove. She would never be able to share this part of her life with them. Thank heavens for Grams and Peyton. They were lifesavers for her.

The sound of the guys' heavy footsteps coming down the stairs gave her thoughts a reprieve. "Did you find anything else?" She stopped in front of Matt at the bottom stair.

"You could say that. We'll talk about it later." Matt reached for her hand. "See you tomorrow." Matt waved at Kip and Gary. "Dinner at Antonio's and then home sound good?" he said to Frank and Jessie. "We can drop Carlene off at the house. Jaxon and Peyton will reserve us a table."

"Works for me. I'm hungry." Jessie waved at Audrey and Heather as she walked out the door. "Please, be sure to check that the back door is locked when you close up."

Chapter 35

During dinner, Jessie listened to Matt explain what they had found in the attic. Anticipation built inside her along with a healthy dose of hesitancy. She couldn't wait to explore, and yet traipsing along the edge of her mind was an endless round of questions. Some were louder than others, and far more demanding of answers. The loudest of all was, how had the items got there when Matt hadn't seen them this morning?

"How is this even possible?" she asked Matt.

"I was hoping you'd be able to tell me. Any ideas, ladies?" He glanced at Jessie and then at Peyton.

"I wonder if they've been there all along hidden until the time for their discovery. I know it doesn't sound logical, but neither did being sucked through a book back in time." Peyton shrugged her shoulders.

"Or seeing a girl in a mirror calling from the past to solve her murder. When I picked up that old key, I was sucked through the mirror and yet remained here in a coma. I was in two dimensions. I know you remember that incident. That could keep you up at night, trying to figure out how it was possible." Jessie took a sip of the water after the waiter refilled her glass.

"How could I ever forget it?" Matt frowned.

"Most of what we've experienced since moving here has nothing to do with logic. I would call it urban fantasy," Jessie told them.

"What about the door in the forest not far from here and those who have come and gone through the door into the invisible world? The possibility for what we think of as magic, belief, or others might think of as mystical might really be the unseen helping us to see what we cannot." Peyton smiled. "After all, if what we learned on our trip is true, it is not rare for those who are born in the chime hours to see spirits."

"True, Peyton. Everything we did seemed to build on the idea of our gift being in our ancestral line." Jessie toyed with the corner of her napkin in her lap. "We did a walking tour of the medieval mile in Kilkenny. It was like going back thousands of years. Over five thousand years of history runs through Kilkenny's laneways, stairwells, walled city gates, towers, and stone-clad landmarks. We were able to climb the tower and visit the castle. Those laneways connect to the modern streets of the city, but as I walked them, I felt connected to our past. We went from old to new and back into the old. It was rather amazing."

"You're right, cousin. If anything, it makes what you found in the attic seem more like a family show and tell than some great mystery. There must be a reason for them being there, and they will be gone when what Jessie needs to know is over." Peyton squeezed Jessie's hand.

"It's rather exciting, isn't it?" Jessie glanced at Peyton.

"Remember the moment we walked through the archways down Butter Slip Lane, we all had goosebumps as though something significant had happened in our lives? Especially when we arrived at

St. Kierens where Kytelers Inn was located. Matt, you didn't simply give us a trip. You gave us an amazing life experience."

"That was a significant moment," Jessie said. "I found it hard to wrap my mind around the idea that we were walking around the city on some of the same streets that Johanna walked. Somehow, that part of our trip is important for what is happening now. I'm more excited than ever to put the pieces all together in my mind. We discovered the past has answers and keys for what's happening today."

"I would like a few of those answers," Matt told her.

"Me too," Jaxon chimed in.

"Hey, don't leave me out." Frank chuckled.

After the bill was paid, Matt and Jessie walked out of the restaurant hand in hand. "Where's Frank?" Jessie slid into the car when Matt opened the door.

"He must have gone with Jaxon and Peyton. He wanted to let Carlene out." Matt closed his door.

"Frank takes good care of his dog. And rightfully so; she's worth her weight in gold. Carlene has solved a lot of cases already, and she's at the beginning of her work years."

"Yeah. Too bad every police force can't afford a tracking dog. More crimes could be solved, and quicker too. Of course, it helps to have you as part of the package since he is your friend. Jeremy, who is also your friend, was an added bonus. It doesn't hurt to have your somewhat strange ability working on our side too." Matt glanced at her and then started the car. "I never stood a chance that day you walked into my office for the first time."

"You're such a sweet-talker. I'd say we are both better off for that turbulent meeting. But if I remember the whole story, you came to my house unannounced to find out what had happened to me at the church. When I told you about the ghost, you were quite uncomfortable and thought me a bit kooky." She raised her hand to stop him from saying more. "In your defense, I thought I was odd too and didn't know what to think about it all."

"We've come a long way over this past year, haven't we?" He stopped at the light. "Hey, give me some credit for at least hearing you out. It's not every day a beautiful woman tells me she saw a ghost and looks like you did." He chuckled.

"Yes, we have." She smiled. "I'm quite proud of you. All you do now is grumble, shake your head, and tell me you'll think about it. You are a prince among men."

"What are we going to do about the attic?" Matt asked.

"I'm going to check it out tomorrow. When you can be there, of course." She reached over and touched his arm. She felt his arm twitch.

"Thank you." He turned into his driveway and pulled into the garage.

"You told me you didn't want me to open the box without you there. I do listen sometimes." She unlatched her seat belt.

"For that too, but first and foremost, I love when you touch me." Matt traced her lips with his finger.

She smiled at him. "That's good to know." She opened the car door and jumped out. She ran into his unmovable form at the back of the car.

"You can wait for me to open the door." He tipped her chin up and gazed into her eyes.

"I know. Sometimes I get in a hurry. I've been opening my own car door for years before you." She let him take her hand. "This waiting drives me nuts. I want to know what's going on and how to deal with it. I'm not sure we've seen much yet."

"I'm sure you're right." He tugged her toward the house and closed the garage door. "Did I tell you the man who shot Bristol and dumped his body has been arrested? Another gang member who was once his friend. The police have an eyewitness who was in the car when Bristol was shot and dumped ready to testify against the suspect. Keeping him alive will be paramount for the case."

"That's scary to think about. But I'm glad there's an arrest. Bobby wasn't nice, but no one deserves to be dumped unceremoniously at the side of road. It's sad. I've wondered if there is something that might have been done to change him or his choices. Such a waste of a young life." She walked through the door he held open into the house. "Purpose, a reason to live, something bigger than your own wants might be a good starting point."

"Good luck with that idea. These kids grow up in extreme and stressful situations. It's a wonder they make it as long as they do." He headed for his recliner. "I want to catch up on the scores, if that's okay."

"Works for me. I'm writing an article for Neil, my old boss, about the mass shooting in Elm's Spring from my personal perspective. I have some more research to do tonight. I'll kiss you goodnight now." She leaned close and kissed him. "Goodnight, everyone."

****

Matt watched her walk away. If he knew his girl, she would review everything in her mind and come up with a plan of action. He hadn't told her all his concerns tonight. There were too many to count. He couldn't wrap his head around how the items came to be in the attic that he checked daily. It frustrated the hell out of him. The idea that she would have to face this traveler bugged him. At least he knew what the potential suspect looked like. Jessie was convinced from the beginning that he would confront her again. Although, who he might be was even a mystery to her.

He hadn't told her about the threatening notes that arrived at the station nor the threats at city hall. He didn't want to concern her, which seemed right at the time but dumb now. She had more than earned the right to be kept in the loop. He put his feet up and flipped through the stations. Tomorrow would be soon enough.

"Did you decide what to do about the artifacts you found?" Jaxon asked as he plopped down onto the couch.

"Jessie is going to check them out with me in the morning. I wouldn't mind if you were there too." Matt muted the volume on the TV.

"Sure, I'm curious. I'll admit it. I talked to Peyton about the threats on our walk tonight. She didn't seem to be surprised." Jaxon leaned his head back and closed his eyes. "Did you tell Jessie your concerns."

"We talked, but I was just castigating myself for not being upfront with her. It's this ridiculous need I have to protect her, and after the shooting, I'm in an overprotective mode." He shook his head. "Yes, I know how lame that sounds. I'll tell her on the way to work tomorrow."

Jaxon chuckled. "Good idea. She won't be happy if Peyton tells her."

"I seem to be pulled several directions at once. Maybe that's the purpose—to keep our eyes off what's the real crime." Matt flipped the remote back and forth in his hands. "Has Maxwell said anything? I know you'll have to be back in the field office as soon as you finish the investigation on the girls."

"Maxwell said the same thing to our team earlier on a phone call. Maybe this is about getting law enforcement to be overworked and caught off guard. The chatter online suggests something big on the horizon. They're speaking in some kind of code, and we have agents trying to infiltrate and learn the encrypted language."

"Which brings us back to Jessie's dream. A rising tide, taking anyone who can't fight its force into the depths of discontent and anger. Could it be similar to when the Normans rode into Kilkenny, killing everyone in their path until a woman challenged the madness? Hmm, something to think about." Matt rubbed his temple. "At the moment, I need an escape. How about you?" He lifted the remote, pointed it at the television, and unmuted it.

Chapter 36

Matt talked to Jessie as he took her to work. He included the threatening notes his department had received and any other negative event that he could think of. His sleepless night taught him one thing—he had to trust her capabilities to handle what was thrown her way. Which in the past year, had been a lot.

"Thanks for letting me know." She smiled at him. "I can't wait to start running outside again. The summer is winding down, and thanks to Bobby, I haven't had much time to run besides at the gym. It's simply not the same. I loved my early morning runs in Ireland."

"You don't seem too worried about all this." Matt pulled into the open spot in front of her store. "I'm aware how much you love to run. I'll try to make time to run with you outside. Sound good?"

"Yes, thank you. But it makes me mad every time one of these guys thinks they can make us a target. I don't like to have to change my life each time." She took off her seat belt and pulled her keys from her purse. "After Bristol, I get it. I mean the incident could have been lights-out for me. No one likes to think about that. Still, I like my freedom to drive, run, or even work in my store without being someone's mark."

"I hear you. Not to change the subject, but did you see the email that Jeremy sent?" Matt asked.

"I haven't opened it yet. I was too busy going over

the scrolls last night. I'm not sure if I will have them much longer. Frankly, I don't understand how I have them now. I'm not complaining; seeing them has been a great gift to me. I had no idea how many others have been called upon to be a part of something beyond themselves. And as far as I can tell, those are the people who seemed to be the happiest in life. Not without troubles, mind you. That's something we all share."

"A purpose for your life is important." Matt started to open his door. "Are you concerned about what you will find upstairs? Wait." He got out and walked to her side of the car.

"I'm excited, as strange as that may seem." She placed the key to the store in his outstretched hand. "What amazing new truth am I about to learn from the past that will enlighten the present? It gives me goosebumps thinking about it." She walked through the door he held open.

"Stay here until I check out the store, and while you wait take a look at the email Jeremy sent. You need to see the suspect's face." Matt started up the stairs.

He wasn't sure what he would find this morning if anything. Was any of it real to begin with? No way would any of this go into a report—something he had said many times over the past year. Matt looked around the space. At least at that moment, nothing had disappeared. Jessie was obviously supposed to see the artifacts.

Matt started down the stairs. "Okay, sweetheart, it's your turn." He waited for her to come to where he stood. "Are you ready?"

"I can't wait." She took the steps two at a time, saluting the ghost as she passed where he hovered.

Jessie exhaled her breath in a slow steady rhythm. Her eyes lit up as she glanced around the attic. The first place she went was to where she had placed the box. She lifted the ornate case out of the insulation where she placed it the night before. The tingling warmth spread from her fingertips, up her arms, and through her body. When she felt Matt's breath on her neck and his hands squeezed her shoulder—that was all the encouragement she needed. She lifted the lid of the small chest with care. Nestled inside on a worn fabric was a beautiful silver medallion and chain. A note written in Gaelic was tucked inside underneath the necklace. She knew what the silver ornament on the chain meant. "Isn't it beautiful?" She turned to show Matt. "This is an ancient symbol for a warrior." She ran her finger over the same symbol on the box. The same warmth moved through her fingers with each pass.

"What does the note say?" he asked.

"It's in Gaelic. I will have to see if I can have the message translated." Jessie moved on to the dagger behind the beam. "I saw a drawing of this on one of the scrolls. Look at the size of the emerald. It's beautiful, and I can't imagine its worth in today's currency. My grumpy friend must be keeping watch over these treasures."

"When Kip tried to open the chest, he was knocked on his backside. You must be the only one meant to open the chest. Do you want to?" Matt reached for her hand. "You don't have to."

"Oh, but I want to." Jessie lifted the lid and got down on her knees to inspect the contents. "Look, Matt. These are all from the drawings on the scrolls. They must have been passed down from one generation to the next, and each one added their treasures to the collection. I will someday add mine." She placed the dagger, the Celtic Cross, and the beautiful carved box into the chest. Instinct told her they belonged there. But the note and the pendant she withheld. She closed the lid. "I'm going to see if I can find the meaning to this before I put it back. Peyton needs to see all of this too."

"What do you think? Why is it here?" Matt took her hand.

"I'm about to find out." They started down the stairs together. "Did I really see that?" She wiped a tear from her eye. "Magic of the best kind, and I got to be a part of history and so did you. One of the things I learned about marrying from Johanna's life and the scrolls was that the man I should marry would accept this part of my life. You have in the past year and still do. That means everything to me."

"I guess that's because I know the real you is amazing and genuine. I know that in the beginning, it shook you too. You've learned to accept yourself, and I have learned to do the same." He walked with her to the counter. "Did you see the photo?"

"I did. I'll be on the lookout for him. I'll tell you if I find out what this means." She walked him to the door. "Have a good day." She pulled his head down and kissed him.

"Now that's a good way to start my day." He kissed her and walked out the door.

Jessie watched him drive away. She needed to get Jeremy to help her with finding the translation. She snapped a photo of the paper and sent a text to her friend.

—*Wow, girl, what are you into now?*— *Emoji*

smiley face.

—I'll call you later and fill you in.— Emoji waving hand.

Jessie smiled to herself when Peyton and Reba walked in together. Perfect. The day was bound to get interesting. There was enough time before the store opened to take them upstairs.

Jessie was thrilled all over again when she saw Reba's and her cousin's reaction to the chest and the treasures inside. This time she remembered to bring her phone and take pictures. For her use and eyes only and as a way to remember the items. She wanted to check them against the drawings on the scroll. There had to be a backstory for each item and, given her personality, she wanted to know every detail she could find. Who had they belonged to and what was their gift during their lifetime?

"My dear girls, I've never thought I would live to see a day like this. Thank you for sharing this moment with me. The day will remain one of my cherished memories as long as I live." Reba wiped the tears from her eyes. "With that said, you know you've been allowed this for a reason. It's not to make you feel good but to remind you of your ancestral heritage and to encourage you to remain true to it."

"You know, cous, I'm proud to be in this amazing family line and to be a chime-hour baby. I want to understand how all of these beautiful artifacts came to be in our family's possession." Peyton placed the Celtic cross back into the trunk. "Do you think the scrolls must be returned to Johanna?"

"Yes. We don't have a lot more time to view them. I have one you must see. I believe you are like Reagan who came a few generations after Johanna. I could see you in her writings, at least those I understood."

"Someday, one of your daughters, if you're blessed to have them, may be gifted in some way as well." Reba smiled at them. "I told you girls you'd be on a journey of self-discovery, didn't I? But you can't rest on your laurels. It's about to get interesting around here."

"Sheesh." Jessie slapped her hand to her forehead. "About to? It's been more than interesting and overwhelming already." She reached for their hands. "I don't know what I would have done without you two. Now, it's time to open the store and get to work." Jessie started down the stairs.

Chapter 37

Matt's morning got off to a fast start when a bomb scare was called in to the station. After a thorough search of the evacuated city hall, thankfully nothing was found. Was it a hoax or a diversion? His gut told him something wasn't right. Carlene seemed restless and Matt trusted the dog's instinct. He could relate. He found himself searching the area and wanting to get people back inside and away from whatever he couldn't see.

"Are we in the wrong place?" Jaxon walked up to Matt. "All these people milling around are sitting ducks and I don't like the sensation. My thoughts keep going from this isn't where the bomb is to the purpose for the call was to get these people outside and pick them off."

"I had the same thought. Let's move them inside." Once the all-clear was sounded, Matt went from group to group encouraging them to return to their offices. Jaxon helped and when the last group was inside the building, that's when the explosion rang out. The city building's windows rattled, but the structure seemed to be unscathed and still standing. But a black plume of smoke and debris rose high into the air from the direction of the harbor. Matt knew what the possible target was and found himself rushing to his car speaking expletives under his breath followed by Jaxon. Damn, he should have known. Talk about a cause for anger spreading. If he was right, that explosion could be a trigger. The sinking feeling in the pit of his stomach intensified as he sped toward the harbor.

"I thought they had brought their own security." Jaxon glanced at Matt.

"They did. Whenever a high-profile figure in government comes, they do unless they request the locals to take charge. We're always here to be backup. The yacht arrived last night. One can hope the passengers were not on board."

"I know they booked a whole floor in the seaside resort for a couple of nights." Jaxon unlatched his seat belt. "Well hell, there's not much left." He pointed at the yacht on fire with debris floating in the water around the burning hull.

"I'm there now," Matt told Kenny on the phone. "There's nothing left of the yacht. Ask Gary to see if he can find any chatter online taking credit for the bombing. Do we know if there was anyone onboard?"

"I'm waiting for confirmation but the owner and his passengers, which as you know included a Supreme Court justice, were at a wedding celebration until late into the night and slept at the resort. Some security and crew were supposed to be onboard. The FBI is sending an investigative team."

"I'm sure the place will be crawling with Feds." Matt got out of his car. "Stay in touch."

"Maxwell has a bomb squad on the way. They're monitoring the chatter and will let us know what they hear. Town hall was a diversion, I guess," Jaxon said.

"What I want to know is how did they get explosives aboard if there was a security detail? Divers, perhaps?" Matt and Jaxon walked out to the end of the dock. The police boat was ready for them to board. They were waiting for the divers and rescue units to arrive. What seemed like hours all happened in minutes. They were fast and professional because in their line of work time was of the essence.

"I can see someone floating near the wreckage." A young man, binoculars in his hands, pointed to the spot. "I'm not sure if the person is alive or not," he said as the group boarded. "Let's go."

The first man they reached couldn't be helped nor could a few more. One crew member was found clinging to life in the water and was rescued. The team members gave aid until they could get him back to shore and transport him to the hospital.

Matt spent the afternoon talking to witnesses who saw the explosion from other boats in the harbor and from restaurants where they ate. A woman remembered seeing a man standing on the dock with a cell phone. Not in itself an unusual sight, but the fact that he threw the cell phone into the water right before the yacht exploded seemed strange to her.

A few crew members who were on the bow of the ship survived along with two in the security detail. They talked with agents, telling them in detail all they could remember.

"Do you remember hearing anything before the explosion?" Matt asked the leader of the security detail that survived.

"No. The bomb didn't come from underneath the ship. The way the ship blew makes me think that the explosive was planted somewhere near the stern. My detail never left the ship, and there were three of my guys on duty around the clock at any given time. The only way this could have happened is if someone in the crew planted the bomb, or there's a traitor among my men. We were aware of threats, and that's why we were vigilant. The owner has had his ship checked in several ports by bomb-sniffing canines."

"Sounds like he was covering all the bases. How likely is it that someone could detonate the bomb using a cell phone?" Matt leaned against the rail on the pier.

"It seems to be a method of choice in a low-cost operation." The man scrunched his face.

"A lone wolf or a two- or three-man operation, perhaps?" Matt asked.

"Quite possible." The man folded his arms across his chest. "Which has me wondering if one of my guys was bad. To keep the judge safe, few if any details of the trip were known by anyone. Only those on a need-to-know basis were included."

"Could someone get hold of the log with info on the travel plans?"

"Anything is possible, but it makes me sick to think about it. Another hour, and the guests would have returned to the ship, ready to move on to another destination."

"I wonder if our would-be suspect knew those details," Matt mused. "Or was he even aware they weren't on the ship at all? Something to think about. Agent Kincaid has some more questions to ask." Matt walked away and called to talk to Jessie. She must have heard the explosion and was wondering what happened.

****

He felt no remorse watching the yacht explode and the smoke rise into the clear blue sky. Almost like the good old days, when the cause coursing through his veins made his actions not only justified but heroic. At least, this host was passive and didn't seem to battle his will. He could get a few things done, place the blame in a few places, and just like that, he could start a war. Isn't that what he lived for—to divide, destroy, and conquer? These were different times, of course, but human nature hadn't changed much over the years. Pride, greed, and hate could motivate many men to treat others with little regard for their life. With the right words anger could be ignited by the simple act of cutting in line in front of someone. Yes, things hadn't changed much.

A small wave of lies here or there mixed with the strong winds of discontent and an even larger wave of anger, and soon you could control many minds with a less-than-dynamic leader. History was filled with the bones of such men. He knew all too well—he followed one, became one, and died an unknown, only to live on through others and still try to control their minds and actions. He was great in his own mind, and that was better than nothing, he supposed. The problem he ran into more often than not was that there were some people easy to control and others who held to principles he couldn't understand. But there still were those who lusted after what didn't belong to them and were willing to sell their soul to attain what was not theirs. That's where he and those like him came in. Kaboom! He watched them scurrying about trying to piece together what had happened. To him it was almost like old times.

****

"Can you believe what happened?" Peyton stood at the counter. "I swear, no one will want to come to Blue

Cove if these crimes keep happening. Jaxon said they're busy in Hanover too."

"Matt said the same thing. I talked to Sally, and she said the bomb scare this morning was frightening. I would be worried about our town too, if it weren't happening in other places as well." Jessie pointed at the headline on her computer screen. "What we sensed on our trip seems to be playing out in front of our eyes."

"Do you think what we saw upstairs has anything to do with all the anger around us in some way?" Peyton looked at the computer and to where Jessie pointed.

"I do, and I'm sure we'll know how in short order. We may slow down the process of what is happening, but it may take time for there to be a major change. Each generation has to do its part to fight the chaos of the age in which they live. Or maybe a better way to look at it is to decide what kind of people they want to be." Jessie shrugged.

"What's your theory?" Peyton asked. "I know we've always said there are no simple murder cases, but the strange twists to this seem beyond my ability to navigate."

"I'm working through my ideas now. One fact I know for sure is that online chat rooms, misleading information on the web, and the often-political tribal circus that foments spin makes this time prime for troubles. Remember as a teen when a crisis made you think it was the end of the world, only to rebound the next day?" Jessie raised her hand to forehead dramatically. "Oh, the drama of those days. This reminds me of those times."

"I can see that. People are overreacting." Peyton

nodded.

"Johanna had issues in her lifetime, great-great-grandma Kathryn in hers, and Grams did too. Sadie told me about burning her bras, marching for civil and women's rights in her youth. I believe we are dealing with something or someone who knows the weakness of our humanity and how to exploit us." Jessie waved at Molly through the open doors. "She's just so cute pregnant, don't you think?"

"Yes. We should give her a baby shower early this fall. I wonder if they are going to find out the gender of the baby or wait." Peyton fiddled with the bookmarks in the basket.

"Molly hasn't told me their plans in that regard. I've already mentioned to her that we are going to give her a shower. I have some great ideas that should include those who come into the coffee shop." Jessie leaned against the counter and explained to Peyton what might work. "With any luck she'll get enough gifts to clothe her baby for a long while."

Jessie spent the rest of the day with customers who were abuzz with gossip about the bombing of the yacht. Everyone had their own idea as to who was responsible, and it didn't take long to see people becoming more agitated and divided as the day went on. To her way of thinking, there was probably a small element of truth in each idea. A constant parade of news trucks and journalists rolled into town, and the news blasted out the events of the morning on a continuous loop. Included in the updated version of the stories were photos of the people who weren't on the yacht and those who lost their lives. Was this another diversion or part of the waves coming ashore? She wished she knew.

Chapter 38

Matt's morning enlightened him. Happy the FBI bomb squad was on the job, he was free to spend time with survivors and those who had come on the yacht. Finding the person who posted the itinerary of captain's log on the internet was important. Gary had assured him it was easier than he might think.

"Chief, we can track the person's online footprint even if it's encrypted. It may take a few hours, but with all the people working on the case, we should have an answer in no time."

"Sounds good. I have no idea how you'll do that, but I'm glad you can."

"Jeremy's working on the code, along with the FBI. Some of the best! We've already found the chat room where the schedule was first posted," Gary told him. "It was posted several times after that."

"Not good about the itinerary being reposted, but I'm glad they are zeroing in on the chatrooms moving this stuff. Divers found the burner phone that was thrown into the water. These guys always think of them as an easy way to evade detection, but they're not foolproof. True there won't be fingerprints, they're cheap, and the signal can be used to detonate a bomb, but they can be tracked to the store where the phone was bought. They may have a record, and the cellular provider will most likely have credit information. That part of the trail is being followed as we speak." Matt leaned his hip against the open door of his cruiser.

"Criminals are getting smarter, but they still can't cover all their tracks. Forensics is keeping up, and in some cases is far advanced by predicting what someone might think up. The movie industry helps with out-of-the-box thinking. If you can imagine the crime, it's possible. I can't wait to see how we can solve this crime by following the tech trail."

"Enjoy the moment, as bizarre as that sounds when I say it." Matt chuckled.

"I will. This is my dream case. I'm working with some of the best nerd techs in the world. I'll call you soon as we have any details."

"Okay." Matt disconnected the call.

Dylan took over working with the press. Matt liked him in front of the camera. He had a better stage presence. Matt preferred to investigate and not be interviewed. Of course, he had to do his spiel as the local chief of police, but he turned the microphone over as soon as possible to Dylan and the FBI agents trained to deal with the press. He understood they were simply doing their job too. He would stick around after the scheduled press conference to answer questions.

The day was a long one. He was happy to get the owner of the yacht and his guests on their way safely out of town, along with a small contingency of their security detail that were well enough to travel. Matt went over the details of the day that he knew to this point. Those who were allowed to leave had had their stories checked out and were clean. He wasn't as sure about a few members of the crew.

To say the owner was in a state of shock was an

understatement. His cabin cruiser was a beauty. Worth a cool five-hundred million, the four-hundred-and-fifty-foot cruiser was pure luxury. Matt found himself coveting the ship when he first saw her in the harbor gleaming in the waning sunlight last evening when he left work. How sad it was seeing the burned-out hull, personal effects, and pieces of the yacht floating in the water. Everything that could be recovered would be tagged, tested for explosives, and returned to the owners if possible.

When push came to shove, would they find anyone guilty, or had the bad guy in this case also been victim of an overarching conspiracy that would need to be unraveled? His mind moved through each detail but got stuck on the whole Bristol, Digby, and artifacts in the attic at the store aspect. To his way of thinking, they had to be connected or Jessie wouldn't have needed to see them.

"Joe, I'm heading home. You know how to reach me if I'm needed." Matt passed by his officer's desk on his way out of the station. "It's been a long day, and I have an early start tomorrow."

"See you, Chief. It's been some day. The whole town is buzzing about it."

"I bet." Matt stepped out the door and stopped to take a deep breath of fresh air. Jessie was probably hungry. It was damn near eight. She didn't complain when he told her he'd be late. She had mentioned that if she had her own car, he wouldn't have to worry about picking her up at all. He chuckled. She always found a way to remind him she was capable of taking care of herself. She was right, but he still liked to think she needed him in some small way. Call it his inflated ego but he wanted her to need him. Maybe after they were married, he'd be happy she had this independent streak.

"Hey, Matt, wait up," Jaxon called to him. "Tom wanted to let you know they're closing in on the type of explosive that was used. At this point they have a lot of traceable residue to work with."

"Any progress is good news." Matt stopped until Jaxon caught up with him. "I feel bad that the girls had to wait this long. Jessie seemed to take it all in stride. She used the situation to remind me they could have left for home if they could drive." Matt shrugged. "I still don't think they're out of the bullseye yet."

"This morning reminded me to remain vigilant. We still have no idea what we are dealing with. Was this a part of a plot or a loner with a grudge against the justice?"

"Buckle up. We're about to find out." Matt opened his car door. "We'd better get the ladies; they've waited long enough."

"We should take them out to make up for making them wait," Jaxon said as he passed Matt on his way to his car.

"We can ask."

****

Jessie smiled when she read the text from Matt that he was on his way. The day had been a trying one. She let Audrey and Heather leave early. There was no need for the four of them to be there to close. Peyton closed the doors into the coffee shop and locked them. She turned the closed sign around on the front door and then sat next to her cousin to wait until their rides arrived.

"What a day! Every customer had some version of the day's events to tell." Peyton pushed her hair back off her forehead. "Whew."

"I hear you, cous. It's been some day." Jessie twisted a strand of hair around her finger. "My mind is going into overdrive as I try to place the incidents of this day with all the other events that have happened both in Ireland and since we've come home."

"I do wonder at times if our lives will ever slow down. I mean, will mayhem and chaos follow us everywhere we go?" Peyton reached for the phone in her purse.

"That's a depressing idea." Jessie pursed her lips. "Or maybe it's the other way around—we are the ones following trouble."

"That's not much better." Peyton chuckled. "Either way, trouble seems to like to hang out with us. Even more when you add Reba to the mix."

"I often wonder why this ability never fully manifested in either of us until we moved to Blue Cove. I know there were signs of it early on."

"We were too young, maybe," Peyton said.

"True. Our great-great grandmother Kathyrn had connections in this area, and of course Mila and her sweet sister have worked this area since Cara Cassidy came from Ireland with her family during the great famine. But why here and not New York? It does cause me to think."

"I hear you." Peyton glanced at her phone and the incoming text message. "Jaxon says they are on their way, and they will take us to dinner for having to wait."

"Good idea on their part. I'm hungry." Jessie reached for her purse and stood when she saw Matt pull up with Jaxon right behind him. "I'll be nice. I know they've had a rough day." Jessie opened the door for her cousin and turned the lock when she closed it.

She slipped into the passenger seat and latched the belt. "I want to hear the details of what happened today from you. Everyone, and I do mean everyone, who came into the store had something to say about what they heard. Tell me what you can." She reached over and touched his hand.

"I can fill you in on the details that I'm allowed to share." Matt explained what he knew to this point. "Jess, once we got the idea something wasn't right, I can't tell you the sick feeling that came over me. Then, when I heard the explosion, that sensation only grew as we rushed to where we saw the smoke plume rise. Nothing prepared me to see that burning hull of the beautiful yacht, the bodies, and the personal belongings of people floating in the water." Matt pulled into traffic. "Does Mindy's Waterfront Grill work for you? It's a quiet place to talk, and after the day I've had, a bit of downtime with you sounds perfect."

"I'm good with that. Where you lead, I will obviously follow because I'm riding with you. You do know if I had a car, I could have gone back to your place and made dinner." She put her hand to her mouth in a gesture to not say anything. "I'm just saying, is all."

"Yeah, but then I would have worried about you on top of everything else." He grinned at her.

"Okay, you win for now. You know what that smile of yours does to me," she muttered. "Mush. That lopsided grin of yours turns my mind into mush."

"Nice to know. I'll use it more often. Thanks, sweetheart. You have a way of making days like this seem almost normal when I'm with you."

"I'm happy to oblige." She smiled at him. "We must be past the dinner hour. This place is almost empty for a summer night."

"Party of four," Matt told the host. "Jaxon and Peyton will be here soon. Frank went back to my place to let the dog out. Thankfully, he stayed on a few extra days, or I would be calling him back tomorrow. Secretly, I think he wanted to get in my recliner and put his feet up. That chair calls to every man within a few feet of it." Matt chuckled. "

"I heard Peyton was encouraging Jaxon to buy one, as she's been helping him decorate his new place. I have to start refurnishing mine." Jessie twisted a strand of her hair around her finger. "That night and what happened in the store that morning still haunts my dreams. I don't think I'll be able to forget that moment. Neil Dempsey is going to publish my article that I wrote about how a shooting affects your psyche."

"I'm glad. Maybe it will make someone stop and think. One can hope." Matt made eye contact with her over the menu.

"I'm still trying to figure out why Bobby Bristol went down the path he did. Take the stranger elements out of his story, and he had already made decisions that landed him as shooting victim on the side of the road."

"I hope you understand, sweetheart, you can't fix everyone. Sometimes there is no rhyme or reason. When I see Bristol's record, I see a young man who made choices that were destructive. How do you fix that?" Matt waved at Jaxon when he walked in with Peyton.

After they gave their orders, Jessie reached for Matt's hand. "What's on your mind?"

"No fair. That's the question I was going to ask you. Tell me if you can, what the hell is going on?" Matt frowned.

"I'd like to know too." Jaxon took a sip of his iced tea. "I know it isn't only in Blue Cove by any means, but the intensity of today's events makes it seem unique to us."

"I understand. I keep going over each detail of the past several days in my mind, but today was more about anger at the justice than at Blue Cove. This is where they caught up with him."

"Okay, I can see that," Matt said.

Jessie took a bite of her salad the waiter had placed in front of her. "Having said that, I believe because there is such discontentment and anger right now that people are looking for something or someone to blame. Everything going on seems more about a strange influence clouding the minds of people than about any one crime. How else can we account for all the global unrest?"

"I agree. People in general seem unhappy," Peyton said. "For the most part, we aren't thinking beyond our own anger and passion." She took a sip of her water. "Some unseen force seems to be stoking all the anger."

"We've seen this throughout history. How else did neighbors turn against neighbors and send them to their deaths? It seems it's our turn to face some hard choices. People will have to make some tough personal decisions on what kind of person they want to be." Jessie glanced at Peyton.

"And our country and town will have to decide what kind place we want to be." Peyton toyed with the napkin on her lap.

"You had to ask, Matt. Sounded a bit depressing to me." Jaxon frowned.

"But not hopeless." Jessie took a bite of her grilled chicken sandwich.

"Ever the optimist, sweetheart." Matt shook his head.

"Who, me? Not really. I'd be hopeless too if I hadn't seen how our ancestors rose to the occasion and made a difference in their time. My store attic has the proof within its walls. At least for the time. I'm sure there's a reason why it showed up at a time such as this." In her heart of hearts, she knew that was true.

Chapter 39

Matt stacked his hands behind his head and stretched out on his bed. Tom Maxwell had informed Jaxon and him earlier that the Supreme Court justice was the target of the bombing. They were following the cyber trail and had gained more information as the day progressed. A personal vendetta played into the assassination attempt. What a mess.

He couldn't imagine how it must have been during the Civil War. The politics of the day became so vitriolic that the division split households, sending brothers off to war to fight against each other. Matt shuddered. His brothers were his best friends. He couldn't imagine taking up arms against them. His dad had a rule when they were growing up that they couldn't talk about religion or politics at the dinner table. That rule still applied whenever they got together.

"Dad, you're much smarter than I ever gave you credit for," Matt mused. "Not that three ridiculous boys talked much about religion, but our politics could get heated at time." His dad often told them no politician could live up to all their promises, but family would always have your back. They'd seen you at your best, worst, and still loved you. What Jessie was talking about was aspirational. Policing oneself is the first choice, but laws were designed to protect us and others from our own worst instincts.

That's why he chose the career path he had taken. Maybe that's why Jessie was walking the strange path she was on. There had to be a reason those artifacts arrived at this time. As strange as their arrival was to him, he knew Jessie at some point would put all the details together and blow him away. How he loved her and thanked his lucky stars that she walked into his life.

He wanted to believe the bomb threat at city hall was only a diversion, but his gut told him there was more there. He had no proof of the fact, but when they were standing outside, he was sure there was someone observing the process. Maybe a trial run perhaps. The whole event didn't sit well with him. He rolled over onto his side and closed his eyes.

The smoke was thick and rancid. He couldn't see his way through the darkness. His gun was drawn as he rushed toward the sound of the screams. Adrenaline gave him the strength of two men as he fought off the clawlike hands grabbing as his legs and feet. Still, he pushed forward into the unknown with his pulse racing with each step. The sounds seemed to come at him from every direction as he spun around, trying to find the one voice he could hear above all the noises filling his head. Her sweet faint cry called his name. On he ran, hoping for enough light to see. The tree root sent him sprawling to the ground while unseen creatures pulled at him. He scrambled to his feet, kicking and calling her name—"Jess, keep talking to me. I'm coming for you."

The sound of his own voice yelling awakened him. The sweaty sheen covered his body tangled in the twisted sheets. What the hell?

"Matt, are you okay?" Jessie called through the closed door.

"I'll be there in a minute, sweetheart. Don't go anywhere." Matt got out of bed and slipped on his jeans and a tee. He opened the door, his hair tousled and his feet bare.

"I heard you calling my name. Did you need something?" Jessie asked him.

"I was trapped in a dream unlike any nightmare I've ever had. I don't dream or have premonitions; that's your department." He sat on the edge of the bed and pulled her down beside him. "Jess, it seemed too real to be a dream." He retold the nightmare. "I couldn't find you." He raked his hand through his hair. 'You called me, and I couldn't find you. I couldn't save you."

"I'm here. Right now, that's all that matters." She tugged his head down onto her shoulder. "You've had a rough day. Was something troubling you before you went to sleep?"

"I was thinking that the bomb threat at town hall today wasn't a diversion but maybe a practice run. Now this. What if I can't keep you or the town safe?" Matt's hands fisted at his side.

"You can't keep us all safe every minute. Such is life. That's too much stress for any one person to bear. All you can do is your job the best way that you can." She rubbed his back. "We'll get through this together."

"Yes, together. Jess, these last few weeks have been too intense. You were shot at twice. Seeing those bodies floating in the water, not unlike your dream, was a wake-up call for me. I'm sure they had no idea when they got up this morning this would be their last day. I don't want to waste my time when I can be living." He lifted his head off her shoulder.

"I know the feeling. Life is too short not to enjoy

those you love. I've been thinking about that a lot. I've called my parents so often lately my mom is getting suspicious." Jessie took his fisted hand in hers. "We'll figure us out too."

"Are you guys all right?" Jaxon asked while Peyton peeked over his shoulder.

"Yes, it's been a rough day, as you know, which makes for a rough night." Jessie stood. "We should probably all get some sleep. You have another long day tomorrow." She kissed Matt goodnight and whispered into his ear, "I love you."

Matt didn't want her to leave, but he let go of her hand reluctantly. "I love you too."

"I'll be right back. I have something I want you to read."

He watched her as she came back into his room with a notebook in her hand. She was lovely, this woman of his. Her curls tangled and wild looking, her skin soft and glowing in the night light, and she loved him. He shuddered. He'd better marry her soon.

"Read this. I think it will put you to sleep." She smiled at him. "If not, you'll get a good idea what your gift did for me. As soon as we can, you and I need to have our talk. Our future together won't wait forever for us. I'm ready, Mr. Parker, to seal the deal. See you in the morning."

The room seemed empty, and the light left when she did. He propped up the pillows behind his back and began to read her notes. Her descriptions transported him to Ireland, London, and Paris. He could almost see the Eiffel Tower and taste the amazing pastries at the sidewalk café. The description of her dream was like walking through his own. He marked the place where he stopped reading, turned off the light, and closed his eyes. Her beautiful face, soothing voice, and stunning blue eyes made falling asleep easy. He could see himself visiting all the places she had written about—as long as she was his tour guide.

****

After Matt told her his dream, Jessie knew he needed to read her writings. At best they were disjointed thoughts, personal observations, and her emotions spilled out on paper. She hoped something in her musings would speak to him. She wanted to help him in some way. His dream hit too close to home. A different take but in the same spirit of her dream. She understood his helplessness and felt the same sensation every time the scene of the rushing waves invaded her sleep. There were no solutions to help those being caught in the waves in her dreams, only their cries for help. Yes, she knew what he was feeling. A dream could leave her listless and fighting to change the outcome of what she saw at the same time.

Matt didn't have many dreams, and the intensity of this one caused her to wonder what it might mean. She wrote down what he had shared, hoping that maybe Reba would have an answer for her.

They always seemed to be in search of answers. Which always took time to reveal themselves. But eventually they showed up and the case was solved. Why did this time feel different? Maybe it was because she was different. There were changes taking place inside of her. She was no longer afraid of the gift she had, nor of her heritage. For the first time in her life, she was content with who she was becoming. Sure, it was only the beginning, and she had more room to grow. She'd be learning for the rest of her years, but this short journey changed her life in more ways than she could count. Where she went from here was yet to be seen and hers to choose. The one thing she was sure of was Matt was the one she wanted to walk beside. Life was a constant flux of change and growth, and she wanted to be a part of all of it—marriage, in-laws, and babies—the whole enchilada.

She laid her head back on the pillows and closed her eyes. Maybe the dream was simply to give Matt a taste of her life. There was a thought. Bless all those women who wrote their knowledge for future generations. From them she learned that dreams could be used to gain insight into the spiritual world. They could receive guidance and gain knowledge of the future.

From the moment she sat with him on the bed with his head on her shoulder, Jessie discovered within her a deeper love for him than she had ever known. In that moment, they were connected to something greater than themselves. The ancient Celts had a name for what she had experienced with Matt. They called such moments the thin places. The scrolls had described some of those places. Like the door Peyton discovered in the woods known by Cara, whose journal Peyton had found, and Katima, whose child had been lost to the boarding schools when taken from the reservation. There were times and locations where the boundaries between heaven and earth or the natural and the supernatural grew a little more porous or thin. The unseen but very real world hidden beyond the door or veil of reality became clearer, and the sacred could be seen. She had no idea if Matt had sensed the strong bond between them, but she had. She wrote a few more of her thoughts down, shut off the light, and closed her eyes. She dreamed of the past, the present, and the future that all seem to collide in Ireland's magical mystical thin places.

Chapter 40

The morning light hit Jessie's eyes through a small space in the closed curtain. Stretching her legs, she swung them over the side of the bed. Her hand pushed the curls falling into her face with a few strays making it to her mouth. Odd as it may seem, her late night wasn't affecting her disposition this morning. Refreshed would describe her feelings best. She peeked out the curtain at what was shaping up to be a beautiful day.

She rushed through her morning shower and routine, ready to get moving. Her future was waiting, and she wanted to be on time. She smiled at the image in her mind of her as a warrior rushing into battle with a sword in hand and an ill-fitting suit of armor. "Jessie, I swear your imagination is leading you astray," she whispered at her reflection in the mirror.

She looked in the drawer where she had hidden the scrolls beneath her clothes. They were still there, and she couldn't wait to spend more time with them tonight. She wanted to understand the locations that her sisters designated thin places. Confident with her thoughts that she would add the portal that she was pulled through to see the locations of the murdered Native American women. Peyton would have to add the door in the woods. That's why the scrolls were in her possession for now. They would add what their gifts allowed them to see. She wondered how many other thin places there were around the world. Closing the drawer, she reached for her purse and phone and made her way to the kitchen.

"Good morning. I thought I would get here before you and make you breakfast. Did you get any rest?" She kissed Matt's cheek as she reached around him for a mug.

"You know, Jess, I learned something new about you last night." Matt spread cream cheese on his toasted bagel. "These are pumpkin spice, if you like that. Add a bit of honey walnut cream cheese, and they're hard to beat."

"Don't leave me hanging. What did you discover?" She popped half of a bagel into the toaster.

"You're a great writer even when it's only your personal notes. I could see the places you were talking about. I think we need to go there together at some point."

"I couldn't agree more, and now I have all kinds of new places I want to see." Jessie placed her bagel slathered with cream cheese on a plate, picked up her full cup of decaf, and followed him to the table. Once they sat down, she explained to him all about what she had learned about the thin places.

"And you think we have one of those here?" Matt asked.

"Maybe more than one. Don't forget Cara, her grandmother, and Katima who visited us from beyond the door were all travelers on some level. Some from the visible world and others from the invisible." She took a bite of her bagel. "Yum, you're right—this is good." She sipped her coffee to wash the bagel down.

"I mean, all the artifacts in my attic along with the scrolls should tell us that something is not ordinary about Blue Cove. Remember, Peyton went through a book she found in the attic at the inn back to the early nineteen-hundreds. That's not normal."

"If what you say is true, what does it mean for us?" Matt's brows furrowed.

"Other than the occasional strange visitor who comes to disrupt our lives? For most folks they won't notice anything different. Peyton and I are a different subject. We will continue to see and be called upon to do our part in the ongoing battle for our town."

"As noble as that may sound, doesn't it bother you?" Matt finished his bagel and the last of his coffee.

"Yes, and no. Of course, the idea brings a lot of uncertainty with it, but I find a sense of purpose too." She wiped her mouth with her napkin. "As you know, I've continued to write articles for Neil. The other day a lady came into the store who has read many of them and wanted to talk to me. I found that quite satisfying. You're a cop, a good one, and you're making a difference. That's what I want to do in my own small way."

"And that's why I love you. We can leave early if you want. Jaxon is taking Peyton, and I want to check out your store. I'm still trying to logically figure out how someone managed to carry that large chest up those stairs." He grinned at her.

"Don't strain your brain." She laughed. "I'm ready when you are." She put her dishes into the dishwasher. She followed him out the door to his car and her ride for now.

Jessie's early arrival gave her plenty of time to read

emails, total her sales for the week, and put together her order for the month based on requests from some customers, which included fourteen books for the Cozy Mystery Club. She not only enjoyed the group meeting there, but appreciated their business. With a good thirty minutes until she opened, she could do a little research on the concept of the thin places and a few of the names she had copied off the scrolls. She opened her computer and got lost in the pages she read. When it came time for her to open, Jessie was sure of one thing—her theory made more sense now.

****

Matt's conversation with Fred Hinkley, the driver of the white car, left him scratching his head. Fred told Matt that he had no idea how he came to be in that accident or in the hospital. He was leaving the barber when he got shoved in the back into his car. By the time he righted himself, he was barreling down the road at a high speed. He said at first his hands weren't even on the wheel until he realized he should have them there. As far as the gas pedal was concerned, he was sure it had to be stuck. He couldn't remember putting his foot on it. His take from the event was it was like someone else was driving the car, and did Matt think he needed a shrink?

Fred knew nothing about Ashley or the other kidnapped girl, and he had a strong alibi for his whereabouts at the time of their abductions. Hinkley didn't know Gordon or Howard either. Fred couldn't understand how no one was killed when he saw what was left of the mangled cars. Neither could Matt. The big question left for Matt to find the answer to was who was actually driving the car since it appeared that

Hinkley wasn't. Gordon couldn't be questioned because he conveniently left the hospital late at night and he wasn't discovered missing until morning.

"Hell." Matt shook his head.

"I know I'll regret asking you, but what's up?" Jaxon walked in with Dylan following him.

"I have no idea where to begin." Matt pointed to the chairs. "You may need to sit for this." As soon as they did, Matt told him about his earlier conversations with Jessie and Fred Hinkley. "The thing is, Fred sounded like Howard Digby. He had no idea what had happened to him or how he wasn't dead. The missing Gordon Miller has me wondering if he is somehow involved."

"I'm at a loss. How do you write that piece of info in a report?" Jaxon asked.

"I should be used to this, but it still takes me by surprise. Do you think Hinkley was telling the truth?" Dylan frowned.

"He told it as he thought it happened. He even asked if he needed to see a shrink." Matt frowned. "If he didn't before, he might after this."

"His is a strange story, which makes me wonder if it will be the same with whoever blew up the yacht," Jaxon said.

"Jessie has a theory about all this, but damn it's confusing. It doesn't make sense on any rational level but it's as good as any I've heard so far. Figure that one out."

"Are you going to tell us?" Dylan asked.

"Hell no. I wouldn't even try. You'll need to hear it from her, but I'm not sure you'll understand it either."

"It's worth a try." Jaxon stood. "Does that mean

lunch at Joe's later?

"I guess it does." Matt saw someone rush past his door. He stood and rushed out into the hall to find out who it was. No one was there. How had they moved so fast?

****

His suspicion was correct. The conversation he overheard confirmed his wariness. Women had been a thorn in his side through several generations, and it seemed he would have to contend with another one of Johanna's descendants again. There was good reason for his growing concern when he followed her in Ireland. He sensed trouble when he first laid eyes her. She was no ordinary tourist. Nor the other two with her. If the cop boyfriend was concerned enough to tell the others about a theory she was developing, then he needed to move fast. Most of his existence he spent searching for the source of their ancestral strength. In some strange way, they passed their gifts down to one another without needing to have a host. In their family line, the power seemed to go through the mother or the woman's line, which seemed strange to him. He had been at war with Johanna Murphy through many generations. But no woman or one of her descendants would keep him from his mission this time. He needed to get his hands on what belonged to him. The old man had affected him like Johanna had. Their goodness threatened the darkness in him.

Chapter 41

Matt finalized the details for the afternoon track with Carlene. All of the agencies involved in the investigation wanted to be in the loop and to find the guy who blew up the yacht and left five people dead and several injured. A key witness and evidence pointed to the cell phone as the source of the bomb's detonation. The security camera showed a blurred image of a man talking to someone on the phone right before he tossed it. As he walked away from the dock, it was only thirty seconds later that the bomb blew.

Matt's morning consisted of a news conference, and conversations with Tom Maxwell for updates from the FBI lab, and with Dave Lewis, the coroner for information concerning the deceased. Glancing at the clock, he was ready for his break. He had a short window for lunch and a busy afternoon ahead of him.

He made his way to Dylan's office through a maze of extras using space wherever they could find it. He motioned for Dylan and Jaxon to follow him. With some fancy maneuvering, they managed to evade the press and make their way to the car undetected.

They arrived at Joe's for lunch. As soon as he had placed his order, Matt went to see Jessie. "Hi, sweetheart." He glanced around the store before he pulled her into his arms.

"I didn't know you were coming today." She

smiled at him.

"I want you to tell the guys what your working theory of the case is. I had a talk with Fred Hinkley this morning, which might interest you." He told her the conversation. "I'll let you think about his story while I get my lunch." He nuzzled her neck before he released her.

When Matt returned with lunch, Jaxon and Dylan followed him. They went to the table in the middle of the room. "Tell them your theory. As crazy as it sounds, it makes more sense after talking to Hinkley and Digby. They still have no idea what happened to them, and I believe them both." Matt took a sip of his iced tea. "Gordon Miller still hasn't been found. I'm hoping Carlene can find him this afternoon. Okay, Jess, you have the floor." He took a bite of his sandwich.

"All right, but you need to understand this is only an idea for now. I'm learning more every day and should have a working theory closer to the truth before long." Jessie explained to them about the difference between a traveler and an influencer and what she knew to this point.

"Let me get this straight. You think this spirit, or whatever an influencer is and not a traveler, is involved. Am I hearing you right?" Jaxon asked. "You make it sound like a possession when you say they look for a host."

"Yes, I guess it sounds a bit that way. I'm not sure how best to describe the difference. Maybe with time I'll be able to. Right now, this is the best I can do, but I do believe we are dealing with an influencer this time." She went on to explain why she thought the way she did. "There is much more we could get into, but this isn't the time or place. My store is getting busy. I'll fill Matt in, and he can let you know. You can always ask if you have questions." Jessie jumped up to wait on the next customer.

"If I have questions, how could I not? I have no idea what she is talking about." Dylan stood up, shaking his head. He threw his trash away.

"That makes two of us." Jaxon followed Dylan, but stopped to give Peyton a kiss goodbye.

"You may not understand her idea, but you need to listen. She's closing in on the truth," Peyton whispered in his ear.

"I'll keep an open mind; you know that. Even if it doesn't make a lick of sense to me." He kissed her again before he left the store.

"Thanks, sweetheart, they'll come around." Matt kissed Jessie goodbye.

"I'm not worried. We'll all have to." She stood in the open door.

"Frank and Carlene are doing another track this afternoon. I'm hoping we can find the bomber before he leaves the area. If he is not gone already. I'll keep you in the loop."

"Thanks. See you later." She waved at him.

****

Jessie spent the afternoon waiting on customers and with her eyes glued to various sites on the computer. She took a couple of trips upstairs to look at the items tied to her history. The locket she wore was hidden underneath her shirt until she understood the reason she was told to keep the necklace until it was her time to pass it on.

The more she read on the mysticism surrounding

babies born in the chime hours and the thin places, the more she realized she had experienced life beyond the veil. Yes, she could see the invisible world literally at times, but she wasn't the only one. Besides Reba and Peyton, there were many before her and many who were living, which meant there would be more after her too.

After she saw the almost superhuman strength of the Norman leader who fought for possession of Kilkenny, the more she understood there were influencers that affect people for good and evil. But knowing the possibility didn't make it any easier to explain.

"I've been thinking about what you told me about the thin places. I've experienced one, and I know you have too. I was wondering if upstairs might now be one like Katie's inn. I mean, how else did those artifacts come to be there?" Peyton stood beside her and talked softly. "Is that why our grumpy ghost remains on the premises?"

"Strange, but I thought the same thing," Jessie told her. "Between the scrolls which we are supposed to add to before we pass them on and my dream, I believe we are being set up for our future. I want to go on the record as saying I would love to go back to Ireland and find some of the thin places that they speak about."

"I'm right there with you, cousin." Peyton's phone went off at the same time Jessie's did.

"Hey, sweetheart, I promised to let you know what happened. I'll tell you later because the details are mind-bending to me. Get your theories warmed up; we have some investigating to do, and I'm going to need your input," Matt said.

"Sounds to me like you've had an interesting afternoon," Jessie responded.

"Yeah, and it's not over yet. See you soon."

"Jaxon said they've had an unusual afternoon. I can't wait to hear more details." Peyton put her phone back into her pocket.

"Looks like our evening should be eventful. Matt said something similar." Jessie walked to the front of the store when a customer came in.

The closer she got to the man, the more apprehension ran through her. Something was off about him, and her grumpy spirit was of the same mind. He hurled himself through the air and hovered in the space between the man and her. When the man took a step toward her, a shield with a light emanating from the center was raised, and the man stepped back with an angry expression on his face.

"May, I help you?" Jessie's voice trembled when she spoke. She wasn't sure how she was able to get the words out at all. What was happening?

The man nodded his head. "I believe you have something of mine." He waved his fist in the air.

"Hey, Jess, do you need any help?" Peyton stood beside her and placed her hand on her shoulder.

"No, I believe this gentleman is leaving now," she said forcibly.

"I'll be back," he shouted as he left the store. "I will take what is mine."

"And he will, and he'll try but he won't succeed." She watched him until the man was no longer in sight. "I don't know who you are, but I thank you," she said to the ghost. "We thank you."

"Who was that man?" Peyton asked.

"I don't know who the man is, but I believe we have seen an influencer from another era, and our ghost has dealt with him at some point too. Our grouchy in-house spirit saved our necks this time. But we need to know how to deal with others like him in the future."

"How do you know?" Peyton asked.

"I'm theorizing, but the more I've learned from the scrolls and from what I just saw happen, it seems there is an influencer or an entity that battles for the hearts of people in every generation. Some of our ancestors said they were battling with the spirit of their age. Influencers challenge a nation or a generation for their minds and hearts. They divide and turn us one against the other. We've read about their work in our history books but never knew what to call them. We simply thought of them as bad men, but maybe they were only men influenced by evil. At least that's how I see it at the moment. I'm sure I'll understand more in time."

"What was that strange light in front of you?"

Jessie explained to Peyton about the ghost inserting himself, and the shield with light coming out of the center. "The man backed away when he saw it, which leads me to believe they have met before."

"Talk about thinking outside of the box. Here's another entry into our notebook of the strange and unusual."

Jessie was happy when another customer came in and all they wanted was a book. Books she could handle with no problem at all. Every time she turned to look at the stairs, she was happy to see the ghost standing guard. Having him there gave her a sense of security. Though she wouldn't mind having a plan and knowing how to deal with the situation herself. Because she knew she would have to. The challenge had been given, and the guard might not be with her when she had to face the entity again.

Chapter 42

Jessie spent her time waiting for her ride deep in thought. Matt was sending Kip to take them home because he was tied up at the station with another news conference. He promised to fill them in on all the details as soon as he got back to the house.

Kip went through the same routine that Matt did. He made them wait until he checked out the house before he let them go in. Kip was such a handsome and nice guy that Jessie had no idea why someone hadn't snatched him up already.

After he left, she searched for something to make for dinner. She had no idea when Matt would be home, but the least she could do was make something for them to eat and keep it warm. With a chicken casserole in the oven baking, she went to get the scrolls. Jessie wanted to count how many times she saw her ancient sisters talk about the thin places and what they saw behind the veil. She also wanted to understand the back story on all of the artifacts and why they showed up in her store's attic at this time.

The place on her chest where the symbol rested was continuously warm. Today, when the man came in the store, it tingled. The amazing thing she noticed was the shield her guard held up had the same symbol in the middle, and that's where the light came from that stopped the man in his tracks. She understood the ancient symbol to mean warrior, but there had to be more to the story. Hopefully, Jeremy would find a person who could translate what the note said soon.

Jessie went over the scrolls one after another. Each of the artifacts in the attic was drawn and pictured on the parchments. Now all she needed was for someone to explain it all to her. It may as well be Greek, or any foreign language for that matter, because she couldn't understand the words, but she would. She had to trust that the insight would come, or why would any of this be necessary? One idea that came through loud and clear to her was Johanna and the others understood what they wrote but the experiences they shared had been strange and unusual to them at one time too. She had a hard time tamping down the excitement that came as she studied each scroll.

When she heard the timer, she went to check on dinner. The kitchen smelled delicious, and a peek inside the oven had her stomach grumbling and ready to eat. Peyton had made a salad and heated some crusty bread. Jessie pulled the casserole out of the oven as the guys walked in.

"Something smells good in here." Matt kissed Jessie's cheek on his way to the sink to wash his hands. "I'm starving. How about you, Frank?"

"I can always eat." He smiled.

"This is too hot to pass. If you hand me your plate, I'll give you some."

"Thanks, ladies." Jaxon handed Jessie his plate for a scoop of the casserole.

She smiled to herself. The table was quiet, and no one talked much, which was a good sign to her that everyone was enjoying the food. Boy, guys could sure eat a lot when they were hungry.

****

"We'll clean up in a minute," Matt said. "I promised to fill you in on all the details. Carlene was amazing as always. She impressed even some of the agents."

"I was proud of her. In the second track she didn't have much to go on." Frank ate the last bite of his bread.

"Carlene found Gordon Miller. He was as confused as Fred Hinkley had been. He told us that he had no idea why he left the hospital in the middle of the night until he found himself sitting outside his house. The strange thing to him was how he had ended up in the car in the first place and how he had survived such an awful crash," Jaxon explained. "No one is a good enough actor to pull off what he told us. He was genuinely dumbfounded."

"The second guy, the man who used the phone to set off the bomb, was given it by someone he had never seen before. He dialed the number he was told to dial. He said he knew what would happen and read about the throwaways being used to detonate a bomb and was given a stash of cash to do what the man told him. He found it kind of exciting, and he will be charged in the crime." Matt frowned. "To be truthful, he reminded me of Bristol. A loose cannon and a bit out of control."

"How did Carlene track him?" Peyton asked.

"His scent remained on the dock where he had leaned against the rail. Carlene was able to pick up the same personal scent on the phone he had handled. She tracked him to a motel. He was packing up and getting ready to leave." Frank nodded. "She did great."

"I thought if a person went through water, the trail could be lost." Peyton finished her salad.

"That's not always true, as Frank taught us today. A TV celebrity tried to bust the bloodhound's tracking ability using several methods. They ran through water, doused themselves with coffee and cologne, and even tried changing their clothes. There was so much scent it confused the dog for a moment, but within minutes the dog picked up the person's personal scent and found him within minutes." Matt smiled. "I'm a believer and a big fan of Frank's dogs."

"Wow, you must be proud, Frank." Jessie squeezed his hand.

"I am, but I'm still perplexed about how these crimes have played out. Matt said that's your department and not ours." Frank grinned at her. "You'll have to send me an email or call when you solve this case. I'm going home to see my wife tomorrow."

"I will for sure because I'm getting closer to understanding all the moving pieces. I'm waiting on some info from Jeremy." She sipped her water. "I bet you'll be glad to get home. Tell your wife hi and thanks for sharing you with us. I, for one, can't wait to meet her. You need to bring her with you some time."

Matt stood and started to clear the plates. Jessie helped him. "How was your day?"

"About as interesting as yours." She loaded the plates he handed her in the dishwasher and went on to tell him about the man and how the ghost became their guardian.

"What do you think the guy wanted?" Matt asked. His voice sounded weary to his ears.

"I'm close to finding out. He's challenged me, and

I have to find a way to stop him."

"We both can use some downtime. What do you say we plan a special date when things settle down a bit? I think we deserve it." He kissed her. "I can't to seem to find any time alone with you."

"Sounds perfect. Let's join the others. This is Frank's last night."

Matt took her hand and walked into the living room and sat on the couch. He pulled Jessie into his lap. Frank had beat him to his chair, but heck, he earned it. Matt rested his chin on Jessie's head. In his arms was where he wanted her. He would worry about what she told him later. For now he would enjoy this time with her and his friends. He hoped he would have many more moments like this one.

Chapter 43

After Jessie kissed Matt goodnight, she got ready for bed. Opening her computer, she finally got the one piece to the puzzle she had been waiting for. Jeremy had sent her an email.

Here is what I found per your request, my friend. All I can say is wow! "I give you my medallion with esteem and honor for you are the only one who dared to stand in my way. Wear it as a warrior who changed the course of the battle and saved her people. Pass it on to the next in your line deserving of the title you earned."

Jessie was stunned and wrote a quick note back to Jeremy to thank him.

You're welcome, my little warrior. I guess I can call you that after reading the professor's translation. He wanted to know who had found such an amazing note and how they had come by it. I didn't give him your name. I explained the note was passed down in your ancestral line. He was impressed and now so am I. You lead an interesting life, my friend.

Jeremy didn't know half of it. Jessie spent the rest of her awake time putting pieces together in her head, starting with something Reba had told her and moving on to Johanna. Little by little, the picture made more sense and so did her dreams. She shut her computer off for the night and stretched out on the bed. She would be happy to get home to her own bed. This one wasn't the same. Closing her eyes, she smiled into the dark room. "A warrior, me. Who would have ever thought?" she whispered. Well, maybe her mother, who had to deal with her strong will day after day. To know that an ancestor saw the fire that still burned in her and thought she was worthy of the medallion was pretty freaking awesome.

She could be content knowing that while Matt worked the logical facts of each of the crimes, she took up the mystical side. To even think that seemed strange to her, and yet there seemed to be a supernatural side to everything that helped to make the invisible visible. And this case had a lot.

****

Jessie didn't argue with him about not driving. As a matter of fact, she hadn't said much all morning. Matt took one last look around the attic before heading down the stairs. He knew his girl, and it was time for a chat.

"You're quiet this morning." He wrapped his arms around her waist and pulled her back against his chest. "Anything you need to tell me?"

"Thinking is all." She relaxed against him. "You'll be the first to know as soon as I work it all out."

"I'll hold you to that." He turned her around to kiss her. "I have a full day ahead of me. We are working on the charges against Casey Craven, and what to do with Fred Hinkley and Gordon Miller. Once we figure out who was at fault, there will be traffic tickets for sure."

"What about the bomber? Any plans yet for him?" She walked with him to the door.

"The suspect who detonated the bomb knew what he was doing. He gave us quite a story, but as we dug deeper into his past, we learned he had a run-in with the judge. The FBI took charge of him, and the DOJ is working with them. I was happy to see the back of him. With all the calls my officers are going on, we have court dates for the charging officers lined up for weeks. Any help you can send my way would be appreciated." He kissed her again.

Matt drove to the station when the call came over the radio about a shooting at city hall. His car sped in that direction with lights and sirens on. That sick sensation returned. He knew in his gut that this hadn't been a diversion but a possible trial run.

He pulled in the area at the same time as Dylan and jumped out of his car. He put on his tactical gear and grabbed his long gun. "Any more details yet, Joe?"

"We have a hostage situation in the mayor's office. Chad Bennett and his secretary were in a meeting with the mayor when the gunman stormed the office. We are getting people into place and opening a line of communication to try to talk the guy down."

"I'm on scene along with Dylan. Others are arriving as we speak. Keep a channel open. I want to hear how negotiations are going."

"Will do."

Damn, Chad was in there too. He couldn't imagine what the guy's beef was with the mayor. Hell, the guy was a politician—he could make a lot people mad without even trying. Matt strained to hear the mediator talking with someone in the mayor's office. He could hear the guy screaming and cursing in the background. His business was with the mayor and nobody else. The others were his insurance to get out of there safely.

Matt started running when he heard the gunshot. He positioned himself in the hall outside the mayor's office. Matt listened to the man yelling behind the closed doors.

"The next bullet won't miss. Sit down and shut up." The man cursed. "I'm tired of you guys never listening. You yap promises you never intend to keep. Liars, every one of you. I'd do the world a big service by killing you now."

Matt motioned to Dylan to get into position and wait. The man became more agitated as he spoke to the negotiator. His voice rose in anger, and expletives flew. Matt knew the moment he snapped. He hit the secretary who had started to cry and screamed at her to shut up.

"Matt, I have eyes on our shooter. He's got a gun at the mayor's head. I'll let you know if he moves," Kip told him over the phone.

Matt's hands fisted at his sides. Tension coiled like a cobra in him, and he was ready to strike. He wanted to save them all. He didn't want another person to die on his watch. The man had become too quiet. Not a good sign in his book. Seconds ticked by that seemed like hours, and Matt crouched low ready to spring.

"He's pacing, swinging his gun from one person to the next. You'll have to move fast, and the door might be locked."

"Well, hell." Matt stood. "Can you get a clean shot if we shock him by trying to kick the door in?" Matt asked Kip.

"Yes."

"On the count of three." Matt counted down. Matt and Dylan kicked the door together to divert the attention of the suspect. Matt was surprised when it flew open right after two shots rang out followed by screams.

Matt rushed into the room and kicked the gun away from the suspect writhing on the floor. The secretary had fainted, and Chad was trying to help her. The mayor was as white as a sheet and slumped against the wall. The suspect was bleeding and had shot a hole in the ceiling on his way to the ground. Another mess to deal with and unpack.

Once the ambulances arrived, the suspect was loaded into one and taken to the hospital with a police officer escort. He would have police around him until he was released and in jail. The mayor and the secretary were tended to, and the mayor ended up being transported with a cardiac issue. Matt spent the morning questioning Chad and several others. How was the man able to get into city hall carrying a weapon?

"Thank you both." Chad walked up to Matt and Dylan. "I thought we were goners. The guy was touting one conspiracy theory after another and got stranger as the time went on. He wanted to know where the blood was that mayor took from kids to drink." Chad shook his head. "Nothing he said made any sense to me."

"With his name, we should be able to see if he's on any online chat rooms connected with anyone else we have been dealing with." Dylan frowned. "Gary is on it now. I gave him the name on his ID in his wallet."

"The suspect we arrested yesterday had threatened the judge online several times. He had been on the FBI's radar for a while. Which made his story he made up the other day all the more ludicrous He had tracked the yacht's travel log through an online channel for ship captains. It's used around the world to stay in touch and keep abreast of weather changes," Jaxon informed them when he walked into town hall. "He bragged about what he was going to do. I wonder if he'll brag about spending time in prison too."

"I doubt that. Prison isn't a great place to hang out." Dylan leaned against the wall. "I'll finish up the interviews here if you want to get back to the station.

"Once the search warrant gets in our hands, I'll send a team to the suspect's house. I'm interested in his computers." Matt shook hands with Chad. "I'm glad we got to you in time. Kip took a great shot."

"Now that it's all over, I can let my stress out and find a release valve for the anger still building inside me. I don't think I've been that scared since I was a kid. I had to keep it in check in the situation. That guy seemed wound tight enough to shoot any one of us at any second." Chad walked to the door. "Thanks, and later, guys. I need to make sure my secretary's okay and give her the day off. I, however, need to work." Chad waved at them as he walked down the hall.

Matt drove back to the station while processing what had gone down. Blue Cove had experienced its share of bad luck lately. The minute he walked in the door, Joe handed him the warrant that had come from the judge's office. He took Gary, Kenny, and one of his new guys along with the forensics team to Walter Henderson's house. His brother, Evan, was taking crime photos at town hall and promised to join them as soon as he wrapped up there.

"Are you Mrs. Henderson?" Matt asked the woman who answered the door.

She nodded, eyeing them suspiciously. "What's he done now?" she asked when they handed her the warrant.

Matt told her a small amount of information. "We

need to check the premises."

"Be my guest. I never know what the man is up to. Besides drinking, cussing at the TV, and sitting in front of his computer, he doesn't do a damn thing."

When they left in the afternoon, they carried out several weapons, a computer, and several bags of incriminating evidence.

Whew, what a morning. Mrs. Henderson was a talker, and she gave them an earful. After a quick stop at Joe's for a sandwich, he would stop by the hospital to have a chat with Walter, who the nurse said was lucid and resting comfortably.

Chapter 44

Jessie couldn't believe the morning that Matt obviously had. Hers must have been in competition or at the very least tried to keep step with his. She only saw him for a few minutes at noon when he dashed in to pick up a sandwich, give her a quick kiss, and hurry back out to his car, with his promise to give her details later. Her strange morning began with Reba's arrival.

"Good day, girls." Reba rushed into the store, breathless. "Something is going on at City Hall. There are lots of police cars, and I saw our dear Chief Parker all suited up in tactical gear. It doesn't look good." She sat down and didn't bother to straighten her dress as she did. "I was on my way back from the dentist's office when I saw it."

Peyton reached for her phone. "I'll check the local radio station and see if they know what's happening."

They listened while customers came in and out of the store. Everyone was talking about what was happening. When news came that disaster had been avoided at town hall, Reba wanted to see the artifacts upstairs. Reba was in awe and even more amazed when Jessie told her how the note translated. Jessie carried the cross and dagger down. She wanted to check online to find any details about the time period they came from. She tucked them safely out of sight behind the counter.

"I believe I told you, dear girl, this time would be about discovering why you have your gift and how important it is. I also remember mentioning that with the rising tide there was a possibility of a rise in violence. This morning proves that out, as well as the bombing the other day. We've seen a few things here in the past few weeks, and believe me, the news tells us it's everywhere," Reba said.

"Yes, I remember you told me." Jessie smiled at Reba once they were seated at the table again.

"You hold an important key to push back against the tide. It won't stop the troubles altogether, for the waves will continue to give setbacks until people wake up to what's happening around them." Reba pulled a tissue from her purse. "My daddy fought in WWII and believe me, no one wants to live through another dark period like that again. He told us stories of liberating the death camps."

"Not a period anyone wants to repeat." Peyton patted Reba's hand.

"Hard times will continue to plague us as long as there are people who are swept away by the anger in their hearts. We are in the midst of another rising tide. But we can't let others dictate to us how to think or what to believe. We must think for ourselves. As my mom used to say, we need to treat others the way we want to be treated." Reba dabbed at her eyes.

"I'm not sure how my cousin or anybody can stop her dream from becoming reality," Peyton mused aloud.

"Those scrolls and artifacts tell a different story, my dear girls. You are only two, but there are more like you. Anything is possible." Reba grabbed her purse.

"Ta-ta for now. I can't wait to see how this ends. Remember to wear that medallion with pride, Jessie girl. You've been given a great honor. And you, my sweet Peyton, are about to discover more yourself." She waved on her way out the door.

Jessie understood a lot more than she had told Reba and Peyton. The first person she wanted to share the whole story with was Matt. He looked tired, and she wanted to do whatever she could to help him. She took the artifacts out from behind the counter. Peyton had asked her to get a closer look at the dagger and the jewel embedded in it. She was sure she had seen it somewhere before.

Jessie touched the medallion under her shirt. The same warm sensation traveled through her fingertips and up her arms followed by a strong sense of dread. Without turning around, she knew he was back. This time his appearance was different than before, and the ghost on the stairs had moved beside her.

Jessie pulled the medallion from her shirt. "You know what this is, for you were defeated by the one who wore its likeness on the battlefield." Then she pulled out the Celtic cross and held it before him. "Though you searched in vain to defeat the one who carried this into battle, your attempts to raise a movement died at the hands of a woman. Your influence along with others like you have sought to spread destruction through many generations until you come against the one voice joined by a chorus of others saying, 'No more.' You are defeated once again by those who have regard for their neighbor as their brother and refuse to take your bait. Those who won't be caught in the tide that seeks to divide and take them to their own destruction."

"And you think you can stop me? That's mine. I will take what is mine." He sneered at her. His eyes filled with rage and fury. "You are no match for the anger that is building."

She stood firm, not wavering, when he got closer to her, looked him in the eyes, and shouted, "Enough! I may be only a small voice, but like in the day of your first defeat, there are many others. You have no power over me or those who know that good triumphs over evil and love over hate. I will fight your influence over my life, my friends, and my town with every ounce of my strength." She lifted the medallion, and the light that had been in the shield flowed through the necklace, causing him to retreat. She glanced around to see Peyton standing beside her holding the jeweled dagger.

"You haven't seen the end of me because I have others too. That dagger should be mine," he said as he slithered away.

"Thank you, cous." Jessie hugged her. "You know that dagger once belonged to our ghost. I've figured out who he was. While that guy"—Jessie pointed at the man's retreating form—"was the one who tried to kill his leader during a struggle for power because Johanna received what he thought should belong to him." She sat down next to Peyton and explained all that she knew, making her promise not to tell anyone, even Jaxon, until she could talk to Matt.

"Do you know how strange we must have looked?" Peyton smiled at her. "Or sounded, for that matter."

"I do, but I don't care. What this morning taught me is there is nothing new. The battle for the hearts and minds of people has been around as long as people have been. The tactics may have changed from battlefields to internets, but the reasons remain the same. The struggle for greed and the power to control will keep the tide ebbing and flowing like the sea. We pushed him back for now."

"Yes, for now, but for how long?" Peyton rubbed her hand across the jewel in the dagger. "As Reba reminded us, this is our time to discover why and how we came to have the gifts that we do. At least I can find happiness in knowing I'm not the only oddball, besides you and Reba, of course. We belong to a long line of them. Look." Jessie pointed at the ghost, who seemed to have a smile on his ever-grumpy face.

"I wonder how long he'll be here?"

"As long as he's needed." Jessie surmised.

****

That symbol and dagger had been his downfall many times. How had he wound up in the same area as that woman's relative? He needed to regroup. He had won some rounds and lost some, in this outing. But the tide was rising, and she wouldn't be able to hold it back forever unless she got reinforcements. He could ride the waves. It still amazed him the power one person influenced for good or evil. She was a strong one and wouldn't be easily defeated, nor would the one standing beside her. But the force of the tides in a storm were strong, and with the right thoughts carefully hidden inside others, a person could be worn down. *Lull them to sleep before they realize they've been carried out on the waves* was his motto. Still, he knew the human instinct to fight against the wave could be strong. He could sense himself succumbing to the good in Digby. Hell, he had found a way to let him live. He wasn't proud of himself. Who would win the day?

They would soon find out. Actually, along with all those he worked with on this earth, he found it quite stimulating and rather fun to challenge these humans. Some would bend with every wind that blew at them, but others could put up a good fight. Then there were the stories of loving acts of selflessness that moved the masses and turned hearts of stone to flesh. He had seen more than his fair share of them and been defeated by their acts of kindness. That's when he would leave for a period of time until he saw someone else he could influence and build another movement through. He would bide his time, but no doubt about it, he would be back, and the war would continue on. She was young, and the commander wouldn't always be there to save her.

****

Once Matt heard what happened at the store earlier, he decided it was safe for Jessie and Peyton to return home. He would be working late the next few nights, and Jessie was getting antsy. After dinner, he followed her home and walked her to the door.

"You know, sweetheart, we still haven't had our talk. Once I get past the next couple of days at work, I want our special date night. I have the night planned, and I'm looking forward to spending time alone with you." He held the door open for her.

"Sounds perfect. I have a few plans of my own." She smiled at him. "Plus, I have quite a story to tell you." She glanced around her space which smelled like fresh paint and flooring. "It looks pretty good compared to a few weeks ago." She shuddered. "That was an awful night."

"Will you be okay alone here?" he asked.

"Yes, I need to do this. Katie did a nice job decorating the space. I don't need to do much."

"Peyton had a hand in the process too." He led her over to the couch and pulled her down beside him.

"I thought I saw her handiwork in all of this. She did a beautiful job." She rested her head on his shoulder. "Who paid the upfront money?"

"I'll never tell." He kissed her. "I've missed being with you, only you, the last few weeks. Something tells me I've missed a few stories that I need to hear. I'll be by tomorrow after work to hear all about it and to fill you in on what's happened with the cases. Because on Friday, we won't talk about anything but us."

"Works for me." She turned to look at him, and he took advantage of it with her lips so near to his.

"I missed that more than anything else." He traced her lips and kissed her again.

Chapter 45

Jessie left work and couldn't wait to get home. She had ordered two of Molly's specialty salads with grilled chicken and some of her wonderful desserts. She spent the day contemplating how to tell Matt the story she had figured out. Of course, she had no way to prove the details, but she would give her rendition her best shot. There was only so much research she could find on the times of Johanna and the others. Waiting for Matt to come seemed like old times to her. How she loved the man. She smiled to herself, glancing around the room which looked perfect, and went to stand at her favorite place. The view of the cove was a peaceful and beautiful reminder of how she loved her cottage by the sea. She turned when she heard the door open. Matt had a key and couldn't lecture her for not locking her door anymore.

He came in looking better than any one man had the right to. She took his hand and walked with him into her freshly painted, sparkling kitchen. She filled his glass with iced tea.

"Hmm, just what I needed, Jess. Thanks." He sat at the table.

"Even though it's rabbit food?" She chuckled.

"There's some manly meat too." He poured dressing on his salad. "Do you want to go first or should I?" he asked.

"You should. I want to know the factual side of the case first." She took a bite of her salad.

"We charged Ria Craven's husband Casey with her murder. He's been charged and is being held without bond until his trial. Bobby Bristol's shooter is also awaiting trial. Now, as to who Bristol was when he shot up your place, I have no idea. I know that same Bobby went on a shooting rampage and killed six people and wounded fifteen at the store in Elm's Spring. He will go down in the records as the kidnapper and mass murderer, and the book is closed on him. Ashley is getting help, along with the other girl, and as far as they are concerned, Bristol was the guilty party." He took a bite of his salad. "Not bad."

"But what about Howard Digby?" she asked.

"He's doing well and with his family. He still doesn't remember much about the whole event. You know that from the time you talked to him." Matt took one of the sweet treats she offered him. "Both Hinkley and Miller got speeding tickets, which seemed appropriate for them. Neither one of them argued with me, given the situation."

"What about Henderson?" Jessie asked.

"He's being charged with attempted murder, assault with a deadly weapon, and calling in a false bomb threat, to name a few. He was a real piece or work." He raked his hand through his hair. "Jess, when I walked into their house, I almost lost my stomach contents. The place was filthy, and the smell was atrocious. I've watched a show on hoarders once, but had never been in the home of one. I'm not sure how a person can live like that." He took a big bite of his brownie. "I do love Molly's brownies." He removed his glasses and slipped them into his pocket.

"Let's go into the living room and get comfy, and I'll tell you my story." She sat beside him on the couch. "I don't remember if I told you or not, but while we were in Ireland, I felt like someone was watching me. In the morning during one of my runs, I knew it. Come to find out, he was the man who ended up in the hospital the night Bobby died. He saw me searching the records in Kilkenny and seemed to recognize me as someone he had dealt with in the past. An influencer, as I've come to know them, has need of a human host to work through on a small scale. The grand scale is to influence large groups of people by whispering his or her lies, whatever the case may be. Like my dream people are sucked into the tide before they realize it."

"How did that impact Bobby?" Matt looked perplexed.

"With Bobby, it went both ways. An influencer has to work with the free will of the person who can go rogue at times and be hard to control. The rampage at the store was Bobby's response to the lies he heard in his head."

"Was that true with Digby?"

"I believe Digby couldn't be influenced, so the influencer found a way to dump him and still let him live. Digby's good nature was starting to affect him. I found that surprising. He staged the accident. Henderson and the other suspect were easier to manipulate because they had already bought into the lies."

"Wow." Matt shook his head. "What about the scrolls, artifacts, and the ghost in the store? How do they fit into all of this?"

Jessie told him about what Reba had told her and Peyton at the beginning. "Going to Ireland and finding my family line changed everything. Johanna and I had a connection, and she entrusted me with important family heirlooms. I will study the scrolls and add to them what I learn. Someday I will pass them on. The necklace around my neck"—Jessie touched where it sat on her chest—"was given to her by the Norman warrior who attacked Kilkenny after she stood up to him. The dagger he carried with him was used destroy the one who tried to kill him. A power struggle of sorts." She handed Matt the translation of the note to read.

"I knew it all along. Only now you're my warrior." He squeezed her shoulder and added, "Symbolically."

"There is great strength in the women in my family line. If we have a daughter someday, it could be passed to her. Knowing the power that comes with the gift was important for me to discover. I can use it to push back against the darkness that threatens humanity. I can never use it for my own purposes. I must walk a fine line, or I would be on the other side."

"No pressure there." He shook his head.

"I can't stop it by myself, but as you told me, one voice added to another makes for strength. The ghost in my store was the Norman warrior, and he was there to protect me until I understood what it all means. The other day in my store, he actually smiled." She glanced at Matt. "Do you have any questions?"

"I'm sure at some point I will, but for now I'll try to soak in what you've told me." He turned to face her. "Let me get this straight. Johanna really stood up to the man as you saw it that day, and he gave her the pendant you are wearing. She passed it down to you along with the items in the trunk which also belonged to him and to others?"

"That's about it." She smiled. "Look at it this way—I'm a chime baby, I've experienced a few of the thin places where heaven and earth meet, and I'm blessed with a gift. You fight the criminals your way, and now I'm learning to fight them another way."

"One more question," he told her. "Do you think the other guy will be back?"

"Of course. Are there humans to influence, trouble to make, and nations to topple? He'll definitely be back and more like him, and we'll be ready. There is a rising tide, and we must speak truth to combat it. You in your way, and me in mine. In the process, some will see the truth, and others will not."

"I get that. I felt the effects of the discontent and anger rising these past few weeks. It doesn't seem to want to slow down either," Matt told her.

"Like the tide coming in, troubles will follow in waves until the darkness is pushed back and goes underground. There it will wait for another generation to decide what's worth fighting for."

"Babe. You live an enchanted life." He squeezed her shoulder. "I'll be by for you at five tomorrow. Can you be ready that early?"

"Yes." She stood when he did and kissed him goodnight. She would be ready, and she knew exactly what she would wear. She also had a plan. Racing to her closet, she reached for the dress. She would pull out all the stops. Her gorgeous dress from Paris of blue silk shot through with silver threads was only the beginning. Peyton described it as her way-to-seal-the-deal dress. She told her that she looked like a runway model when she came out of the dressing room to show them.

"Cous, your eyes are breathtaking in that color. Matt doesn't stand a chance." Jessie smiled, remembering her words. She sure hoped that was true. It was time for her to seal the deal.

****

Matt left the station early. He rushed home to shower and dress. He had found what he hoped was the perfect spot for their night out. Dinner yes, but also dancing. He couldn't wait to move to the music with Jessie in his arms. Tonight was their night. He was sure of it. Running the comb through his hair, he sprayed a light touch of cologne, straightened his shirt collar, and he was ready.

Walking the familiar path to her door, he hoped he wouldn't have too much longer to wait. He would do everything he could to convince her they belonged together. She was the one for him. He knew how she loved this place, and who could blame her, but she would like their place together too. With fingers crossed, he knocked on her door. No key tonight—she was his date.

When she opened the door, he had no words but looked her up and down. "Damn, Jess. You are stunning." His mouth went dry. The dress was a knockout on her, and the color made her eyes seem bluer than he had ever seen them. Beautiful came to his mind.

"You have such a way with words." She twirled in front of him. "Do you like my dress? I got it in Paris." She ran her hands down the rich silk fabric.

"I can't put two thoughts together with you looking the way you do." He reached for her hand, set the alarm, and locked the door as they left. "I hope you like what I have planned, but man, sweetheart, you're not making it easy on me looking the way you do. I want to show you off to the world." He opened the car door for her and drove to the special place he had made reservations at.

"Matt, this is perfect," she told him when they turned into the parking area of the Seaside Restaurant. "I've heard customers mention this place more than once."

"Perfect are my sentiments exactly every time I look at you." He placed his hand possessively on her back as they walked through the doors.

The ambience was romantic with the soft glow of candlelight and dimmed lighting. They feasted on steak and lobster with a wondrous chocolate creation for dessert. Small talk gave way to dancing and the sparks that came with being close to each other. Especially with the memorable slow dances where they moved as one. His world felt right when he held her tight in his arms, and he drank in the scent of her sweet perfume.

Afterward, they walked hand in hand near the waterfront, on a path behind the restaurant. The stars aligned themselves in the heavens, filling the night sky with their brilliance, and the moon glowed, casting its light onto her hair and making it shimmer. She was his warrior, like her ancestors before her, and he couldn't be more proud to call her his.

"Jess, I know you have to know how much I love you. And I bet you can imagine what I want to know." He stopped walking and turned her to face him. "Did my bribe work?"

"Yes, oh my, yes. You didn't need to bribe me, but

I'm ever so glad you did." She put her finger to his mouth. "Before you say more, can you really live with me and all the crazy family skeletons I've told you about?"

He kissed each of her fingers. "You bet I can." He grinned his lopsided grin. "I keep thinking of the medallion you wear and the words your ancestor wrote for you to read. You're my warrior. You've saved me on more than one occasion." It was his turn to put his finger to her lips. "Let me have my fantasy. I know you belong only to you, but I like to think of you as mine."

"I can live with that." She smiled. "I used to like to think of you as my handsome prince." She ran her hand down his cheek. "Now it's more like my handsome, fierce protector." She gazed into his eyes. "How does four months work for you? I've always wanted a December wedding."

"Two would be better, three at the most, but I'm willing to wait for you to have the wedding of your dreams." He took her in his arms and rested his chin on the top of her head. He would give her anything when she looked at him that way.

"We can negotiate. I could do three if that works for you." She pulled his head down and framed his face with her hands.

"I'm thinking two and half tops." He leaned close and kissed her.

"The first part of November, it is," she whispered in his ear.

"Really?" He saw her nod, and he took her into his arms and danced under the starry night to the music they could hear through the open window. "No matter what day it is, ours will be a wedding to remember, my little warrior. He kissed her passionately.

"A love that is swoon worthy to tell our children about," she said breathlessly almost touching her lips to his before he captured her mouth again.

A word about the author...

I am a multi-published, award winning Amazon bestselling author who writes romantic suspense with a touch of the paranormal. I enjoy writing fiction. The character development, their stories, and the twists and turns in the plot intrigue me. Once I let the characters loose, I can't wait to see where they take me. I'm hooked from the first words on the paper, and I have to keep writing to see how the story ends.

I live in Colorado with my husband and family. I am a member of the RMFWPAL (Rocky Mountain Fiction Writers Published Authors League) and have enjoyed becoming involved in my community as one of the many authors living in Colorado. I invite you to read one of my Blue Cove Mysteries and see for yourself why Blue Cove is a special and unusual place. http://www.ionamorrison.com

Thank you for purchasing
this publication of The Wild Rose Press, Inc.

For questions or more information
contact us at
info@thewildrosepress.com.

The Wild Rose Press, Inc.
www.thewildrosepress.com

Milton Keynes UK
Ingram Content Group UK Ltd.
UKHW030908141024
449705UK00012B/464

9 781509 258338